BLOOD
TIES

BLOOD TIES

A NIK POHL THRILLER

ALEXANDER HARTUNG

Translated by Fiona Beaton

THOMAS & MERCER

Text copyright © 2019 by Alexander Hartung
Translation copyright © 2019 by Fiona Beaton
All rights reserved.

Previously published as Vom Gleichen Blut by Edition M, Amazon Media EU S.à r.l. in Luxembourg in 2019. Translated from German by Fiona Beaton. First published in English by Amazon Crossing in 2019.

Published by Amazon Crossing, Seattle

www.apub.com

Amazon, the Amazon logo, and Amazon Crossing are trademarks of Amazon.com, Inc., or its affiliates.

ISBN-13: 9781542015837
ISBN-10: 1542015839

Cover design by @blacksheep-uk.com

Printed in the United States of America

First edition

BLOOD TIES

Prologue

The pain in her lower abdomen made her eyes water. Blood ran down her inner thigh, all the way to her bare feet. Her hospital gown flapped around her, exposing her back. The only source of warmth was the hand towel she had quickly grabbed and thrown over her shoulders. Step after cautious step, she placed her feet on to the cool lino. Making a noise wasn't an option: the women's hospital was always deserted at this time of night and the men would notice every sound.

The baby in her arms was sleeping. Wrapped up warm in a blanket, a woollen hat on its head and shoes on its little feet. A tiny new human being. Helpless and fragile. And the most beautiful thing she had ever seen. Nothing in the world was more important than this child.

It had been a difficult birth, with the contractions lasting seven hours. But when she had looked into her baby's eyes for the first time, all the suffering had vanished. Any pain and fear forgotten. And as the child had lain on her chest, looking up at her, she'd been powerless to hold back her tears.

She had only been asleep for two hours when her phone rang. Just once, as had been discussed, and the flashing moment of joy was gone. She pulled the tube out of her hand, twisted out of bed and lifted the child from its cot. And then, as a night nurse was called into another room, she set off.

She had already carried out a thorough search of the hospital months before the birth: locating emergency exits and following dark basement corridors that led outside. And now the time had come to put her knowledge to use. She made no attempt to use the main entrance or to see if the side door was clear. There was every chance the men were waiting there for her.

Every metre was torture and the staircase in front of her seemed to stretch down endlessly. So she concentrated on one step at a time, until she finally reached the ground floor. She slipped through a side door into a small room where she knew there was an unlocked window and climbed up on to the slim ledge. Clenching her teeth, she squeezed both herself and the child through the narrow opening, suppressing an excruciating need to scream. Once on the other side, she sat down and let herself fall to the ground. The rain had stopped but the grass still felt damp underneath her feet. With its rectangular lawns, the hospital's inner courtyard resembled a small park, and the only light came from the glinting stars in the clear sky above. A fountain splashed softly and invitingly. How she would have loved to sit on a bench and listen to the water as it whispered. But there wasn't a second to spare.

She squeezed the sleeping child tightly to her chest one more time and kissed its head, taking in every curve and dip of its face: the small lips, the peaceful eyes and the tiny nose. It was an image she would never forget. Then she knelt down and carefully placed the mini bundle underneath a bench. Dawn wasn't far off and the park was starting to show signs of life. Some birds had started to sing and a squirrel was scurrying up an oak tree. The early risers among the patients would soon want to stretch their legs and the nurses would need a quiet place to smoke. Someone would find the baby and give it a better life than she could. Away from violence and fear and suffering.

She was struck by another spasm in her abdomen. Standing, bent double, she clenched her fists. Blood started running more heavily down her thighs and she realised her legs wouldn't be able to carry her for much longer. But for as long as they could, she would draw those men away from here; away from that hospital, and away from her child, whom she loved so dearly.

Chapter 1

The bar's interior was alluring. High leather stools stood before a dark cherry-wood bar, while to the back of it were towering mirrored shelves, stocked with expensive single-malt whisky. Each of the small tables was occupied and a Premier League game was playing on a television. The game's commentary had been turned off and in its place rolled the smoky tones of Tom Waits, telling the story of a prostitute from Minneapolis. At one of the tables, deep within the bar's dusky yellow light, an attractive red-headed woman moved sedately with the melancholic music. Her eyes were closed and she held a tumbler of ice in her hand. Jon had always enjoyed coming here, but not anymore. Nowadays, he didn't like to be around other people. Come to think of it, he didn't even like venturing out of his flat and only did so if he really had to. But the informant he was meeting today was of the old school. Details were never given over the phone and emails and texts were strictly avoided. As such, the only option left had been to meet face-to-face in a public place. Jon sat down at the bar, ordered an eighteen-year-old Talisker and picked a pretzel stick from a glass.

'I don't have much time,' came a voice from behind him; a voice so deep and raspy, it would have made for a perfect duet with Mr Waits himself. An older man sat down beside him, drink in hand. His creased, bearded face told of a life of alcohol, and his hair, shaggy and grey, hung down to the frames of his dark sunglasses. He looked older than his forty-nine years.

'And I don't want to be here long,' replied Jon, passing the man an envelope under the bar.

'You asked me to look out for strange cases and incidents at the police,' said the man, accepting the envelope with trembling fingers.

'That's right. Not everything gets uploaded on to the CID server,' said Jon as the bartender set down his whisky in front of him. 'So I need someone on the inside.'

'And why are you so interested in these cases?'

'Sometimes, there are lines that the CID can't cross and that's when I come into play. To right some wrongs, you might say.'

'And how do you do that?'

'Probably best you don't know.'

The man emptied his glass in one gulp, clearly in need of the courage. The ice cubes clinked as he placed his glass back on the bar. 'Did you hear about the abduction of the girl this evening?'

Jon nodded. 'It's the top news story.'

'Well, it's normally Unit 11 that deals with abduction and extortion. But people from Unit 7 and homicide were also at the meeting.'

'What do corporate and homicide have to do with abduction?' asked Jon.

'That's exactly what a lot of us are asking,' answered the man. 'But nobody on the case will say a word.'

'OK, so there's more to the abduction than they're making public?'

'Looks like it.'

'And d'you know why?'

The man shook his head. 'As I said, nobody's talking. It's as if the chief of police has imposed a vow of silence.'

'Does this kind of thing happen a lot?'

'Not in recent years.'

Jon stood up and put down a twenty-euro note on the bar top. 'Thanks for the tip,' he said, sliding his untouched glass to the informant. He then made his way to the U-Bahn.

Accessing the CID server to download details about the abduction wouldn't be a problem, but after that, he'd need someone well versed in working dubious cases. Luckily, he had just the man for the job.

◆　◆　◆

It was a heavenly Saturday afternoon. Nik raised his face to the seamless sky and let the rays warm his skin. He was sitting in Munich's Olympic Stadium, watching the rugby match between Germany and Argentina. Every bleacher was full and the atmosphere topped that of many a football game he had watched at the Allianz Arena. The spectators were a diverse bunch, clearly stemming from all corners of the world. In the row in front of him was a group of Fijians, who were dancing with a man sporting the green South African Springboks shirt. Then beside them, complete with sun-scorched faces, were three men from England, bawling and bumping jovially with plastic beer glasses in their hands. A German player on the right-hand side of the pitch caught the ball and started bolting towards the try line. Everybody sprang out of their seats.

'Come o-o-o-on!' cried a man dressed as a banana two seats down. A bull-necked Argentinian was now running after the German but it was no good. The ball was passed right to another German player, who then dived gloriously into the end zone.

'Ye-e-e-a-ah! Fantastic try!' screamed the banana. A woman to the right of Nik, dressed as Pippi Longstocking, hugged him in ecstasy. The mood in the stadium was intoxicating and Nik couldn't help but laugh and reciprocate the hug.

The commentator's voice sounded loudly over the stadium speakers. 'Twelve-nil to our home team, ladies and gentlemen.' Music started to play and more people jumped up to dance in the stands. Just as Nik was raising his glass to the English trio, his mobile started to vibrate in his breast pocket. He pushed his way through the elated masses and managed to find a small clearing where the music was slightly quieter.

'Hello, Jon. To what do I owe the pleasure?'

'Hi, Nik. Sorry to bother you . . . I know you're at the rugby, but something's been on my mind since yesterday evening.'

'Let's have it then.' Nik moved further away from the crowds.

'Did you hear about the abduction of fourteen-year-old Greta Grohnert?'

'Hard to avoid it,' replied Nik, before taking a swig of beer. 'Only story the press seem to care about at the moment. Abducted yesterday evening from her home. I read a special commission's been set up and the search is in full swing. Child abductions are never good news but I can't say I noticed anything particularly unusual about the case.'

'Did you know that the family's chauffeur was shot during the abduction?' asked Jon.

Nik let out a high-pitched whistle. 'No, I didn't. Where did you hear that?'

'An informant told me about a few discrepancies with the case so I downloaded the files from the CID server . . . I've still got back-door access.'

'Right, well, that level of violence isn't typical for an abduction,' commented Nik, 'and certainly doesn't suggest it was down to some kind of internal family conflict. And it also doesn't sound like some random kiddie-snatcher who just happened to be passing.'

'Yeah, well, whoever it was put a lot of effort into planning it,' added Jon. 'And victims rarely get out of that kind of abduction unscathed. If at all.'

'The CID were smart to keep that piece of information to themselves,' said Nik. 'Was there a ransom note?'

'Not yet,' said Jon. 'And that's the next odd thing about the case.'

'OK, listen, I'm heading home.' Nik placed his glass on the ground and started making his way out of the stadium. 'Send me everything you've got.'

◆ ◆ ◆

Nik had considered Jon's flat his home for a long time now; it had a lot of perks that made it far more attractive than his own place. A large living room with a home cinema projector, access to every streaming service possible, surround sound, a brand-new kitchen with a large fridge and a Salamander broiler – which even Nik could use to cook a steak – and not to mention the cleaning woman who came once a week. And all of that with no rent and no bills. There was no way he would have been able to afford anything close to that with his last job as a CID inspector.

Nik used the bare white wall in the living room to hang up information on the case. Right at the top was a photo of Greta Grohnert sitting on a garden swing, her face framed by curly brown hair. Her red cheeks and innocent smile might have still been those of a child but her features had already started to hint at the beautiful woman she was to become. To the right of her photo, Nik had written 'Suspect?' in red marker. This area of the wall was still bare. Next to that were photos of the Grohnerts' family home: a two-storey villa, painted bright white, with a pointed roof, upon which solar panels had been mounted. A large balcony projected from the front of the building, looking out on to a garden lined with beech and oak trees. The property was surrounded by a wall of about six feet and at the very front was an entrance gate, made of dark wood.

Nik's phone rang. He answered and put the call on speakerphone.

'How far along are you?' Jon asked.

'I'm just sorting through the first bits of information. Would be good to have a bit more on the sequence of events.' Nik pinned another photo of the crime scene on to the wall.

'OK,' Jon began. 'At 6.37 p.m. the family's chauffeur set off to take the Grohnerts' only daughter to ballet class. As the driver was leaving via the gate, the kidnapper shot a bullet through the window. The bullet hit the driver in the temple, causing him to die instantly. The kidnapper proceeded to put the girl into another car before driving away.'

'OK. Let's go through all those stages bit by bit,' said Nik. 'Did the daughter go to this ballet class on a regular basis?'

'Driven there every Friday. Why d'you ask?'

'Because an abduction is easier when the target follows a planned routine. The fact the kidnapper was waiting at the gate at exactly that time suggests good planning. The Grohnerts are wealthy and live in an expensive neighbourhood so it's possible money was the motive.'

'They're wealthy, but according to the father's statement, nobody had threatened to do it and he doesn't owe anyone any money. That's why he never installed any far-reaching safety precautions at the house. Just the security system. Although it's no run-of-the-mill security system, I might add.'

'Abductions are only very rarely announced before they are carried out and no businessman has ever owned up to having dubious connections. The father's statement is of little use.' Nik pinned the photo of the shattered windscreen to the wall. 'OK, let's talk about the weapon. What was used to shoot the driver?'

'According to the autopsy it was an HK P30. The bullet was left in a bad state so it's hard to tell, but chances are high it was a Heckler & Koch.'

'Then no one would've heard the shot.'

'Right. According to the report, nobody did,' said Jon. 'How did you know that?'

'The P30 loses next to no precision when it's used with a silencer. It would have been stupid to attract attention from the whole neighbourhood by making loads of noise. A shot from a P30 without a silencer can be heard two hundred metres away.' Nik looked at a photo of the dead chauffeur. His head was slumped on top of the steering wheel. The entry wound on the left temple was clearly visible and blood had sprayed on to the headrest, the dashboard and the front window. The fingers on the left hand were still seized up around the steering wheel, while the right hand was on top of the gear stick. 'The driver's murder was planned,' continued Nik. 'If the kidnapper had threatened him, his head would have been turned to the side and the shot would have been in his forehead, not the temple.'

'The guy sounds pretty ruthless,' Jon remarked. 'Not good at all.'

'Any witnesses?'

'A delivery guy had just come out of the house next door. He didn't hear any shots or see a gun so he didn't think twice when he saw Greta getting into the VW with a man. He got in touch with the police as soon as he heard the news.'

'Did he see the kidnapper?'

'Only from behind. He described him as particularly tall and slim . . . wearing dark jeans, a sweatshirt and brown trainers. He was dragging his right leg behind him.'

'Number plate?'

'Nope,' Jon replied. 'But a search for the car has gone out anyway.'

'For a dark blue VW . . . in Munich?' Nik asked sceptically. 'Fantastic.'

'That was the only witness.'

'Six thirty to seven p.m. on a Friday evening . . . in good weather . . . and the only person on the street was a delivery guy?'

'Apparently so.'

'Has the family's social circle been questioned?'

'According to the interim report, the family's closest friends were questioned yesterday. And then this morning it was the parents' work colleagues, Greta's friends and her school teacher.' Jon let out a groan of frustration. 'A whole load of records and not a single bit of new information. They're all in shock and nobody has a clue why anyone would want to kidnap Greta, or who might have done it.'

Nik pinned the last photo to the wall and took two steps back. 'Still no word of a ransom demand?'

'Nothing. The CID have bugged the family's landline and mobiles, but the kidnapper hasn't made any contact.'

'Are you sure *all* phones are being bugged or does Grohnert maybe have another one he used for less official business?'

'Well, I know he doesn't have any other contracts with German service providers. I checked.'

'Doesn't make any sense,' mumbled Nik. 'If we're taking greed to be the motive, there would have at least been a demand for money.'

'Maybe there was but it slipped past the police,' suggested Jon.

'Possible. But if Grohnert doesn't have a secret mobile, then it could have only happened via email or letter. And the CID will be monitoring both. So let's forget ransom for the time being and say she was abducted for another reason.'

12

'Maybe the kidnapper's a child molester?'

'At fourteen, Greta's slightly too old to fit that target group,' said Nik. 'Sexual violence is still a valid possibility but the violence during the abduction seems abnormally severe for that to be the case. Plus, there are so many other corners of Munich where it would have been far easier to find vulnerable minors . . . the main station to name one.'

'So what other options are there?'

'Well, the children of rival gang leaders are sometimes used in organised crime to apply pressure. But I don't know enough about the Grohnerts for that.'

'From what I can tell, everything seems pretty kosher. Clemens Grohnert is a qualified civil engineer and earns a couple of hundred thousand a year. The villa is paid off, as is his wife's car, so it's just the Maserati to go. But the money in his account more than covers that. He also has an impressive number of shares so pressure from a loan shark seems unlikely.'

'And what about his wife?'

'Vanessa Grohnert is an architect. They got married nineteen years ago. Nowadays she only works occasionally on sporadic projects in Munich and most of her clients come from Munich's high society. I took a look at her WhatsApp messages but didn't find anything that hints of a lover or stalker . . . or anyone else acting crazily.'

'You hacked Vanessa Grohnert's mobile?'

'One-two-three-four isn't exactly the best PIN.'

'Did you hack any of Clemens' devices?'

'The server at his construction company is well protected but he reads his work emails on his mobile so I didn't have to hack the system. His PIN was as ridiculous as his wife's,' explained Jon. 'Anyway, long story short, there was nothing to suggest why someone would want to kidnap Greta.'

'Then the only person left is the daughter herself.'

'Already looked. As you might expect with a fourteen-year-old, she was in more groups than I have hairs on my head. Each one full of the same trivial nonsense. And her Instagram wasn't any better.'

'Any problems in school? A dubious boyfriend perhaps?'

'School seems trouble-free. She goes to a humanist high school in the Ludwigsvorstadt borough. Doesn't have a boyfriend from what I can see. And her hobbies are ballet and astronomy. She goes to ballet every Friday. And other than that, she likes to post the photos she takes with her telescope on Instagram.'

'This is getting us nowhere,' said Nik with a groan. 'Never seen a case with so few leads before. Had it been a robbery, it wouldn't seem so suspicious; but not for a kidnapping without ransom.' He heard Jon typing in the background.

'That's strange,' mumbled Jon.

'What is?'

'I ran a search of newspaper articles and press portals and I've found a tabloid photo from 2016 showing police in front of the Grohnerts' house. They are carrying cardboard boxes. All it says is that public prosecution carried out a search.'

'Was he arrested?'

'There's nothing on his record to say he was. It doesn't even mention any house search,' replied Jon. 'And I can't find anything apart from that headline. Not a single article.'

'This might be our missing lead.'

'I'll look into it and be in touch as soon as I find anything.'

It was a bright and mild early autumn morning and the cloudless sky was reminiscent of the summer just past. Just right for a walk through Munich's English Garden. It was too early for the beer garden to be open yet, and Jon sighed regretfully. He was wearing black jogging bottoms, blue trainers and a white T-shirt that sat taut over his protruding belly. He had been too tired to shave and hadn't even bothered to comb his short, dyed-blonde hair. Sullenly, he rubbed his fingers over the stubble on his cheeks. 'Seven o'clock,' he said under his breath. 'Who the hell gets up at seven o'clock on a Sunday morning to go jogging?'

A woman running up the side of the park caught his attention and he turned to look at her. A pair of toned legs in tight running trousers strode comfortably, while her black crop top exposed her midriff. Her long blonde hair was tied up high in a ponytail and it was evident from her speed and technique that she was a frequent runner. With a grumble, Jon started to run after her.

'Good morning,' he said as he approached her, attempting to sound friendly. The woman he was running beside worked for the Munich public prosecution service.

'Jon.' She gave him a quick nod of recognition.

'Could we not have just met up for a nice chat in a cafe?'

'You are fully aware I should arrest you, aren't you?' she responded, glancing towards him while maintaining the same swift pace. 'There are people behind bars who have broken fewer laws than you managed to break last year alone.'

'That's true,' said Jon nonchalantly. 'But I'm sure all that anonymous evidence I sent you more than balances it up.'

'You *know* we would have got there ourselves.'

'C'mon. You don't really believe that,' said Jon. 'I delivered you a psychopathic serial killer on a silver platter. The media went wild praising you for your speedy investigating abilities. You even got a personal note of congratulations from the prime minister himself.' Jon wiped his brow with the back of his hand. 'And not to mention the raise that went along with your promotion . . . If you ask me, I think a case of champagne is more appropriate than a threat of arrest.'

'How do you know about my pay rise?'

'Oh, please,' Jon retorted, his ability to keep up with the woman now seriously flagging. 'So, before I have a heart attack, I'd actually like to get around to the real reason for our meeting.'

'You know, I actually considered just deleting your text.'

'Understandable. But the thing is, we're talking about a teenage girl here, and you know even better than I do that Greta's chances of getting out alive are getting slimmer with every passing hour. So really, you should be taking every ounce of help available to you . . . Even if it means turning a blind eye to a few unlawful actions.'

'And don't forget, the girl's well-being is the *only* factor at play here,' said the woman. 'Don't think you can bother me with every little speeding ticket from now on.'

'I have a fake number plate,' Jon said with a wry smile.

The woman looked at him snidely before upping her pace in retaliation. 'OK. Clemens Grohnert belonged to a consortium that was responsible for building a new bypass in the north of Munich. The new route opened in 2012 but it took until 2015 for all its connecting roads to be linked up. An enquiry found that unused materials were never accounted for. The planned construction involved the renovation of a train station. But then a lighting system with a budget of eight hundred thousand euros was never installed.'

'Hence the home search?'

The woman nodded.

'Apart from one headline, I couldn't find anything on Grohnert in the press. And he has a clean record.'

'We were trying out a new hush-up method. We needed someone from the inside.'

'You mean you made Grohnert a deal?'

'Look, I'm not going to go into the details, but charges were pressed in 2016 against the people responsible. We found a man called Ulrich Sasse to be the ringleader. A repugnant bastard of a criminal who we've run into on various occasions in recent years. But finally, with the help of Grohnert, we were able to catch him. He was sentenced to three years in prison at the end of 2016 and a few weeks after that, his construction empire completely disintegrated.'

'Plenty of grounds for revenge there then,' Jon commented.

'That's what you'd think. But Ulrich Sasse was found hanging in his cell six months into his sentence.'

'He killed himself?'

'Not according to his ex-wife, who'd been to see him in jail the day before. She was convinced Sasse was murdered. Which was why she sued Munich Prison Service. Unsuccessfully, I might add.'

'Who might have wanted to kill him?'

'Even Frau Sasse didn't know the answer to that one. According to an external inquiry, there was nothing to suggest he was suicidal. But if you ask me, it's certainly plausible he was depressed. I mean, look at the circumstances: before the conviction, he was part of Munich's high society, and afterwards, he had to sell his house in Starnberg and didn't have a penny to his name.'

'Shouldn't someone be questioning her about the case?'

'Eva Sasse is Argentinian,' explained the woman. 'After her husband's death, she went back home. Going by the rumours, the grieving didn't last long and she was married again two months later.'

Jon wiped the sweat from his forehead. 'What did the autopsy results say regarding suicide?'

'Nothing particularly remarkable. Ulrich Sasse hanged himself with his TV cable. Video footage of that night was checked three times and nothing indicated anyone else was involved.'

'Yeah, but that kind of thing can be covered up.'

'You should stop reading so much crime fiction,' she replied indignantly.

'So if Sasse didn't arrange the abduction, then who did?'

'Are you seriously asking me to tell you inside information pertaining to a current investigation?'

'Oh, come on. You know perfectly well if it doesn't come from you, I'll get it somewhere else,' said Jon. 'Why not spare me a bit of time.'

For a moment, the woman felt a surge of fury and squeezed her eyes tightly shut, but as suddenly as it had arrived, the anger dissipated, to be replaced with sorrow. She herself had a three-year-old son and the case was affecting her on a personal level. 'We're getting nowhere,' she finally admitted. 'No clues as to why Greta was abducted or where she might be. And nothing on the kidnapper either.' She paused for a moment. 'Maybe you'll come across something. Do whatever you can.'

'I promise I will,' replied Jon.

'So Grohnert snitches on his business partner so he can get off scot-free,' Nik concluded. He picked up the croissant from his plate and dunked it in his coffee. 'Good enough reason for someone to want revenge.'

'Yeah, but then our would-have-been main suspect dies in jail.' Jon's voice sounded over the loudspeaker.

'Yeah, and under pretty dubious circumstances too,' added Nik.

'Let's talk it through,' said Jon. 'Why would someone murder Ulrich Sasse?'

'Maybe he had secret information,' Nik speculated. 'Maybe he knew things about other people who were involved . . . things that would have got them chucked in jail.'

'Perhaps he worked closely with the public prosecution, saving him from a long prison sentence – and in doing so gave evidence against his partner.'

'Maybe he kept something to himself.'

'But there's no reason why he would then suddenly reveal it, is there? The case was closed and nobody else had been prosecuted.'

'OK, well, maybe Sasse's murder doesn't have anything to do with the case,' said Nik. 'I mean, you did say he wasn't a particularly respectable guy.'

'Yep. Along with all the fraud, he was also a notorious cheater, was caught doing coke twice by the tabloids and had loads of points on his licence. There's no doubt he would have definitely pissed off a fair few people in his lifetime.'

'Perhaps he'd had a fight with a fellow inmate.' Nik took a sip of coffee. 'But if that was the case, then his death wouldn't have anything to do with Greta's abduction. So maybe we should just stop trying to link Sasse's suicide with the case.'

'OK, but that still leaves Sasse's employees who lost their jobs because of the fraud. And not to forget the tradespeople who are still waiting for their money. It's also possible *they're* angry with Grohnert. I mean, they know he was in on it, even if he wasn't charged.'

'How many people are we talking here?'

'Hard to say,' said Jon. 'Around a hundred employees were left without work after Sasse went bankrupt. He ran numerous other subcontracted companies which got next to nothing during the insolvency proceedings. I know of three companies that flopped because of it.'

'And how do we make the connection to Greta's kidnapping?'

'Sasse maintained throughout the proceedings that Clemens Grohnert was the man behind the fraud.'

'And was he?'

'Hard to say, isn't it, since he bought himself out of jail,' said Jon. 'If Grohnert was the real scammer, then the kidnapper might really be a victim who's looking for justice.'

'Nobody simply mutates into a cold-blooded killer and child kidnapper because their business goes bust or they didn't get paid.' Nik looked at the wall. 'There has to be something else.'

'Maybe we don't need to worry about it anymore,' said Jon. 'Turn on the TV. Greta's kidnapper just made an announcement.'

The TV time slot was normally reserved for a Bavarian soap opera but the kidnapper's announcement was apparently more important. A female newsreader sat at a large desk. On the wall behind her was the image of a world map. She was reading from a sheet of paper.

'*Two days ago, fourteen-year-old Greta Grohnert was abducted from her parents' house. Despite every effort being made by a special committee set up by the police, there is still no trace of the girl. Today, however, the case has seen a significant development. We will now go to our correspondent at police headquarters, where a press conference will be beginning in just a few minutes.*'

The scene changed to a man in his forties with short black hair. He wore a white shirt and a grey jacket that had gone out of fashion years ago. His forehead was beaded with sweat and the microphone in his hand was shaking. It was obvious he hadn't had enough time to prepare. Reporters were running around frantically in the background, cameras were being brought into the room and police officers were checking IDs.

The man began to speak. '*Thirty minutes ago, the presumed kid-napper in the Greta Grohnert case sent a voice message that went out to all police departments, including the CID, as well as to all national and regional TV channels and newspapers. The message circulated so quickly on the internet that the police were obliged to call a press conference at short notice.*'

'*And is there any other new information on the Greta Grohnert case?*' The newsreader's voice sounded over the scene.

'*Until now, the only new element has been the voice message but perhaps the press conference will provide some new details.*'

The picture returned to the newsreader in the studio. '*According to our experts, the message is not a hoax and we are able to broadcast it to you now.*'

A photo of Greta Grohnert appeared on the screen and a sinister computer-generated voice began to speak.

'*Clemens Grohnert is a criminal. He got rich at the cost of others and broke laws. People lost their jobs and livelihood. They have been left with nothing, while Clemens Grohnert sits in his villa, planning his next holiday and laughing about his exemption from sentencing. This injustice can no longer be tolerated and I demand that a fund of three million euros is set up to provide for those affected by the building scandal. As well as that, I demand that Clemens Grohnert comes clean about his role in the hush-up and takes responsibility for the crimes he committed. If these demands are met, Greta Grohnert will be released unharmed.*'

The shot returned to the studio. '*I'd now like to welcome to the studio an expert on . . .*'

Nik turned down the volume on the TV and picked up his phone. 'Such a strange case,' he mumbled, deep in contemplation.

'So I was right with my initial suspicion then,' said Jon. 'It's all to do with the building scandal.'

'I don't believe it.'

'But the kidnapper has given the embezzlement as the reason for the kidnapping,' Jon said, confused. 'Doesn't get any clearer than that.' He paused for a moment. Nik could hear him typing in the background. 'Looks like the special commission is meeting up right now to discuss the case while everyone's waiting for the press conference to start. They've invited Unit 7 along.'

'What? This has got nothing to do with corporate crime.'

'You're confusing me, Nik. How many more clues do you need?'

Nik reached for his coffee. 'OK, let's say the kidnapper is a Robin Hood type who wants to lend a hand to the weak – in this case, the people harmed by the construction scandal. Let's say he's ready to do anything for justice. That kind of person would never shoot an innocent driver or kidnap an innocent child.'

'The Red Army Faction never had an issue with killing their victims' drivers.'

'Yeah, but they were all about the struggle against the system,' Nik said. 'This guy only talked about Grohnert; not about the construction mafia or anyone else involved. The kidnapper could have abducted Grohnert himself with all the effort he's gone to. Then he could at least get the money out of him by taking him hostage.' He took a sip of beer. 'Plus, that ransom demand doesn't make any sense. How is it supposed to work with the funds? Who gets the money? How much are the pay-outs? And three million euros? Come on! That's not enough! Even if we presume a comfortable yearly salary of fifty thousand euros, that would only just be enough to reimburse sixty people for twelve months' work.'

'And what about the demand for Grohnert to come clean on his part?'

'Just another distraction . . . like the funds.'

'All right. I'll play along,' said Jon. 'If this is all a load of crap, then why is the kidnapper taking such a risk by making the demand? If he sent the message by email, it could be traced. CDs or USBs have to be sent by post and can have fingerprints or other clues on them.'

'The kidnapper is trying to distract the CID and the public,' explained Nik. 'By focusing on Grohnert, all eyes are on him and the construction scandal. It means all the other traces become insignificant. If the abduction is indeed for another reason, this was the perfect diversion.'

'Diversion from what?' asked Jon. 'Other than the scandal, we've got nothing that would justify an abduction with murder.'

'I can't answer that. But I'm sticking to my theory,' replied Nik. 'I need to find out more about the Grohnerts. And by that, I mean information that not everybody knows or that can be found in the tabloids.'

'They'll be better protected than Fort Knox. We won't get to them.'

'OK.' Nik had another sip. 'Well, Clemens Grohnert isn't going to tell me any more than he's been telling the police. Does the family know anyone in Munich's high society?'

'They're always at the larger events. What d'you need?'

'An old friend or business partner. No flashy It girl, but somebody Grohnert knows well. Greta wasn't kidnapped because of the construction scandal and I want to know what the kidnapper's planning.'

'Today's your lucky day then,' said Jon. 'There's this swanky event on tonight. Lots of big names will be there and I was thinking earlier how it would be a good idea for you to get in with that kind of crowd. It cost me a lot of money and effort to get two tickets, you know.'

'Why two?'

Just then, there was a knock at Nik's door. 'Oh, Ni-i-i-k!' Balthasar's cheerful voice rang through from the other side of his front door. 'Slop yourself into those ugly boots and that rancid leather jacket of yours. It's makeover time!'

Nik groaned. 'You're joking. I'll get you back for this one day, you know that, don't you?' He stood up and shuffled to the door. With a long sigh, he reluctantly let the pathologist into the flat.

Chapter 2

Nik looked at the blonde streaks in his otherwise dark hair. He wished he was working a case from Munich's underworld, where he could stick on his boots and nobody would give a damn if he had three-day-old stubble. But instead, here he was, being sent to wine and dine among Munich's most exalted circles, after having a mandatory haircut from Balthasar's friend, Charles, whose real name was Bernd Hackel. Charles came from a small village in Lower Bavaria and had moved to Munich after completing his apprenticeship. The man loved sweet perfumes and eccentric clothing, had eyelashes most women would kill for, and his teeth were so white, it was as though he'd taken a Tipp-Ex pen to them. Nik wasn't fussed about Charles's somewhat unconventional appearance. What he couldn't stand, however, were his constant comments on Nik's lack of hair care, paired with the endless tips on how to give the best manicure. The incessant jabbering had almost driven Nik to the edge of insanity.

And as if the makeover hadn't been humiliating enough, he now had to accompany Balthasar to a reception being held by some rich art enthusiast in honour of Oktoberfest. Since this particular host had no desire to mix with the usual Oktoberfest riff-raff, he had decided to rent out a large hall near to the Sendling Gate, where, in order to make the place feel more like a tent, large canvas sheets had been hung from the ceilings. But there the similarities ended. All the benches and tables were of the best quality, cushions had been strewn across the benches for extra comfort, and an orchestra from the Bavarian Oberland played soft music. Instead of chicken, there was duck with baked-apple risotto that had been cooked by a Michelin-star chef, and the beer was from the host's private brewery. In one corner of the room was an expansive table overflowing with lavish starters. Catering staff hovered over the food, and as soon as a dish started to run out, they would mutter solemnly into a microphone on their lapel. Two seconds later, a man dressed in a white chef's jacket would appear and replace any almost-empty plates. Dotted around the room were attractive women in matching dirndls, each one eager to show guests to a free seat, direct them to the toilet or take a drinks order.

All in all, the evening actually had the potential to be very pleasant – if Nik had been able to choose his own outfit, that was. Even a tailored suit would have been better than his traditional Bavarian get-up, which included short lederhosen, a plaid linen shirt, knee-high white socks and uncomfortable Haferl shoes.

And of course, Balthasar wouldn't have been Balthasar if he hadn't enriched his own outfit with an individual touch. He wore an elaborately embroidered waistcoat with a pocket handkerchief, ankle socks with traditional leg warmers around his calves, and finally, a green hat with a yellow feather instead of the usual Gamsbart.

'It doesn't get better than this, eh?' Balthasar called out to Nik, raising his Mass glass. The pathologist was certainly doing his best to immerse himself in the Oktoberfest spirit. In the half hour since their arrival, he had managed to pack away two portions of duck and rice, two servings of Bavarian cream dessert, and had washed each one down with a Mass of beer. Nik was in no doubt as to why his stomach was the size it was.

'We're here to find out more about Clemens Grohnert. Not to stuff our guts until they burst,' said Nik sternly under his breath.

Balthasar grinned contentedly at Nik and took another gulp of beer. His cheeks were bright red.

'A girl has been *kidnapped*,' Nik whispered furiously in his ear.

'Let me make something clear to you, old Nikky-Boy,' replied Balthasar, his smile not budging from his lips. 'This is the Oktoberfest of the media-shy. Those people, that is, who do *not* want to be featured in the evening paper and do *not* want their photos to be splattered across *OK!* magazine. Loads of these people are utterly paranoid individuals and if they cotton on to our little investigation, we'll be chucked out quicker than you can say Oktoberfest.'

'Oh, come on. Stop exaggerating.'

'I most definitely am not exaggerating. Did you not notice that the invitation came with the request to not bring mobile phones? And do you see a single person in this hall using a mobile?'

Nik took a look around at the guests. 'No, but—'

'No. Because every guest knows exactly how serious the host was when he wrote that. You know, there are some *big* industrial magnates here tonight – very media-shy industrial magnates – who haven't had their photo taken in over ten years.'

'OK. But it doesn't mean you have to act like a blithering Bavarian fool, does it?'

'You see the man over there with the broad shoulders? Black lederhosen? Grey hat? Sitting at the end of table four?'

Nik looked at the man. 'Yeah, fit-looking guy. What about him?'

'That's a security guard,' explained Balthasar. 'There are four of them walking around here, monitoring the crowd. And if they suspect anyone of being a journalist, the party is more than over for them.' The pathologist sipped his beer. 'So what are they going to think about an ex-CID officer who wants to question guests?' Nik remained silent. 'Exactly,' Balthasar continued. 'So we are going to play along and have fun until every guest is so drunk they can't even stand up. So for God's sake, get that beer down you and stop being so fucking serious, because with that cat-arse face, you're sticking out more than a Prussian general on parade.'

Nik grudgingly lifted the beer and placed the glass on his lips.

'And cheers to the handsome couple over there!' Balthasar called out to an elderly couple, raising his glass. The couple laughed and raised their glasses back to him.

'So who is it we're meeting?' asked Nik, after draining the Mass in one.

'Our main target is Herr Julian Nooten. A kind of éminence grise in the construction industry. Doesn't have his own company, but he does hold a whole load of shares in other firms. He has an extensive network of important connections and would have earned a fair whack with the bypass, and probably with every other building project in the region.'

'Was he also charged?'

Balthasar laughed heartily. 'God no. Nooten's far too clever for that. He's never *responsible* for any of the projects . . . He just rakes in the profits made by the construction companies. He leaves the dirty work to small-timers like Grohnert.' The pathologist set down his beer and picked up another glass of Bavarian cream. 'If the rumours are true, Nooten employed a group of snoops to delve into the life of each one of his business partners until they found something unsavoury. If there's anyone who knows Grohnert's secrets, it's him.'

'And how do you know him?'

'I don't,' replied Balthasar. 'But we're going to ask him if he'll help us.'

'Are you taking the piss?' said Nik. 'You think a big shot like Nooten's going to happily tell us all Grohnert's secrets?'

'Happily . . . no.'

'What, so you brought a gun and you're going to use it to get him to speak?'

'Oh no. Violence is a technique resorted to by people like yourself,' replied Balthasar with a side-long glance. 'My methods are more subtle.'

'Oh, please do enlighten me, wise master.'

'I'm going to get under his staunch Catholic skin. His parents disinherited his brother eight years ago because he got divorced.' Balthasar scraped the dessert glass clean with his spoon and placed it on the table. 'The Nooten family donates more money to the Archdiocese of Augsburg than the Bavarian Church collects in tax.'

'And how's that going to help us?'

'You'll find out later.' Balthasar gave his outfit the once-over and pulled up his leg warmers. 'Try not to hit or shoot anyone in the next five minutes, would you? I need to do a bit of networking and have a look for our man.' He beamed a smile at Nik and walked over to a couple, who greeted him warmly. Seconds later, they were all immersed in conversation. Minute by minute, more and more guests approached Balthasar until he was surrounded by a cluster of giggling guests. Making use of his booming voice and taking advantage of the convivial atmosphere, the pathologist managed to keep his audience profoundly entertained.

'How the hell does he do that?' Nik asked himself, shaking his head. Just then, he noticed a familiar face. The man was wearing an expensive traditional Tracht, a hat with a magnificent Gamsbart, black patent shoes, and socks that went up to the middle of his calves. His face was a strange mixture of orange and brown, and his gold Rolex sparkled in the light.

'Good evening, Herr Naumann,' Nik said, approaching him from behind. The man jerked with shock and turned around from the dessert buffet.

'Good evening, Nik . . . Herr Pohl,' answered Naumann, clearly surprised. He quickly put the glass of Bavarian cream back down on the table, like a child who had just been caught stealing.

'Not here with your wife then?'

'She's um . . . a bit under the weather.'

'Really?' said Nik, feigning surprise. 'I heard she arrived just after you finished flirting with that nice busty commissioner who's worked in your department for two years now.' Nik looked blatantly towards the man's bare wedding ring finger.

'What are you doing here?' asked Naumann, changing the subject. 'Wouldn't expect to see you socialising with such an elite bunch.'

'I'm not staying long,' Nik replied. 'Just need to speak to a couple of people.'

'Word is you're a private investigator now?'

'Ah, that's the word, is it?'

'It is. And that you're getting mixed up in cases that are the CID's responsibility.'

'Only in cases where help is needed. Like the one with the kidnapped girl where the police haven't found a single trace.'

'And that's exactly why we've formed one of the biggest special commissions there's been in years,' said Naumann defensively. 'And why I've got the best men from Unit 11 on the job too.' He moved closer to Nik. 'If you know *anything* . . . you tell us, you hear me? I'm sure I don't need to remind you of what happens if you interfere in ongoing investigations, do I?'

Nik laughed. 'You don't really think that's going to scare me off, do you?'

Nik noticed Balthasar had said his goodbyes to the group and was beckoning him over.

'Oh! Please excuse me. Must be off,' he said, patting his ex-boss cordially on the shoulder.

He made his way over to Balthasar. 'Did you find our man?'

The pathologist nodded. 'Time to wash our hands.' He tipped his head in the direction of the toilets.

'But my hands aren't dirt—'

'My God, just be quiet and follow me.'

The music was much quieter in the toilets and the rumble of the party-goers was barely audible. The entrance area consisted of six washbasins, each with chrome taps and an exquisite mirror on the wall above it. Cheap paper towels had been replaced by plush, mini hand towels that sat in piles on a shelf. Nik squeezed soap out of a white dispenser and noticed the scent of lilac. At the basin beside him, a man of about fifty was also washing his hands. He had a full head of white hair and was tanned, as if he'd spent a lot of time on holiday that summer. In spite of the Tracht, he still exuded a certain aura of authority. Balthasar moved to the sink on the other side of the man and turned on the tap.

'Good evening, Herr Nooten,' Balthasar began in a friendly manner, running his hands under the water. 'Wonderful party, don't you think?'

The man turned his head to look at Balthasar. 'I'm very sorry, but do I know you?'

'Actually no, we've never had the pleasure, but I'm a friend of Florian Knape.'

Nooten stopped moving instantly. For a moment he looked insecure but his demeanour quickly turned serious again. 'And you are?' he asked, drying his hands. 'Let me guess . . . a bloody dirty reporter maggot? What d'you want . . . money? A job?'

'Just some information on Clemens Grohnert,' answered Balthasar.

'I don't know who that is.'

'Please, Herr Nooten. You are offending my intelligence.' Balthasar turned off the tap and nodded towards Nik. 'If you would just answer my friend here's questions about the man, you'll never see or hear from me again.'

Nooten moved up close to Balthasar and looked him in the eyes. The pathologist returned the look calmly, drying his hands.

'You must be absolutely insane to antagonise me,' said Nooten.

'I think the word is "venturesome",' said Balthasar. 'I know a lot about you, Herr Nooten. About your wealth, your power, your little troop of dirt collectors . . . all the way back to your time at that Catholic boarding school.' Balthasar paused. 'I can tell from your face you're wondering if I'm bluffing . . . or if I might pose a threat.' Balthasar shrugged. 'Well, we don't actually care in the slightest about you. It's Clemens Grohnert we want. And if you tell us one or two secrets about him, we'll be out of your hair in no time.'

Balthasar threw the hand towel in a basket. The businessman looked him up and down with no emotion, as if trying to uncover his weakness.

'You've got five minutes,' Nooten said finally. 'And after that I'd better not run into you *ever again*.'

Balthasar nodded. 'And that's how it will be.' He turned to Nik. 'I'll be waiting at the buffet. Good luck.'

◆ ◆ ◆

There was an emergency exit beside the toilet. It had been covered by a large flag of the Free State of Bavaria but it was no surprise to Nik that Nooten knew about it. He didn't seem like the kind of man who ever left anything to chance.

'What do you want with Clemens Grohnert?' began Nooten.

'I'm only interested in the well-being of his daughter, Greta.'

'And you're blaming me for that?'

'If we go along with what the kidnapper is saying . . .'

'That's all bullshit,' said Nooten. 'The construction industry is rife with embezzlement and unlawful goings-on. Happens all the time. On the one hand, people lose their job, but on the other, it just means new companies have to open up. If every frustrated builder kidnapped a kid, the place would be like Sodom during the fires.'

'An abduction is always personal so it has to have *something* to do with Clemens. According to the court reports, Grohnert was only one of many involved in the scam.'

'He was at the head of it all,' said Nooten. 'He was smarter than the others – in particular, smarter than that dipshit, Ulrich Sasse.'

'So Sasse was the scapegoat?'

'He certainly wasn't innocent, but no guiltier than any of the others. He was just more foolish because he trusted Grohnert.' He shrugged his shoulders. 'Even the hardest of men turn soft when faced with the threat of a sentence from the public prosecutor.'

'Is it possible Grohnert arranged Sasse's murder?'

'Grohnert doesn't play in that kind of league. Yeah, he might be talented when it comes to slipping money past the tax office or faking a bill, but getting a man murdered in prison? That requires a professional. And Grohnert doesn't have those kinds of connections.'

'But you do?'

The question made Nooten laugh sincerely. 'There was no reason to have Sasse murdered . . . not for me or for Grohnert.'

'And what about the demand for Grohnert to come clean about his role in the scandal?'

'Yeah, of course he deceived people and embezzled money. But I can give you the name of ten other construction giants who've done much worse. And their kids were never abducted.'

'So what *is* the motive for Greta's kidnapping then?'

'Listen, Clemens Grohnert doesn't exactly come across as a nice guy, but I don't know of any dark business secret that would justify abducting his daughter. Either the kidnapper has some personal conflict with Grohnert or the abduction has nothing to do with him.'

◆ ◆ ◆

After letting Nik move into his flat, Jon had got used to life in his loft apartment. It was initially only supposed to be an office, with plenty of room for his PCs and Cray supercomputer. But during their last investigation, he'd had to destroy the whole place to get rid of every last clue, so a renovation had been on the cards anyway. He'd spent days laying laminate on the cold concrete floors and painting the walls white. He'd finally attached any loose wires to the walls and bought some lampshades. And now, instead of an old mattress on the floor, he had a box-spring bed, while the kitchen consisted of more than just a microwave. The four electric heaters that he'd attached to the wall kept the place warm, even in the winter.

The one thing he did have to rebuild was a metal cage to house all of his computers and the two monitors he used to keep an eye on the area surrounding the loft and the front door. On top of the Cray sat two canisters full of an aluminium-based fire accelerant that would burn through the computer like acid if Jon was ever to pull the release mechanism.

He'd bought the flat above a bogus company and all his post was delivered to a PO box. He only ever left the loft in the evening, when all the workers from the industrial area had gone home. Other than Nik and Balthasar, nobody knew of the hiding place.

Jon stared at a computer screen, deep in concentration. He was analysing the voice recording from the kidnapper. After meticulously inspecting the waves one by one, he came to the same conclusion as the CID: it was a computer-generated voice. The internet was full of free voice-generators these days which converted text to speech. As a result, it would be impossible to get any clues from the voice on the message. The fact it had been generated also meant he couldn't isolate any background noises. The file had been thoroughly wiped of all metadata, making it impossible to see when the recording had been made or to find any clues about the user's personal information. And to top it all off, the demand had been sent from a disposable email account, on a public Wi-Fi connection, via a popular anonymisation service.

Jon exhaled loudly. Getting rid of electronic traces was a laborious act. It indicated good planning, which in turn proved Greta's kidnapping was not just some spontaneous crime. And even if the free online programs these days could be used by beginners, at least one person involved had to be reasonably IT savvy, suggesting the perpetrators were not just some mob of violent, idiotic criminals.

Jon clicked through the allocated case files on the CID system but it had been hours since any new findings had been entered. He could only hope that Nik and Balthasar were having more luck.

◆　◆　◆

'How did it go?' Balthasar asked Nik as they made their way outside.

'Nooten was cooperative,' answered Nik. 'Your remark about Florian Knape clearly shook him. Who is he? A contract killer?'

'A rent boy,' replied Balthasar. 'One of the best.'

Nik whistled in amazement. 'Now I understand why you were going on about the staunch Catholic parents. But I have to admit, I wouldn't have expected one gay guy to threaten another with a forced outing.'

'I know. It really wasn't my proudest moment,' said Balthasar, sighing. 'But an innocent child is at risk here and that's more important.' He turned to look at Nik. 'And I wouldn't have outed him anyway. It was just a threat.'

'And how d'you know about Nooten's liaison? He must do absolutely everything in his power to protect his private life.'

'It was actually a shot in the dark. Florian Knape is booked because of his discretion but Munich is a village and everyone knows everyone in the gay scene.' Balthasar went to the edge of the pavement and waved for a taxi. 'As I'm sure you're well aware, alcohol relaxes the tongue and Knape was feeling quite chatty last New Year's Eve. Even if he never mentioned Nooten's name, a lot of what he said suggested they'd had contact.' Balthasar shrugged. 'In all honesty, I feel sorry for the guy. He's going to have to wear a façade for the rest of his life and suppress his sexuality, because if he doesn't, his whole world will shatter into tiny pieces. His family would ostracise him, his wife would leave him and his social circles would avoid him. The tabloids would wallow in his suffering and bring out a new scandal every day. And according to his faith, it would all be in the name of salvation.' Balthasar closed his eyes. 'We're living in the twenty-first century but sometimes it still feels like the Middle Ages. Do you know how many unhappy people I've known who were destroyed because they couldn't reveal their sexual orientation? There always comes a point when they can't take it any longer so they go to a rent boy . . . only to feel even worse afterwards. It's not easy,' he concluded pensively. 'Let's just hope your conversation got us closer to getting Greta released. Then I can sleep with a slightly clearer conscience.'

'Unfortunately, I wouldn't say it got us much closer. Nooten just confirmed what I already thought: Clemens Grohnert might have been the main man behind the fraud but it's all too thin for someone to commit abduction with murder.'

'So what does that mean for the investigation?'

'Jon is still working his way through the case records from the scandal. But I'm slowly beginning to disregard Grohnert as the reason for the kidnapping,' Nik answered. 'I'll look into the shot driver tomorrow. Maybe he wasn't the innocent victim we've been thinking he was.'

◆ ◆ ◆

Vanessa Grohnert stood in front of a large window wearing a thin nightdress and holding a blanket around her shoulders, while her other hand clasped a small, tattered teddy bear to her chest. She stood looking at the driveway, which was illuminated in mellow moonlight, as if waiting for someone to arrive.

'Don't you want to come to bed?' came her husband's voice. 'It's three o'clock.'

The woman shook her head lightly.

'I miss Greta too, you know,' said Clemens quietly. 'And I'm doing everything I can to get her back.'

'Why did you have to be so bloody greedy?' she asked spitefully, without raising her voice.

'This has nothing to do with greed,' replied Grohnert. 'If we want to be able to afford the life we have, then we need the money that comes from jobs like that.'

'I'd be fine living in a smaller house . . . or driving a normal car or not always flying first class. But what I can't live without is my daughter!'

'I'm sorry, Vanessa,' said Clemens remorsefully. 'I'm already borrowing against all the securities . . . I've sold all our equity. I've closed the Swiss account. There's nothing else I can do.' He moved behind her.

Vanessa stroked the bear's head. 'Do you think we need to come clean about Greta?' she asked.

'No,' he said, reaching for her arm. 'Then we will definitely lose her, even if the kidnapper does let her go.'

'You're just afraid of going to jail.' She snatched her arm out of his grasp. 'Away from all the luxury . . . all your important friends.'

'That's not true,' he replied. 'We both swore we would never tell. And that was the right decision. It's got nothing to do with the kidnapping.'

She closed her eyes and held the bear tight to her chest. 'I pray to God you're right.'

◆　◆　◆

Setting off that morning, Nik thought about how good it felt to have a modern car and all the mod cons that came with it: the drinks holder with its warming function, the automatic gearbox, which made it easier to deal with the city traffic, and the hands-free system, meaning he didn't have to hold his phone to his ear. And as if all that wasn't enough, he didn't even have to cover the lease payments or petrol costs.

'So, the driver was thirty-three-year-old Milan Urbaniak,' Jon began. His voice was perfectly clear over the car speakers. 'He was officially unemployed but earned extra cash as a chauffeur. He was covering that day for the family's regular driver, Georg Moosen, who's had his own chauffeur company for four years. Moosen doesn't have any employees but his friends sometimes give him a hand. The Grohnerts were one of Moosen's first clients. He used to drive Greta to her extracurricular activities and sometimes took the parents to cultural events.'

'So why was Moosen not driving that day?'

'According to the Grohnerts, he was in bed with the flu. He'd texted the parents that morning to say Urbaniak would cover for him.'

'And what's Moosen had to say about everything?'

'The CID haven't been able to reach him. He isn't at home and isn't picking up his mobile.'

'And nobody finds that a bit odd?'

'The kidnapping only happened three days ago and Moosen isn't the main suspect, since he doesn't match the description of the perpetrator. There's still a search out for him but since the ransom demand, the special commission has been concentrating on other things.'

'And what have we got on the replacement driver?'

'Milan Urbaniak came from Kosovo but had been in Munich since 1998. He lived in a small second-floor flat in Caracciolastraße. He was single and didn't have any relatives in Germany.'

'What about his record?'

'Had a suspended sentence for bodily harm in 2001,' said Jon. 'Some fight at a wedding which got out of hand. He and nine other guests were arrested. But nothing since then.'

'Any cross references to the Grohnerts?'

'No, but Urbaniak never used social media so I can't be sure.'

'Did the CID find anything in his flat?'

'Just a Heckler & Koch SFP9 with ammunition.'

'OK, well, that changes things slightly.'

'Does it?' asked Jon. 'To be honest, a guy on the dole who gets paid cash in hand and has a gun in the house doesn't really surprise me these days. And according to the CID database, the gun isn't linked to any crimes. So it seems pointless using it as a lead.'

'Anything else?'

'They didn't find a computer. Just a large collection of porno DVDs, a cupboard full of clothes, eight pairs of shoes, some books and a middle-of-the-road sound system. Oh, and a reasonable forty-inch flat screen and a battered old leather couch.'

'I'm gonna take a closer look.'

'What are you hoping to find?'

'I want to get a better idea of Urbaniak's life. Nowhere better to do that than his own home.'

'Your ex-colleagues already took the place to bits. You won't find anything new.'

'Maybe they missed something.'

'Pretty wishful thinking.'

Nik turned off the main road into a side street and parked his car in a free spot. 'I'll call you later.' He hung up and got out of the car before making his way through the drizzling rain towards Urbaniak's flat. The building was three stories high and the white façade had been painted recently. The areas of grass between the house and the path were tidy and well kept, while geraniums hung down from the balcony nearest the path. It wasn't Munich's nicest neighbourhood but the rent would have still been too high for someone on long-term unemployment benefit.

A man in a tatty boiler suit was kneeling at the entrance screwing something on to the door panel. His face was red and he was scrunching his eyes up as if he was having trouble focusing on the screws. His sparse dark hair was sweaty, and going by the body odour that was emanating from him, he had opted not to shower that morning.

'Good morning,' said Nik.

The man turned around quickly to look at Nik. 'Can't you see I'm working?' he said, his face turning from its unhealthy pink tone into a deep, angry red.

'Munich CID,' said Nik, showing the man his fake ID. 'I need to have another look inside Milan Urbaniak's flat.'

'What is it now?' blared the man. 'You were there all day yesterday making a total mess.' Unfortunately, the man's oral hygiene was as lacking as his general cleanliness. Nik took a step back.

'I need to check some details.'

'Can't it wait until tomorrow? I'm busy.'

'Afraid not.' Nik's smile was becoming stiff. He clenched his fist and forced himself to stay calm.

The man slammed down his screwdriver into the toolbox and stood up, swearing. He pulled a bunch of keys out of his pocket – there must have been around twenty sets – and led Nik up to the second floor. Urbaniak's front door had been blocked and sealed with tape but the man put the key in the lock regardless, turned it twice and kicked the door open. 'Pull the door shut when you're done, would you?' he said, stuffing the keys back into his pocket.

Nik peered into the flat. The hall was empty and the walls were dotted with holes and marks – tell-tale signs that a cupboard had once been standing there. The floor was covered in dust and bits of plaster. There was one room at the end of the hall and one to the right of the front door. Both were completely empty.

'Excuse me!' Nik called to the man from the front door. 'Could you come back here for a second, please?'

'My God! What is it now?' asked the man, raising his hands and plodding to the flat. 'You want me to fetch you a coffee or something?'

Nik signalled behind him with his thumb. 'Can you tell me why the place is empty?'

'How the hell should I know? I'm just the caretaker. Ask the owner.'

'You must have seen something?'

'Fuck off! You think I look after the one building or something? I've got better things to do than talk—'

Nik grabbed the man by the upper arm and pushed him inside the flat. He took the barrier tape down with him as he fell to the floor.

'Piece of shit!' said the man as he started to get up. But before he could, Nik had his knee pressed firmly into his back and was twisting his arm behind him.

'Listen, arsehole. This is still a crime scene under investigation, which means nobody apart from the police are allowed on the premises. Even the thickest removal guys know it's grounds for arrest to enter a crime scene. Two minutes ago, that tape wasn't broken so someone must have made the effort to carefully remove it, clear out the flat and stick it back on. And there weren't any signs of forced entry, which means the removal guys must have had a key.'

'Let me go!' cried the man.

'We'll start with a simple question: when was the flat emptied?'

'Yesterday evening!'

'By who?'

'No idea!'

Nik pulled tighter on the man's arm. 'Stop bullshitting me.'

'I didn't know the guy. He was here yesterday. Gave me five hundred euros to open Urbaniak's door and look the other way.'

'What did he look like?'

'Tall. 'Bout six foot. Muscular. Dark complexion. Dark hair. Southern European maybe. Wearing a black suit.'

'And he cleaned out the flat all on his own . . . in a suit?'

'There was a lorry parked outside the flat. Four men were waiting inside. As soon as the door was open, they put on gloves and started moving everything out.'

'Did you get the number plate?'

'Of course not! Five hundred euros? Tax free? D'you have any idea how long I'd have to work to earn that? Urbaniak's dead and didn't have any relatives. The flat would've been cleared anyway.'

Nik let go of the caretaker and stood up. He ripped the rest of the tape off the door and fled downstairs, taking out his phone to call Jon.

'The flat's been cleared,' Nik said as soon as Jon picked up.

'Even though it was all taped up?' Jon asked, confused. 'Why would someone want to empty the flat?'

'To get rid of traces.'

'What traces? The CID pulled the place apart and found nothing apart from the gun. There was nothing connected to the kidnapping.'

'I've got no idea. But it just goes to confirm my suspicion that Clemens Grohnert's involvement in the construction scandal was just a diversion.'

'So what now?'

'I'll look into the family's regular chauffeur. The girl gets kidnapped and the driver gets shot on *precisely* the day Moosen's lying ill in bed. That's no coincidence.'

'You think Moosen's behind it?'

'His behaviour's pretty strange, to say the least,' Nik remarked. 'He drives Greta to ballet for years and then on the one day he's not there, she's abducted and he falls off the face of the earth . . . ? Even if the CID haven't got to him, the case is splattered across every newspaper and on all the news channels. There's no way he doesn't know what's happened. So that just leaves the option that he doesn't want to be found.' Nik got into the car and started the engine. 'Send his address to my mobile. It's time to pay him a visit.'

◆ ◆ ◆

While Nik was driving to Moosen's flat, Jon turned on a local TV channel. The regular programme was interrupted by a special broadcast. A news reporter, a court reporter and a former CID agent were all sitting around a table discussing Greta's kidnapping. In the background was a picture of Clemens and Vanessa Grohnert. They were sitting on a couch beside a white fireplace, upon which sat a small silver vase filled with dark red roses. The mother's suffering lay heavy underneath her make-up. She was holding a photo of Greta at the beach, enclosed in a picture frame that was covered in shells. The girl's face was tanned, her hair was pulled back and she had a pair of sunglasses on her head. On that warm beach, beaming into the camera, it was clear the girl was in her element. Vanessa clung to the picture as if it was her daughter herself.

Jon closed his eyes and sighed. He couldn't imagine what hell the parents were going through.

As the discussion came to an end, the presenter introduced a video. It showed Greta as a child, maybe eight years old, romping around on the autumn grass. She was wearing an anorak and wellington boots. Her brown hair was up in a ponytail and one loose curl fell over her ear and down to her shoulder. She was running around a tree with other children, collecting conkers, which she then put into a small basket. She was so excited and her laugh was so pure, it tore at Jon's heart. He picked up the remote control and turned off the TV, drying a tear.

Nik would be at Moosen's flat soon. Hopefully he'd find something on Greta and they could bring this nightmare to an end.

It was still early in the morning. The sun was low and children were yet to filter into the park. The only child on the bike track was a young girl, riding her scooter in circles, while her mother watched her from the side. The girl was wearing a glittery yellow helmet and a cosy red anorak. The back of the jacket was splattered with mud.

Clemens Grohnert was also watching the girl, leaning on a tree with his hands in his coat pockets. He and Greta had spent almost every summer weekend at the track. He could never pull the tiny green bike out of the car boot fast enough for her. It would barely touch the ground before she was jumping on to it and racing away. She would cycle around and around the track, her eyes sparkling with excitement, engrossed in her own world. Only when she got thirsty would she cycle back over to where he waited, holding her Gruffalo flask. She'd gulp her juice, pass back the flask and cycle off again without saying a word.

While she cycled, he would sit underneath a large oak at the top of a little hill. From there, you could look out over the entire park. He usually had his phone in his hand, either to read the news or answer emails. He hadn't watched his daughter nearly as much as he should have; hadn't spent nearly enough time with her. And now that she was gone, he felt a gap in his life and saw all too well the mistakes he'd made.

His work provided no relief from the situation and he could no longer stand the looks of pity everywhere he went; the whispers from behind him as soon as he turned his back, and the way everyone was constantly asking if there had been any news. Since Greta had been kidnapped, he had realised how empty his life had become over the years; how meaningless his success and how worthless his money. He wished more than anything to come back to the park and watch his daughter cycling around the track; to forget about the world around them. He would have given up everything for that. But it wasn't in his hands. Clemens closed his eyes and thought back to the time when he had no worries. He thought about Greta's beautiful face and her curly hair, which would bulge out from under her green helmet. And as the tears streamed down his cheeks, he smiled.

◆　◆　◆

Nik considered pushing every buzzer in the hope that a careless resident would let him in. But there weren't enough flats in the block for that to be a plausible option. And his trick with the CID badge wouldn't work here without a legitimate search warrant.

From the outside, Moosen's flat seemed inconspicuous. There was a balcony with a plastic chair, a small table and a folded clothes horse. The blinds on the window looking out to the balcony had been rolled halfway down. Nik couldn't see any movement or light inside that could indicate whether Moosen was at home. If Nik's latest suspect in the kidnapping really had been involved, it would have been unimaginably stupid to hang around. As such, Nik came to the conclusion he wasn't going to bump into him.

Moosen's red Ford Escort was parked twenty metres away in a residents' parking space. Nik had walked around the car three times before putting his ear to the boot. He hadn't heard a thing. The car bonnet was cool, which indicated the Ford hadn't been driven that day. Nik's urge to break into the car was strong, but he knew that if Moosen was indeed the wanted man, he couldn't risk destroying any traces and managed to resist.

It was just after 11 a.m. and Nik was back in his car. He kept tapping nervously on the steering wheel and checking his phone. If he decided to tell his ex-colleagues in the CID about Urbaniak's empty flat, it wouldn't be long until they also stepped up the search for Moosen. A team of investigators would be at his flat in five minutes, only to pull it apart. The press would soon catch on, and not long after, Moosen would find out they were on to him. Nik didn't want to give him this advantage.

But then, maybe staying silent about it was wrong. Maybe it would hinder the investigation. It wasn't as if they were dealing with a murder case where the victim was already dead; Greta was hopefully still alive and her chances were getting worse with every passing hour.

Nik's quandary was interrupted by the arrival of a yellow delivery van. An hour ago, Nik had arranged for a greetings card to be sent by express delivery to the flat. He hoped that maybe the delivery person would have more chance of getting inside the building. Nik followed the man and waited behind a bush until he'd pressed the buzzer. Not long after, the door buzzed open and Nik slipped through before it closed. He waited beside the narrow lift until the man arrived downstairs again and left. He then took the stairs up to Moosen's flat and put his ear against the door. He closed his eyes and listened for around five seconds. Nothing. No radio. No TV. Nik put on his gloves and took out his picklock. Apparently, high-quality locks were not a top priority for the property management and Nik was inside within a matter of minutes.

He closed the door gently behind him and listened for any noises, but there was nothing to suggest anyone else was in the property. No steps, no snoring, no running water. In the entrance area was a small, scratched-up old cupboard. There were worn-out trainers and a crate of empty weissbier bottles on the floor, and a jacket hanging on a hook on the wall. The air inside the flat was stale, as if the windows hadn't been open in a good while.

Across from the front door was a small bathroom with a bathtub and a stained shower curtain. The toilet seat was up and some faded pyjamas had been thrown over the washing basket. The bedroom was just as untidy as the rest of the flat. The sheets were covered in stains, pillowcases that had once been white were yellow with sweat, and dirty clothes were strewn across the floor. Nik turned right into the kitchen and living-room area. There was a small kitchenette in the corner of the room containing a stove with two hot plates, a filthy oven and a microwave. The microwave door was covered in a white cloudy layer, as if a milk carton had exploded inside. Hanging on the fridge, Nik found a list of people's names. Beside their names was a phone number and their hours of availability. It looked like a list of people who worked for him but there was no mention of Milan Urbaniak. A denim jacket hung over the armrest of a worn-out, fake leather couch, in front of which were dirty grey socks and a pair of slippers. The coffee table was covered in crisps and there was an empty beer bottle lying on its side on the floor. Half the bottle's contents had apparently dripped out, leaving a dark, sticky patch beside it. It must have been at least two days since Moosen was last in the flat.

Nik touched the TV and the hi-fi. Both were cold. And the sink in the kitchen was dry. A suitcase stood in the corner of the bedroom and the cupboard was full of clothes. There was nothing to hint at a trip or a hasty departure. After an hour, Nik had finished his search and hadn't found anything to suggest Moosen was involved in the abduction. But why then had he called in sick on Friday and got someone to cover his shift? Had Moosen known about the planned kidnapping and therefore disappeared out of fear?

Nik looked at a bunch of keys hanging on a rack on the wall. There was what looked like a house key and a car key, and then there was one labelled 'Basement'. Maybe Moosen had hidden something down there. Nik grabbed them, opened the flat door and looked into the hallway. He heard steps on the staircase so waited until everything had gone quiet again before making his way swiftly downstairs.

The rooms in the basement were separated only by wooden planks. Nik opened up the padlock to Moosen's area. There was a grubby shelving unit with a toolbox, a saw and a rusty portable barbecue. Beside the barbeque was a freezer with a beer crate on top. Nik lifted off the crate and opened the freezer lid.

Nik didn't find any food inside. Instead, he found Georg Moosen himself, his wide-open eyes staring up at the ceiling and his lips slightly pursed. His head was twisted unnaturally to the side and his fingers had clawed together in spasm. Going by the jogging bottoms and vest he was wearing, it looked as if his murderer had surprised him while he'd been watching TV on the couch.

Nik took out his phone and called Jon.

'I need Balthasar to come over to Moosen's flat right now,' he said when Jon picked up. 'I've got a body for him.'

Chapter 3

The hands-free phone system started to ring over the speakers in the living room. Nik sat up and answered the call.

'Good afternoon, gentlemen,' came Jon's voice.

Nik picked up his beer from the coffee table while Balthasar appeared from the kitchen with a cup of tea in his hands.

'And a good afternoon to you too,' said the pathologist politely.

'I contacted the CID anonymously and they're currently on their way over to Moosen's flat with a whole team,' explained Jon. 'Let's hope you two didn't leave any traces.'

'Don't worry. I barely even needed to move the corpse,' said Balthasar. 'It was all over with very quickly.'

'You just need to look at a frozen body and everything's clear?'

'Well, since Moosen was found in the freezer, I couldn't determine the time of death.' Balthasar sipped his tea. 'You see, if a corpse is frozen, the usual signs of death are of no help: you can forget both livor mortis and rigor mortis, and there won't be maggots, or any decomposition or mummification. And the body temperature of a frozen corpse also doesn't tell you much.'

'OK. But a rough guess would be helpful here,' said Jon.

'Going by the extent of the freezing and accumulation of ice, I'd suggest Moosen was murdered on Saturday morning at the latest. Probably earlier. Maybe before Greta's abduction. Maybe after.

But a dead body reacts differently to cold than a living one so only a more in-depth investigation will clarify things further.'

'How was he killed?'

'I didn't find any blood in the flat so I'm ruling out brutal force with a weapon,' said Balthasar. 'The skin and face don't suggest poisoning. And I didn't find any marks on his face or neck to suggest suffocation or strangulation. So this, combined with the unnatural position of his head, leaves the option of a broken neck. It's possible that somebody strong twisted his neck around.'

'Any signs of torture?'

'I couldn't get his vest off because of the ice but he didn't have any bruising on the face, no broken fingers and no burns of any kind.'

'Any signs of resistance?'

'The fingernails were frozen but I didn't manage to find any skin or blood particles underneath them. The doctors down at forensics might be able to find some microscopic traces but it looks to me like the man was taken by surprise.'

'I reckon it happened when he was watching TV,' added Nik. 'There were crisps all over the coffee table in the living room as well as a beer bottle on its side on the floor. The murderer must have crept up behind him.'

'How can that happen to a guy like Moosen?' asked Jon. 'He might have been just the Grohnerts' driver but he'd taken plenty of safety training classes and had worked as a bodyguard.'

'Yeah, that baffled me too,' said Nik. 'So I checked the flat for weapons, alarm systems and other security devices but I didn't even find any pepper spray or a gun. No movement sensors or CCTV. The door wasn't reinforced and the lock was really poor quality. Plus, the back of the couch was facing the entrance. Moosen was no amateur; if he'd thought somebody was after him, he would've been better prepared.'

'OK, so it seems he was too relaxed in general to have been involved in any criminal activity,' said Jon. 'Which suggests he also wasn't involved in Greta's abduction.'

'But there was one thing,' Nik continued. 'When I was searching Moosen's house, I found a list of people who worked for him. The name Milan Urbaniak wasn't on the list.'

'So why did he send a text to the Grohnerts saying Urbaniak would cover for him?' asked Jon.

'He must have been forced to do it,' said Balthasar. 'There weren't any obvious signs of torture but that doesn't mean to say nobody held a gun to his head. I know that would be enough for me.'

'Or the murderer used Moosen's finger to open up the phone and then wrote the message himself,' suggested Nik.

'Why would someone break into Moosen's flat and kill him just so he could employ a cover driver?' asked Jon. 'And who the hell killed Urbaniak?'

'Let's go through everything we have,' said Nik. 'For Moosen, it's Friday lunchtime. He's sitting in front of the TV, beer in hand, before it's time to head off and drive Greta to ballet. It's easy to open his front door, the volume on the speakers is up, and since the TV is mounted high on the wall, Moosen doesn't see the intruder's reflection when he comes in the room. Bang. He's dead. And the beer bottle falls to the floor.'

'With regards to the time of death, Friday midday is perfectly plausible,' said Balthasar.

'The murderer gets in easily without a key. It's an apartment block so it's pretty normal to see unknown faces now and again. If the murderer comes dressed as a delivery guy or even the caretaker, he's practically invisible. He listens at Moosen's door, hears the TV and goes inside. I picked that lock on Moosen's door in a minute so a pro could do it in less. He walks into the hall, sneaks towards the living room and sees Moosen watching TV. Two swift paces and it's all over. And Moosen doesn't even notice a thing. Thanks to the finger ID, the murderer unlocks the mobile and sends the Grohnerts a text message.'

'And what about the body?'

'Our murderer calls up a second guy, who's downstairs guarding the basement. They load Moosen into the lift, heave him into the freezer and hang the key back on the hook to avoid arousing any suspicion. Then they take his mobile and ditch it.'

'So now Urbaniak's up,' said Jon. 'But what's his role in the whole thing?'

'That's where I hit a wall,' answered Nik, taking a gulp of beer. 'But whatever the case, there's no doubt this is all part of something big. Nobody commits murder just so they can drive a property developer's daughter to their ballet class.'

'Maybe Urbaniak was involved in the kidnapping,' said Balthasar.

'So why is he shot in the driveway then?' asked Nik. 'And who shot him? If he was just some dispensable henchman, they could have waited until he'd dropped Greta off.' Nik sank back into the couch. 'Just doesn't make any sense.'

Balthasar put down his cup. 'Can you get hold of more photos and videos of Greta for me?' he asked Jon.

'No problem. A few are saved on the CID database. Including two videos from a school outing. What d'you need them for?'

'I realised something when I saw that video of Greta on the TV. But before any speculation, I need to check something. Could be the clue we're looking for.'

❖   ❖   ❖

Balthasar used his hoe to scrape listlessly at the dry earth. The metal tip barely entered the ground and the weed stayed firmly rooted.

'Can't you at least try to look a little bit more like a gardener?' said Nik spitefully.

'I'm not used to this kind of work,' replied the pathologist.

'You've never done any garden work?'

'We always hired people to do the garden at my parents' house. The only plant I've ever had anything to do with is the basil on my balcony.' He let out a theatrical sigh. 'My back is aching. And my hands . . . Oww.' He removed his gardening gloves and inspected a miniscule red area on the tip of his finger. 'You see! Look at that!' he said, turning to Nik and waving his hands in his face. 'These are the hands of an artist. Hands which use fine motor skills to perform work with a scalpel and *not* a garden hoe.'

'I'll buy you an ice cream after, how's that?' responded Nik.

'I wouldn't have expected to get any sympathy from a backward barbarian like you,' said Balthasar. 'Oh God, and just look at this outfit!' He looked down at his green work trousers and black boots and sighed again, loudly.

'Stop complaining, princess. We need to get to Vanessa Grohnert.'

'But why as gardeners? Could we not have just chatted over a coffee?'

'As you might have noticed, the Grohnerts' property is sealed off by the police and surrounded by a swarm of reporters. Only relatives and some close friends are getting in. But thanks to Jon's willingness to pay the gardener, he let us come in with him. So until Vanessa Grohnert appears, we need to look like we're working.'

'I need a break.' Balthasar dropped the hoe on the ground and leaned against a tree.

'Again? You just had one five minutes ago.'

The pathologist pulled a thermos flask out of his bag and poured a cup of tea. He looked up to the sky, shaking his head, as if bemoaning his fate, and took a sip.

The Grohnerts' garden was enormous. And rather than opting for a simple grass lawn, they chose to have their own mini wood, the edge of which was lined with beech trees, while chestnuts and spruces filled the space in between. And towering above all of these was an old oak tree that for years had been spreading its solid, mossy roots over and under the ground beneath it. Lavender, rhododendron and ivy had all been planted in the areas that caught the sun and there was a small path leading past the oak, through a rose bed, and over to the wall that backed on to the street. Nik was still attempting to identify some kind of planting pattern when he noticed Greta's mother.

'Stand up straight, Balthasar,' whispered Nik. 'Vanessa Grohnert's coming.'

She wasn't wearing as much make-up as she had been on the television but she was a very attractive woman and didn't need it anyway. She had shoulder-length red hair and was wearing pearl earrings and a silver neck chain. Her dainty lips were pressed tightly together in contemplation, and worry lines had formed around her bright green eyes. She looked at the rose bed vacantly and let her finger run over the yellow petals. Nik took off his gloves, signalled to Balthasar and started walking towards the woman. Balthasar did the same.

'Frau Grohnert, my name is Nik Pohl.' They shook hands. 'I work for the Munich CID.'

She took in his clothes. 'And you work part-time as a gardener?'

'It's a cover.'

'If you're CID, then why didn't you just use the main entrance and why the cover?'

'Access to you is somewhat . . . limited at the moment,' Nik replied. 'And since I didn't want to waste days waiting for permission, I chose this option.'

Frau Grohnert didn't seem convinced. She turned around as if she was looking for the support of a police officer.

Balthasar stepped in. 'Frau Grohnert, we are not reporters and we are in no way interested in any sensational nonsense. We just want to offer our help, and going by the current state of the investigation, it looks like you need all the help you can get.'

Her eyes welled up and she stared at Balthasar for a moment. 'I can't take it,' she finally whispered. 'I dreamed about her last night. She was still just a little girl and I woke her up so she could see snow for the first time. We went over to the window and watched the flakes falling . . . saw how the garden was getting whiter and whiter. She leaned in close to me and the window and I watched her breath steam up the cold glass.' She wiped her eyes. 'Now when I go into her room, it's so cold and empty. And dark. Just a room of memories. No more life. I lie down on her bed and look up at the ceiling and ask myself where on earth is she? Is she OK? Will I ever see her again?'

Balthasar placed his hand comfortingly on her shoulder. 'We won't keep you long, Frau Grohnert, and I promise you we'll do absolutely everything in our power to get Greta home.'

She wiped her face dry before standing up straight and pushing her shoulders back. 'OK. What d'you want to know?'

'We can't understand the motive behind Greta's kidnapping,' Nik began. 'We now know that somebody murdered your regular driver, Georg Moosen, in his flat and replaced him with Milan Urbaniak. Urbaniak only just got out of the driveway when he was shot by the kidnapper. Now, that's all strange enough, but then there was the demand to pay off the people affected by the scandal. I've worked on a few kidnapping cases and I've never seen anything like this.'

'Yes, well, if you know about my husband's reputation, then you'll be aware he wasn't always the most law-abiding citizen.'

'Listen, I don't want to discount the pain caused by the fraud . . . but to shoot somebody? And kidnap a child over it? It's seems like an overreaction, in my opinion.'

'What do you mean by that?'

'I mean, I think the construction scandal is being used by the kidnapper as a front,' answered Nik. 'I think Greta has been kidnapped for another reason.'

'OK. Such as?' asked Vanessa. 'D'you think it's some desperate lover or something?'

'Do you know what piebaldism is?' Balthasar asked the woman.

Frau Grohnert paused for a moment and looked at the men sceptically. 'I've got no idea.'

'It's a congenital skin condition. It's evident at the time of birth with a white tuft of hair just above the forehead, and in time, white areas appear on the skin. It's neither dangerous nor contagious but I noticed it on the photos of Greta.'

'And what does that have to do with her kidnapping?'

'Piebaldism is hereditary but neither you nor your husband have the condition. I even looked at photos of both your parents and none of them have it either.'

'I don't understand,' said Frau Grohnert. Her voice was calm but her face told the men she was on edge. She started rubbing her hands together nervously.

'We know Greta isn't your birth daughter, Frau Grohnert,' said Nik. 'Even though you're registered as her mother on her birth certificate.'

Frau Grohnert screwed up her face and clenched her fists. The men waited expectantly for a furious outburst.

'We aren't here to pass any judgements,' said Balthasar reassuringly. 'We just want to get Greta away from the people who abducted her, regardless of whose daughter she is.'

She lifted her head and hesitated for a moment. 'God. Where do I start?' she finally whispered, any trace of anger completely gone. 'My husband and I tried for three years to have a child. I tried numerous therapies but nothing worked. I was just about to give up when our home help got pregnant.' The woman started stroking the roses again. 'Vittoria had a difficult background. Hadn't taken any exams and lived on a run-down council estate. She was thirty-three, unmarried and had no prospects. She'd moved over from Italy when she was six after her parents died in a car crash. Working as a domestic helper looked like the best she could expect from life. She told me about the pregnancy one day. She was in tears. Told me she'd have to get an abortion. And then . . . I saw my chance to have a baby. So I made her an offer. I paid her a generous sum to carry the child to full term and then give it up to us.'

'So Greta *is* adopted?'

She shook her head. 'A good friend of mine is a gynaecologist. He looked after me during my pregnancy attempts and then took on Vittoria when I asked him to. Don't ask me how he did it but one week after the due date, he came to us with a child and I was its registered mother.'

'He faked the birth certificate?'

'The months running up to the birth I padded my clothes, didn't drink any alcohol and told our friends about how lucky we'd been. I stopped going to the gym and . . . well . . . nobody thought anything of it until one day, I was out walking with Greta in a pram.'

'And she's definitely Vittoria's child?'

'She was happy. She knew Greta was in good hands and we paid her two years' salary as a reimbursement. She just had to promise never to contact us again.'

'So you never saw Vittoria again?'

'Not since the day she went on maternity leave,' explained Vanessa. 'She wrote to us a couple of times, once from Ibiza . . . But I never saw her in the flesh again.'

'And where is she now?'

'A month after Greta's third birthday, Vittoria died in a fire at her house.' Vanessa's head drooped with regret.

'Suicide?'

'The police report said it was an accident.'

Nik looked at Balthasar. 'That certainly doesn't make things any clearer.'

'No, but we can rule out her involvement,' the pathologist remarked.

'You haven't mentioned anything about Greta's birth father.' Nik looked again at Vanessa. 'Did Vittoria ever say anything about him?'

'She always kept that a secret,' she replied. 'The man didn't seem to have any interest in the child at all. That was one of the reasons she didn't want to keep it in the first place.'

'Did the birth father ever try to contact you or did Greta ever mention any stalkers?'

'No. Why? Do you think he might have something to do with Greta's kidnapping?'

'I'm only speculating at the moment. But the idea is definitely no more far-fetched than someone looking for revenge after a bodged construction deal.' Nik scratched his head and considered the possibility. 'Do you happen to have anything of Vittoria's that we can take a look at?'

'Just a couple of photos and her former address.'

'The building survived the fire?'

'It wasn't completely destroyed and they managed to restore the bits that got damaged. Vittoria's aunty also lived there. Maybe she still does.'

'Yes. And she might know the birth father,' suggested Nik. 'It's definitely worth trying to find out.'

◆　◆　◆

Nik always did his best not to be prejudiced, but it was proving difficult today as he sat looking at Vittoria's aunty sitting in her armchair in a council house in Milbertshofen. Well over fifty, she was still wearing a short denim skirt with a wide leather belt and a sleeveless pink top that perfectly enhanced her bulging stomach. Her shoulder-length hair had been dyed bright blonde and she had applied a thick stripe of pink blusher to her cheeks. Her fingernails had been painted pillar-box red and she was holding a cigarette between her fingers. The way she was crossing her legs in Nik's direction gave him more than just a good view of her white pumps. The smell inside the flat was a mixture of cigarette smoke, reused cooking oil and body odour.

Nik sipped his coffee and tried to find a comfortable position on the plastic armchair.

'Frau Grassi,' he began. 'Many thanks for taking the time to see me. I just want to ask a couple of questions about your niece, Vittoria Monti.'

'She's been dead a long time now,' replied Grassi in a coarse voice. Her Italian accent was still heavy. She sucked hard on her cigarette before blowing the smoke out of her nose with a wheezing moan.

'Yes, I'd like to know more about the fire she died in,' Nik continued.

'Oh, it was an absolute mess!' she said. 'Couldn't get into the flat for five days and my clothes stank of smoke for months!'

'I see.' Nik quickly began to realise the nature of the conversation to come. 'Well, maybe we could start at the beginning. What kind of woman was Vittoria? What was her family like?'

'Her dad was a total wanker,' she replied.

'Your brother you mean?'

Grassi nodded. 'Left his wife when Vittoria was four years old . . . Ran off to Naples with some whore. His wife couldn't take it and threw herself over a cliff.'

'I thought Vittoria's parents died in a car accident.'

'Who likes telling people that their dad fucked off with another woman and their mum topped themselves?'

'And so the girl was sent to live with you?'

'I was the only living relative.'

'So how did Vittoria cope when she came to Germany?'

'Well . . . she didn't,' replied the woman. 'What can you expect in a place like this?' She puffed on her cigarette. 'Always bunking off school, never sat any exams and didn't care about any work placements.'

'OK. Let's skip the teenage years and talk about her pregnancy.'

'Ha! Stupid idiot,' continued the aunty. 'I couldn't care less if she was fucking around. But come on! At least use a condom! But no . . . she was too fucking thick.'

'Do you know who the father is?'

'She was fucking so many guys, she probably didn't even know herself.'

'Any suspicions? Maybe someone she'd been seeing for a while? Or perhaps someone contacted her after her baby was born?'

'Vittoria wasn't the kind of woman the boys wanted to grow old with. You know what I mean? The blokes had their fun with her for a little while and then moved on to the next one.'

'Any of these men in trouble with the law?'

Grassi laughed gruffly. 'Put it this way: none of them were well-behaved bank employees.'

'Anyone who was particularly dangerous?'

'She had one boyfriend with tattoos over his entire body. Even on his knuckles. He was in some gang and watched every move Vittoria made, like he owned her. He was always with the gang. Right set of thugs. Really terrorised the neighbourhood for a while.'

'And what happened to him?'

'They all got chucked in jail after a police raid. Heroin.'

'Do you know his name?'

Grassi shook her head. 'Stayed well clear of that guy. Creepy bastard.'

'Is it possible – in terms of timings – that he's the father of Vittoria's child?'

'It's possible.' She held in the smoke from her cigarette while she spoke.

'OK. Let's go back to the child,' said Nik. 'Do you know what happened to it?'

'I didn't see Vittoria for a long time before the birth. Don't even know if she was in hospital. But when she got back home, she told me she'd put the kid up for adoption. Thank God.' Grassi made the sign of the cross.

'And how did Vittoria deal with that?'

'She was really tired for the first couple of days and barely spoke. You know, like she was thinking things over or something.'

'Did she ever mention the birth?'

'Not a word,' said Grassi. 'And on the few occasions I brought it up, she clammed up completely. At some point she got back to being her old self again. Probably when she remembered how much money they'd given her for the adoption.' She took another drag. 'But of course . . . instead of saving the money and learning something, she blew the whole lot. Spent two weeks in Ibiza and came home with a suitcase full of new clothes. A necklace here, a pair of new shoes there. Wasn't a single day she didn't buy something.

And then . . . the account was empty and she had to start cleaning again. Wasn't happy about that, I can tell you.'

'What d'you mean?'

'She didn't want to work anymore and got depressed. Started drinking, and after a while, barely even got out of bed. Sometimes she visited me and told me all about how shitty her life was. Went on like that for a long time. And then there was the fire.'

'Can you remember anything strange about that day?' asked Nik. 'Did she seem afraid of anything? Or particularly depressed?'

Grassi shook her head. 'The investigator asked me that back then too. Vittoria was just the same as always.'

'Can you remember the name of the investigator?'

'Nah. But I probably still have his card somewhere.' Grassi stood up and pulled a drawer out from a shelving unit. She emptied all the contents on to the floor. Nik saw unopened bills, various warning letters and old coupons from discount supermarkets. Grassi raked through the pile of papers until she came across a discoloured business card. She passed it to Nik.

'Werner Hunke?' Nik read out loud. 'That was the investigator who questioned you?'

Grassi nodded. 'Nice older man. I'm sure he knows more than me.'

'Thank you,' Nik said, standing up to shake Grassi's hand. 'You've been a lot of help.'

◆ ◆ ◆

When Nik called the number on the card, he was greeted by a young female police officer, who told him that Hunke had retired three years ago. She wasn't able to give him a private number but

Jon was able to hack the CID server to access the personnel department. He found Hunke's current address and home telephone number.

The phone rang twice before someone picked up. 'Werner Hunke,' said a scratchy voice.

'Hello, Herr Hunke, my name is Nik Pohl. I'm working on Greta Grohnert's case and need your help.'

'*My* help?' asked Hunke, confused. 'I've been retired for years. And anyway, I was at Unit 13. Fires. I wasn't involved in a single abduction case in my life.'

'Yes, I know. It's complicated,' replied Nik. 'You see, you dealt with a house fire that might actually be related to the abduction.'

'What did you say your name was?'

'Nik Pohl, CID.'

'The same Nik Pohl who hit a prosecutor because he shelved a case?'

'Yes.'

'And the same Nik Pohl who mugged an innocent man on the street, bringing the Munich Police Force into absolute disrepute?'

'Well, that was a set-up, but . . . yes.'

'I thought you were suspended.'

'I am. I'm working as a private investigator now.'

'Then you're fully aware I can't talk to you about police investigations.'

'Yes. But if you follow the news, then you'll know there's been absolutely no progress with the kidnapped girl and that her chances of living are getting slimmer with every hour.'

Hunke was silent for a moment. 'And how is an old fire case supposed to improve that situation?'

'As I said . . . it's complicated. But give me a chance and I'll tell you everything.'

'I worked hundreds of cases. And my memory is no longer what it was, you know.'

'Not a problem,' replied Nik. 'I've downloaded all the paperwork and printed it out. And before you ask, no, I didn't get permission.'

Hunke groaned. 'My God. You're worse than I even imagined.'

'No time for flattery, I'm afraid. Luckily it's a holiday and the traffic's light. I could be at your flat in fifteen minutes. If you don't have any plans, I'd like to come over straight away?'

'Suppose I'll put on some coffee then.' Hunke sighed and hung up.

Ten minutes later, Nik was at his door.

◆　◆　◆

Hunke was a sturdy, elderly man with an unobtrusive beer belly. He hadn't shaved or combed his hair and it was clear from the stains on his polo shirt that he'd been enjoying some orange juice. The back of his right hand was scarred, as if glowing coal had fallen on top of it at some point. Despite the reading glasses balanced on his nose, he still had difficulty reading the words on the report, squinting as he attempted to focus. He sat in an old armchair, his feet sunk into tattered slippers. His grey jogging bottoms were too short for him and exposed his luminescent white legs. There was a small coffee table in front of him, on top of which were two cups of coffee and a tin of chocolate biscuits.

'The fire in question was in Blodigstraße in 2006.' Nik passed him a photo of the house. 'A woman, Vittoria Monti, died in the fire.'

'Yes, I vaguely remember the case,' said Hunke, his eyes focused intently on the files. 'But what does a fire from eleven years ago have to do with the kidnapping of the Grohnert girl?'

'Vittoria Monti was Greta's birth mother.'

'Greta's adopted?'

'Not officially. Vanessa Grohnert's name was entered in Greta's birth certificate so she is her registered mother.'

Hunke raised his eyebrows in disbelief. 'So you think there's a connection?'

'I'm convinced the ransom note is just a distraction to put the police on the wrong track. That's why I need to find out more about Greta's real mother, and her death is a good place to start.'

Hunke leafed through the files pensively. He then straightened himself up in his chair and pushed back his shoulders. 'After the fire brigade had put out the fire and Monti's body was found, we were called to Blodigstraße.' He reached for a biscuit. 'Most fires occur at the hands of humans. Technical faults and natural causes, like lightning or direct sunlight, are rare.' He pointed to a photo of the burned-out flat. The ceiling and the walls were badly charred, the couch had been burned down to the springs, the shelving units above the kitchen counter had fallen off the wall and the sink was full of broken crockery. Beside the stove sat a dark clump of melted plastic and the floors were hidden by a mass of indefinable debris.

Hunke continued, 'The most important questions for a fire investigator are the following: Who found the fire? When and how was the fire noticed? And in which part of the house were the flames first noticed?'

Nik flicked through the files. 'The fire was first seen at 6.47 a.m. by the building caretaker. The first thing he noticed was a faint smell of smoke. After that, he went up the building stairwell, where he saw smoke wafting from underneath Monti's flat door. According to his statement, he used his universal key to open the door but the fire had already spread extensively by that point so he ran down the stairs and called the fire brigade.'

'Well, that pretty much answers all our questions.' Hunke looked through the files again. 'The only question the caretaker couldn't answer was where the flames first appeared. In the end, the cause of the fire was put down to the washing machine in the kitchen.'

'A technical fault?'

'That couldn't be clearly determined.' Hunke pointed to a photo of the kitchen. 'According to the statement given by the aunt, Monti had stored chemical cleaners on a shelf above the washing machine. Including diluting agent. Packaging remains from the thinner were found in the pile of washing that was standing in front of the machine. The flat had been very untidy and that led to a dense fire load. There were clothes and newspapers all over the place, all of which additionally fed the fire. If the thinner had fallen on to the washing in front of the machine, a small ignition would have been enough to set it alight.' He skimmed through the files. 'The aunt's statement claims the victim was a heavy smoker and ashtrays were found throughout the flat. Evidence suggested Monti even sometimes left a lit cigarette lying on the table.'

'And I read that in the end her death was determined as accidental?'

'The police have the task of eliminating all possible causes of fire until just one is left,' explained Hunke. 'We knew in this case where the fire began and that the thinner encouraged it to spread. And from that came two possibilities.' He stuck his index finger in the air. 'The victim started the fire on purpose. She poured thinner over the clothes, turned on the wash and maybe laid a burning cigarette beside the machine. After that, she lay down in bed and waited to die.'

'It's possible,' said Nik. 'According to her aunt, Monti was severely depressed and it wouldn't be the first time someone tried to kill themselves like that.'

'A behavioural disorder as a motive for arson is not uncommon,' added Hunke. 'But I actually believed there were signs that suggested this fire was accidental.' He pointed to a photo of Monti taken before the post-mortem. She was barely recognisable. Her face was badly burned, she had no hair, and her lips had been burned away, exposing her teeth, and creating an unfortunate, grotesque grin. Two holes sat where her nose had once been and her hands were contorted together into tight fists.

'She died from carbon monoxide poisoning. But large amounts of alcohol were also found in her blood. She would have barely been able to walk in a straight line before going to bed and would have been sleeping off the inebriation when she died. We never found any lighters or other form of igniter, which suggests she would have had to plan the fire very subtly. Not an easy thing to do with a blood alcohol concentration of two. And furthermore, a suicide victim has no reason to cover up the cause of a fire. That's normally what happens in insurance claims or murder cases.'

'Was it possible somebody else started the fire?'

'We investigated that possibility,' replied Hunke. 'The first step was an enquiry into the insurance policyholder. The owner of the building turned out to be financially comfortable, the claimed sum wasn't particularly high, and the sum hadn't been increased before the fire. The owner wasn't involved in any dodgy business deals and he wasn't being threatened, so we were able to rule out insurance fraud or an act of revenge.' Hunke picked up a photo of a badly damaged door from the file. 'There were no signs of breaking and entering, but it is worth mentioning that the locks were of poor quality. This, combined with the fact that there wasn't a burglar alarm, meant it would have been easy for an experienced burglar to enter the flat.' He returned the photo to the file. 'We asked all the neighbours if they'd seen anyone suspicious that morning but nobody had. And when we spoke to people in her social circle, we found nothing to suggest somebody wanted her murdered. So that just left the accident theory.' Hunke laid down the file and reached for his cup. 'And how is this information going to be of help in the abduction case?' He looked over at Nik.

'I was hoping for third-party negligence,' answered Nik. 'Monti was in real financial difficulty at the time and I thought it was possible she might have been blackmailing the Grohnerts.'

'Which would have then led them to have her murdered to prevent the secret from getting out?'

'It's a possibility.'

'So where's the link to the abduction?'

'Well, we still don't know who the father is. He might be the kidnapper.'

'And why only now? Eleven years after Monti's death and fourteen years after Greta was born?' asked Hunke.

'I don't know. And truth be told, I'm starting to run out of ideas.'

Nik looked worriedly at his watch. It was twelve after seven and Balthasar still hadn't arrived at their meeting point. The pathologist was the most punctual person Nik knew and was personally offended by any sign of tardiness. Their gardening friends were already on the premises taking care of the grass. Nik needed to speak to Vanessa Grohnert one more time and so he had thrown on his green work trousers and asked Jon to bribe the boss of the gardening company again.

Nik was taking his phone out of his pocket when he noticed a man in a dark suit walking purposefully towards him, his eyes fixed on Nik. He looked to be in his late forties, and was well built, with a smart haircut and tanned skin. He seemed like a typical businessman but there was something about the expression on his face that made Nik cautious – it was the look of a hunting dog that had spotted its prey, laced with an elusive smile, as though in anticipation of the upcoming encounter. As per his habitual response, Nik's hand started to edge slowly down to his hip, only to realise he was unarmed.

'Good morning,' said the man.

'Morning,' replied Nik glumly.

'May I ask what you're doing here?'

Nik felt a snide remark pushing to escape the edges of his lips but he managed to hold it back. He couldn't risk sabotaging the visit by causing problems with an overeager security guard. 'I'm waiting on my colleague. We work for the gardening company that does the Grohnerts' garden.'

'Interesting,' answered the man, his sly smile not budging. 'You don't look like a gardener.'

'Just got into it recently.'

'I see.' The man paused. 'Wanna know what I think?'

'What's that then?'

'I think you're some investigator, sticking his beak into Greta Grohnert's kidnapping.'

'OK. Or, maybe Clemens Grohnert hired me to keep an eye on his property.'

'Then you wouldn't be waiting around dressed like a gardener, would you?'

'I guess we'll never know, will we?' said Nik, reciprocating the man's smirk. 'And if you wouldn't mind, I'd kindly ask you to carry on with your walk and stop bothering me.' Nik turned away from the man and looked up the street.

'In case you're waiting on your mate, Balthasar, he's been picked up.'

Nik turned around abruptly to look at the man again. 'What did you just say?'

'Oh, I'm sorry, Herr Pohl . . . I wasn't aware you suffer from a hearing impairment.'

'You know what . . . ?' said Nik, starting to take off his jacket. 'Maybe you *shouldn't* be getting on with your walk.'

The man took three smooth steps back, opened his jacket and laid his hand on the gun in his holster. Nik stayed still, weighing up his options. Three steps. Had the man standing opposite him been a novice, he could have got to him quickly enough. But this man appeared too self-assured for that. It would be too risky. Plus, he didn't know what had happened to Balthasar. 'Where is he?' asked Nik, raising his voice now.

'If you're worried about your buddy, you should answer my questions.'

Nik felt the rage mounting in his chest. He ached to pounce on the man; to hit him until every last bone was broken. But his opponent was in the position of power. Balthasar should have been there ages ago. If something had come up, he would have sent Nik a message. Something must have happened to him.

'Let's go back to my initial question. What are you doing here?'

Nik took a deep breath. 'I'm investigating the case of the kidnapped girl, Greta Grohnert.'

'And why are you not leaving that up to the CID?'

'Because the CID are on the wrong track. The compensation demand is a joke. Nobody kills a chauffeur and kidnaps a kid in an act of solidarity with tradespeople who lost their job.'

'So what's the real reason for the kidnapping?'

'I don't know. That's why I want to talk to Vanessa Grohnert. And that's why I'm undercover.'

'OK. I believe you,' said the man, his grin widening.

Nik clenched his right fist. Two steps forward, and he would be in punching distance.

The man put his hand to his ear. 'Bring him over.'

A van started driving along the street towards them. A plain, dark blue Mercedes Sprinter with a Munich registration plate. It stopped beside Nik and the side door slid open. A man jumped out, pulled Balthasar out by the arm and let him fall down on the pavement. Nik's heart skipped a beat at the sight of Balthasar's blood-covered face. He kneeled down beside him and lifted his face gently by the chin. He was still conscious and groaning quietly. His left eye was swollen and the skin underneath the eyebrow was ripped open. His nose was broken and his shirt was covered in blood. Nik pressed his hands down gently but firmly over Balthasar's arms, torso and legs.

'Don't worry. No permanent damage,' said the man. 'Apart from the nose, nothing's broken and we left his delicate pathologist hands fully intact.' He moved closer to Nik. 'This time, that is. But if you two don't leave this case alone, I'll cut off all his fingers next time and let you watch.'

Nik kept holding his friend in his arms after the van and the man had disappeared. 'You're going to be fine,' he said soothingly as Balthasar moaned quietly, barely conscious. 'I'm not going anywhere.'

Only when the ambulance arrived did Nik finally let him go.

Chapter 4

When Jon saw Balthasar lying in bed, he shook his head, feeling responsible for what had happened. Balthasar's left eye was swollen shut and the burst brow above it had been stitched. He had a large plaster across his nose and a tube led from the back of his hand into an empty plastic bag that was hanging from a metal stand. Although asleep, his eyelids kept flickering and he was mumbling quietly. There was the unfortunate chance he was reliving the torture all over again.

The lamp attached to the bedhead was on and in the shadowed corner of the room, a figure sat, utterly still, on a chair, his gaze fixed on the door.

'How is he?' asked Jon.

'Physically, he'll be back to his old self again in no time,' answered Nik. 'There wasn't any permanent damage. A broken nose, bruising on the face and a concussion. The doctor was worried initially because he was complaining of stomach aches but whoever did this, thankfully didn't hit him hard enough to damage any organs. They want to keep him here until tomorrow because of the concussion and they gave him a sleeping tablet for tonight.' Nik grabbed his glass of water and took a sip. 'But it's his mental state I'm worried about. Victims of violence like that keep suffering. I've seen it far too often. The fear on their faces, the feeling they're going insane because they don't understand what happened to them. You never know how they'll react. Some hide it well; others are plagued with nightmares for years.' He shook his head. 'I should've never taken him with me.'

'What the hell's all this about?' Jon pulled a chair over to the bed and sat down. 'None of it makes any sense. The abduction. The fact that not one, but two, drivers are murdered. And then there's the weird demands from the kidnapper.'

The men sat in silence for a moment, contemplating all that had happened. 'Is there anything new on the ransom?' asked Nik.

'The CID reports aren't saying much. Apparently the special commission is saying it's going to open an account for the affected parties so they can win some time. They're using everything at their disposal for the search and dragging things out as long as possible – going from house to house questioning residents, using social media, doing traffic checks. The techies have built a ring circuit around the Grohnerts' phones and linked it up to every police car in Munich. Means they could be near the relevant transmission mast in a matter of minutes if someone gets in contact. The police are doing everything they can. But . . . there's still no sign of Greta, and the kidnapper hasn't been in contact again.'

'Any leads on the guy who beat up Balthasar?'

'I don't have enough information,' answered Jon. 'I never found any criminals on the wanted list that match the description you gave. And you won't be surprised to hear the van registration plate was nicked.'

'Sounds like the guys were pros,' said Nik. 'A van with a fake registration, a gun in a holster and not a whiff of fear. They must've known about our investigation. They wouldn't have taken Balthasar otherwise. Either they got the information from the Grohnerts or they've got the place under constant surveillance.'

'Based on Clemens Grohnert's background, it wouldn't be too surprising if he had contacts like that.'

'But why go to so much bother?' asked Nik. 'All he needed to do was send a message to the CID and they would've taken me straight out of the game.'

'OK. So if not Grohnert, then who? The kidnapper's accomplices?'

Nik shook his head. 'Unnecessary and risky. As it stands, neither we nor the special commission have got a single trace. Why change that?'

'Perhaps it was Julian Nooten looking for revenge. I can imagine a man of that calibre would get pretty upset about his liaison with a rent boy being used to blackmail him for information.'

'He could've just beaten up Balthasar at home. Abducting him and speaking to me was unnecessary. And why would he want us to stop our investigation?' Nik took a sip of water. 'I've gone through everybody it could be and none of them make any sense.' He stuck his index finger in the air. 'First of all, there's the construction mafia. There's every chance my new friends could belong to those corrupt bastards. But Grohnert's construction scandal has been public knowledge for a long time now; our investigations haven't changed a thing.' Nik added a second finger. 'Greta's birth family. But Vittoria is dead and her aunt doesn't have a clue about the agreement with the Grohnerts. So that just leaves the birth father.' He lifted a third finger. 'If the father is involved in Greta's abduction, why would he make such a risky move by getting in contact? Neither Balthasar nor I had a single trace to him. Plus, he could have easily just gone down the legal route: a DNA test would prove Clemens Grohnert isn't the father. So that, together with the statement from Vittoria's aunt, would provide sufficient reason to doubt the birth certificate's authenticity.'

'Maybe we're much closer to the kidnapper than we think.'

Nik shook his head. 'No. There's definitely a fourth party. No idea which side they're on or what their interest is in the whole thing, but we're missing a large piece of the puzzle and I've got no idea where to look from here.'

'I might have found a lead,' said Jon reluctantly.

'To the kidnapper?' asked Nik. 'Where from? The CID server?'

'Probably best if I start at the beginning,' said Jon. 'I programmed an algorithm that looks for similar cases in both the police database and online press portals. The first step recognises strong similarities . . . such as abductions of youngsters where the description of the offender is similar to the one in Greta's case. When I stuck to that step, I didn't get any matches, so I started removing characteristics with each step in the algorithm in order to increase the scope for hits. For example, the offender might have been involved in another kind of crime, so if I only concentrate on kidnappings, any information relating to other crimes wouldn't flash up. And rather than only focusing on Munich, I widened the search to the whole of Germany.' Jon paused and scratched his head. 'In the end, you get a whole load of hits that you need to go through one by one. But yesterday, I came across something really strange. A care worker from a children's residential home got in touch with the police two weeks ago telling them one of the residents had run away. Now, that in itself isn't particularly noteworthy since the boy, Simon, has run away lots of times before. He's been picked up on the street and brought to school by the police on various occasions. The algorithm flashed up the case because Simon is the same age as Greta and also because of a statement given by the care worker in which she explains how she'd seen a tall, scrawny man waiting for Simon outside the home and talking to him on two occasions. Her description was vague but she said the man had limped with his right leg.'

'Like our kidnapper,' Nik remarked. 'Is the CID on the case?'

'No. There's no mention of abduction in the police report and going by Simon's history, it would be easy to assume he's just done another runner. But bearing in mind recent events – and the lack of investigation results – this might be a good lead.'

'What's the care worker's name?'

'Regina Eichert. Works in a home in Neuhausen.'

'Write down the address for me, would you?' said Nik. 'As soon as Balthasar's out of hospital, I'll look into it.'

'D'you not want to get some sleep?' asked Jon. 'It's one in the morning.'

'I don't want him to be alone when he wakes up. And as long as I don't know who the bastards are that are responsible for this, I'm staying here.'

'Have you got a gun on you?' asked Jon.

'In my jacket.'

'Give it to me. I'll do watch duty for the rest of the night.'

'Do you even know how to shoot a gun?'

'It's a small room. At such short range, I'm sure I can't miss. And believe me, I won't let them get Balthasar a second time,' Jon said resolutely.

'OK.' Nik took a short-barrelled black gun out of its holster. 'Safety catch is on the left. Just push it down, hold out your arm and pull the trigger. If anyone comes through that door who doesn't look like a doctor or a nurse, shoot them first and ask them afterwards what they want.'

Jon nodded, taking the weapon. He took Nik's place on the chair in the corner of the room. The cold steel of the gun felt peculiar against his skin, but holding it in his hand, he instantly felt he could take on the whole world.

'I'll head to the kids' care home as soon as it's light.' Nik raised his hand to say goodbye. 'Let's hope that search of yours turns out to be worth it.'

◆ ◆ ◆

The sunny morning clashed with Nik's mood. The sight of Balthasar's smashed-up face was still haunting him. It had even followed him into his dreams. He had kept his mobile beside the bed, terrified Jon would call to say there was a problem. But the phone had stayed silent all night. It was only as Nik was parking the car, still thinking about the call that had never come, that his phone started to ring. It was, of course, Jon.

'How's he doing?' asked Nik.

'He slept for a long time. And then woke up, only to start complaining about the breakfast. So he must be feeling a bit better,' Jon answered.

'Any unwanted visitors?'

'The nurse on night duty stopped in twice to look at him. Other than that, everything was quiet.' Nik heard Jon take a sip of water and the rattle of crockery in the background. 'The doctor wants to examine him once more this morning but then they'll let him out at lunchtime.'

'We'll need to get him somewhere safe straight away.' Nik stepped out of the car. 'Do you have a flat he can go to?'

'Just the one you're in and my loft here in the industrial estate,' explained Jon. 'And I already know that mine will be nowhere near Balthasar's usual standards . . . even after the refurb.'

'OK. Take him to mine. He can have the second bedroom. He'll be safe there – as long as he doesn't throw out my beer again, that is.'

'And you'll take care of the guy who did it?' asked Jon.

'Even if I take the Grohnerts out of the equation, Simon's disappearance might still have something to do with Greta's kidnapping, and if our new friends find out I've not given up the search, they won't be happy. I can look after myself but I'll have to make sure Balthasar's safe.'

'I don't think he's going to be happy about moving.'

'Well, if he says no, I'll tie him up and push him to my flat in a wheelbarrow. Whatever happens, he's moving in with me.'

Jon laughed. 'It'll be the weirdest flat-share in Munich.'

'Don't remind me. But I can worry about that later. I need to deal with Simon first.'

'OK. Let me know how you get on.' Jon hung up.

Nik pocketed his phone and made his way towards the children's home. It was a surprisingly large building: four stories high with a roof extension, blue shutters on the windows and surrounded entirely by large grassy areas. Some children were playing football on a lawn, while others were testing out their climbing skills on an oak tree.

Jon had sent Nik a photo of the care worker, Regina Eichert. It wasn't long before he found her, deep in conversation with a tradesman. The woman was in her late forties, with shaved brown hair and a pair of large square glasses. All this, combined with the monobrow, the lack of make-up and the hair on her arms made Nik wonder if the woman actually cared about her appearance at all. And then there were the red socks that clashed violently with her blue trainers. The look was finished off with a faded old polo shirt and worn-out jeans. Her desire to be alternative couldn't have been more glaringly obvious.

'Good morning, Frau Eichert.' Nik showed her his fake CID badge. 'Nik Pohl from the Munich CID. Would you have a moment for me?'

Panic flared across her face. 'Has something happened to one of the children?'

'Everything's fine,' Nik replied calmly. 'I just want to ask a couple of questions about Simon Fahl.'

'Oh! OK.' She let out a sigh of relief. 'Is the CID dealing with runaways these days?' She signalled towards a nearby bench.

'It doesn't actually have anything to do with Simon's behaviour, Frau Eichert. He might be able to help me with another case.'

'Has he got himself into some kind of trouble again?' She sat down beside Nik on the bench.

'I hope not. But to be sure, I'd need to speak to him first. I saw you filed a police report saying you were concerned about Simon's disappearance . . . especially after you saw him speaking to a stranger?'

'Yes, um. Where to start . . . You see, the kids here can be difficult. You know? It's not always a bed of roses working with them. Most of them come from difficult homes or don't have any parents at all. A lot had to look after themselves from a young age. And a lot of them get into crime before they're even old enough to be prosecuted. So I'm sure you can imagine the kinds of circles they start hanging around in. Some people use the kids as drug couriers, others are violent towards them. So we consider every stranger as a potential risk.' She squirmed uncomfortably on the bench and rubbed her hands on her thighs. 'I *always* try to take people as they are . . . not make assumptions, you know? But the guy Simon was talking to . . . he scared me. He was tall . . . really tall. And he was throwing his arms around all over the place. Looked as if the two were having a fight. And then the next day, he was there again . . . speaking to Simon as if nothing had happened. I tried to talk to Simon about it, but he just fobbed me off with some stupid excuse and went into his room.'

'Did he tell you the man's name?'

'Unfortunately not. And then . . . two days later, Simon never came home. So I went to the police.'

'You said the man had a bad limp. Did anything else occur to you afterwards that you didn't mention in the report?'

Eichert shook her head. 'Sorry.'

'And have you heard anything from Simon since?'

'No. I just cleaned out his cupboard and put his things into storage.' Tears surfaced in her eyes. She wiped them away. 'Haven't seen the man either.'

'OK. Let's talk about Simon's background. What can you tell me about him?'

'Same fate as lots of orphans, I suppose. Doesn't know his real parents. Spent most of his life hopping from one foster family to the next. It never worked out with the families so he'd always find himself back in the home. He was always mouthy with his teachers . . . always bunking off, and he was first caught stealing at eleven.' The woman sighed. 'Simon's clever, you know? Alert and strong-willed . . . But what can you expect from a child who has never had a proper home or got love and security from a good family?'

'What do you know about his most recent foster parents?'

'Lisa Fürste is a paediatric nurse and Timo Fürste works in a thermal power plant,' explained Regina. 'Simon lived with them for seven years but the last few years he was there, it got complicated. Frau Fürste actually stopped working because of it all and ended up needing psychological treatment. Simon and his foster dad kept getting into fights, until Simon finally decided to come back to the home. It was his own decision.' The care worker leaned over slightly towards Nik. 'I actually did a bit of research into Timo Fürste. He's got a clean record but he's allegedly in contact with the Munich drug scene.'

'As a customer?'

'Dealer,' Regina whispered, shaking her head. 'But since there's no evidence of it, Simon's still allowed to visit his foster parents if he wants to.'

'Have you asked the Fürstes about where Simon might currently be?'

'Lisa hasn't seen him for a couple of weeks. But it was barely possible to speak to her last time I called. Her husband keeps staying out all night.'

'OK. Does Simon have any friends who might know where he is?'

'Simon's more of a lone wolf. Doesn't take part in any group activities and avoids contact with the other residents. The only person here he's ever built up a relationship with is Daniela.' She pointed over to a woman who was standing behind a football goal watching a group of teenagers playing football. 'She's actually only a supply care worker but she got along well with him from the start. Whenever he got into one of his rages, she was always able to calm him down. I would have given her a permanent position ages ago if we had the funding. But she seems happy with the supply work. Likes working with kids.'

'Thank you for your time, Frau Eichert.' Nik stood up and they shook hands. 'If you don't mind, I'd like to speak to your colleague for a minute?'

'Of course. Good luck with the investigation. I hope you find Simon.'

Nik said goodbye and headed over to the large field where the woman was standing. He guessed she was in her mid-thirties but the years hadn't taken their toll on her beauty in any way. She had light skin, brown eyes and full red lips. Her clothes were simple – just a pair of baggy jeans and a sweatshirt – but Nik recognised the outline of an attractive figure underneath. Nik gave his fingernails a quick inspection, straightened out his shirt and cleared his throat.

'Excuse me, Frau . . . ?'

'Haas,' answered the woman, shaking his hand. Nik noticed her attractive floral perfume. 'But everyone calls me Daniela.' She looked over at the teenagers, who had started to cheer after the ball flew into the goal. She smiled like a contented, loving mother before turning back to Nik, naturally sweeping her long brown hair over to one side. 'How can I help?'

He showed her his badge. 'Pohl. Munich CID. Frau Eichert mentioned you could maybe answer some questions about Simon Fahl.'

'Has something happened?' she asked instantly. There was worry in her voice.

'Frau Eichert reported Simon missing to the police and I'm following it up.'

'Yes, well, if you've already spoken to Regina, then you'll know what Simon's like.'

'I heard you two are particularly close?' said Nik.

'I try to be a friend to the kids, not just some strict author-ity figure,' explained Daniela. 'Kids like Simon know when they do something wrong. They know stealing isn't right and that they shouldn't skive school. But unfortunately, the more you try to steer them on to the right path, the more they turn the other way. Sometimes they just need a quiet place where they can get away for a while or have someone to speak to.'

'OK. Well, it doesn't really seem like this is the right place for that. Did Simon visit you at home?'

Daniela glanced subtly over towards Eichert, who was convers-ing with the tradesman again. 'It's strictly forbidden to let kids visit you at home.' She lowered her voice.

'Look, I'm not going to judge you here,' said Nik. 'If Simon feels safe with you, he can move in with you for all I care. I'm just trying to make sure he's safe. If you've seen the news recently, you'll know where I'm coming from.'

'God, I know. That poor girl.' She shook her head and looked at the ground.

'Can you tell me anything about Simon that I won't find in his file? Maybe what he was like as a child? And as a teenager?'

'Simon was always a reclusive, contemplative child. Extremely intelligent and wise. But unfortunately, the hurt of being an orphan never left him. He was painfully aware that he was alone in the world.' She sighed. 'And sometimes it would get too much . . . So, he became furious . . . wild . . . barely controllable. But it wasn't actually a violent anger. He only fought when he really had to. And then when he did, it was with the hardness of a kid that's lived in a home and it would go on until he won or until he couldn't fight anymore.' She quickly focused her attention on the football game again, checking everything was all right. 'Simon had to grow up far too quickly, but I know if someone just gave him a bloody chance, he'd turn into a really decent guy. Unfortunately, until that happens, he'll have to deal with a lot more challenges and temptations.'

'Have you seen Simon in the last couple of days?' asked Nik, taking down some notes.

'No. And to be honest, I'm worried about him.'

'Do you have any idea where he might be?'

'No. I've checked all his usual hang-outs and there was no sign of him.'

'And what about his foster parents?'

'God. His foster mother, Lisa, can't even look after herself. And rumour has it that his father, Timo, is a drug dealer. Simon made the right decision coming back to the home.'

'You think Timo might have got him dealing?'

'Well, if he hasn't tried already, I'm sure he will at some point. But Simon's too bright for that.' She looked over at the teenagers playing football. 'You know, one of that lot out there' – she signalled with her head towards the group – 'he robbed coke off a dealer to go and sell it himself. What happens next? The dealers find him one night on the train tracks near the station and leave him with sixteen broken bones. It was a bitter lesson for the boy but a good warning for all the others.'

'Can you tell me where Simon's foster parents live?'

She looked back at Regina. 'Not officially. But if you leave me your number you'll have the address by this evening. Just be careful. Timo Fürste's a . . . difficult guy.'

'Sounds like it,' said Nik with an understanding smile.

Daniela grabbed the tops of Nik's hands and looked him sternly in the eyes. 'Please call me when you find Simon.' Her eyes welled. 'I need to know if he's all right.'

'I will. You've got my word.' Nik shook her hand tightly, trying to reinforce that he meant what he had said.

◆ ◆ ◆

Balthasar still looked terrible and his swollen eye had only gone down slightly. But although the painkillers were making him sluggish, it didn't deter him from scrutinising the flat intensely, apparently already visualising his planned transformation. Looking at the piles of suitcases, bags and boxes in the hallway, Nik wasn't sure how they would fit it all in. But despite the impending madness, he was happy to see Balthasar on his feet. The unknown attacker and his vicious gang were still out there so Nik was relieved to have Balthasar at the flat. He would be safe here.

'Thank God there's a walk-in closet in your bedroom,' said Nik, attempting to make a joke.

'Oh, don't worry,' said Balthasar, ignoring the attempt. 'I'll just take your cupboard as well. What with your three pairs of trousers, two shirts and that pair of worn-out boots, you won't be needing it anyway.' He moved towards the living room table and inspected a half-empty beer bottle like it was an unidentifiable relic from outer space. 'My God, we do have a lot of work to do, don't we?'

Nik groaned. 'Maybe we should set down a couple of rules . . .'

Balthasar took two steps back from the table, giving the bottle a shake.

'Beer is there to be drunk, not thrown out. So, to avoid hurting your Prosecco's feelings, I've divided the fridge into two areas: my beer goes in the bottom, and above that, I don't care what happens.'

Balthasar slid a finger over a side table, checking for dust.

'And then there's the lavender . . .' continued Nik.

'Such a wonderful scent, isn't it?'

'You can put the stuff wherever you want but I do *not* want you washing my underwear with lavender softener. Understood?'

'I was just trying to help,' said Balthasar defensively. 'No wonder you're always scratching your balls,' he mumbled.

'And now, to the live-streaming of football matches—' Nik's next rule was interrupted by a loud squawk. A parrot with dark grey feathers, a bright red tail feather and a black beak suddenly appeared, performing a swooping 360-degree inspection of the room before landing on Balthasar's shoulder.

'Kara, this is Nik.' The pathologist stroked the bird's head. 'He's going to be our flatmate for a while. I apologise now for his bad manners and terrible dietary habits, but the flat does have high ceilings and the park is just down the road.' He turned to Nik and signalled to the parrot with an open hand. 'Nik, may I introduce you to Kara Ben Nemsi.'

'Kara Ben Nemsi? As in Karl May?'

'Yes. The name came to me as soon as I laid eyes on her.'

'On *her*? Kara Ben Nemsi is a man. He's actually called Karl and—'

'Yes, yes, yes,' interrupted Balthasar. 'But my Kara likes the name,' he said with a smile, stroking her feathers. After a short exchange of affection, the lady parrot flew off again and perched itself on a thick picture frame, pecking at the wallpaper and simultaneously letting the digested remains of her breakfast fall on to the floor.

'Isn't she simply adorable?' commented the pathologist, watching her lovingly. 'But anyway. Enough of that . . . We have lots to do.' He turned to Nik. 'You get the suitcases and I'll clean your cupboard. I hate to think about the amount of dust that's accumulated in there since you moved in.'

While Balthasar pulled on some rubber gloves, Nik shuffled out the door and grabbed a red suitcase from the pile. He had to use all his strength to move it. 'I see you brought your library with you.'

'Oh no, that's my shoes!' called Balthasar from Nik's room. 'Please, no sudden movements and keep the case upright!'

Nik had to put the case down twice between the hall and Balthasar's bedroom and only just managed to get it over the threshold. And then, when he thought the torture was over, ABBA started emanating from the stereo system, so loudly even the beer garden across the road would have been able to hear it. 'Everything is much easier with music, don't you think?' Balthasar called out gleefully over the noise. By that point, Kara had discovered Nik's half-full packet of crisps on the coffee table and was doing her best to spill the entire contents over the sofa.

'Maybe not such a good idea after all,' Nik mumbled as he went for the next suitcase.

◆ ◆ ◆

For one of the city's renowned drug dealers, Paddy had an astoundingly normal life. On Thursday evenings, he went to a club not far from the teaching hospital where the customers spent their free time playing pool and listening to loud music. Located within a residential area, the place looked entirely unremarkable from the outside and the regulars looked about as dangerous as the ones you'd find at a bingo club. But Nik still didn't want to take any risks. Paddy was bound to have friends behind the bar and it would be all too easy to become disorientated down in the dark basement room. He would have to catch Paddy on his way in.

The dealer was a passionate and dedicated poser. He drove a black Mercedes-AMG with a subwoofer you could hear three blocks away. Nik stood on the corner of the street smoking a cigarette. Soon, at around 10.30 p.m., he heard the growling of Paddy's engine and the pounding beats of some terrible American neo-punk band. Nik hid himself in the shadows of a driveway until Paddy had completed his obligatory arrival ceremony. The evening was cool, but the car's roof was down, ensuring Paddy's spiky mohawk had space to poke up above the front windscreen. The rest of his head was bald and covered from front to back with a spider's web tattoo. His face was adorned with numerous piercings, and despite the late hour, he was sporting a pair of reflective sunglasses. He parked the Mercedes on the street, not far from the club, and opened the door abruptly. Before he'd managed to get out of the car, Nik had got hold of his mohawk. Gripping it tightly, he smashed his head against the steering wheel and pushed him on to the passenger's seat. He then stepped inside the car and closed the door. Nik reached his hand under the dashboard and pulled out a gun with an ivory handle. 'An HK45, eh?' said Nik approvingly. 'Not kidding around, are you?'

Paddy rubbed his nose. 'Fuck's sake, Pohl. What was that for?'

'Oh, that's just how I say hello.'

'D'you always need to greet me by breaking my face?'

'You deserve a shitload more than that, Paddy, but I need some information from you so it'll have to wait until next time.'

'Maybe you've forgotten, Pohl, but you don't work for the CID anymore.' Paddy took his hand from his face, revealing a smug smile. Distracted briefly at the thought of how one person could have so many lip piercings, Nik swiftly proceeded to throw a punch to Paddy's nose.

'Yeah, well, that's bad news for you, isn't it, Paddy?' Nik fixed his eyes on the man as he groaned in pain. 'Means I can do what I want without worrying about disciplinary procedures.' He lowered the gun down to his lap but kept pointing it at the dealer. 'Do you know Timo Fürste?'

'Who?' The question earned him another punch to the face. 'Fuuuck!' His nose started to bleed.

'Timo . . . Fürste.'

'He's just some small-time prick,' answered Paddy angrily. 'Thick as shit too.'

'Could you be a bit more detailed, please.'

'Look, Fürste's been working with the Somalians for months. Passes on their coke to smaller dealers around the station.'

'And why d'you say he's thick?'

'There's a rumour that he fucked off with a pound of the stuff.' Paddy took his hand from his nose and looked at the blood. 'And these Somalians, yeah . . . they're really sick. They'll shoot someone just for taking their parking spot. If they get hold of Fürste, they'll cut the coke out of him gram by gram.'

'One pound of flesh; no more, no less. No cartilage, no bone, but only flesh,' said Nik under his breath.

'Huh?' said Paddy, dumbfounded.

'*The Merchant of Venice* . . . Course you don't know it.'

'He dealing in Munich?'

'Jesus . . .' said Nik, shaking his head. 'OK. Back to Fürste. What are his chances of surviving?'

'Zero, man! They've not got him yet. If they did, little bits of him would've been turning up in the Isar.'

'And what would the Somalians do to get hold of him?'

'Anything.'

'Would they kidnap kids?'

'Of course,' said Paddy, shrugging his shoulders. 'But to be honest, gory is more their thing.'

'You mean shooting or stabbing?'

Paddy nodded.

'Heard of anyone who's looking for a kidnapper?'

'You really think it's that easy, don't you, Pohl? It's not like some department store. Someone doesn't just walk into a dark pub full of dodgy characters and ask about a kidnapper. This shit only works via connections.'

'OK. Let me rephrase it then: do you know anyone who kidnaps kids for money?'

'Not my field, is it . . . But Munich definitely has its share of sick fucks.'

'I'm talking about a pro here. Not just some junkie who'd do anything for cash.'

Paddy shook his head. 'Sorry, Pohl.'

Nik smacked his palm on the steering wheel. He'd hit another dead end. A second child had disappeared but there wasn't a single link to Greta's kidnapping. Without uttering another word, Nik got out of the car, threw Paddy's gun underneath a parked SUV and headed home. Early tomorrow, he would go and speak to Simon's foster mother. Maybe she could throw some light on the situation.

Chapter 5

Nik was awoken suddenly by a strange noise. Still half asleep, he got out of bed and reached his hand inside the chest of drawers where he kept his gun. Something wasn't right. He followed a low groan into Balthasar's room, which was dimly lit by the moon. The pathologist had kicked his duvet on to the floor and his pyjamas were sodden with sweat. He was hurling his head from side to side, muttering in his sleep. Kara was perched on the back of a chair near the bed, flapping nervously as if trying to understand what on earth her friend was doing.

Nik stood beside the bed and grabbed Balthasar's hand. It was covered in a layer of cold sweat. He squeezed it hard. 'You're OK,' he said. Balthasar tried to free himself of his grip but Nik kept grasping tightly. 'You're safe here,' he whispered. Balthasar remained in this state for so long that Nik lost track of time, but eventually, he started to calm down. His breathing slowed, the thrashing stopped and his fingers fell limp in Nik's hand. Finally, he laid the pathologist's hand down on the bed, picked up the duvet from the floor and placed it back on top of him. He then left the room quietly, leaving both bedroom doors open. He lay back down in bed despite already knowing he wasn't going to be able to fall asleep again.

◆ ◆ ◆

Balthasar was still sleeping when Nik left the house. He had battled with himself for a long time over whether or not to wake him, but in the end, he decided sleep was currently the best thing for him. Besides, Balthasar might have been somewhat embarrassed knowing Nik had seen him in such a state, so he thought it better to avoid the subject entirely. Nik got into his car, turned on the hands-free and called Jon's number.

'So, how was the first night with Balthasar as a flatmate?'

'Difficult,' answered Nik pensively. 'To my face, he's pretending everything's back to normal. But I know for a fact it wasn't just his face that was damaged by the beating. I found him having nightmares last night.'

'Can I do anything to help?'

'Afraid not. He'll feel safe in the flat. That's the most important thing at the moment. Unfortunately, he's the only one who can get to grips with his demons.'

'Maybe you should speak to him about it at some point?'

'Um . . . therapeutic chats aren't exactly my strong suit. But anyway, did you get anything on Timo Fürste? I'm just heading over to speak to his wife.' It was obvious Nik was changing the subject.

'Timo Patrick Fürste,' Jon began. 'Born near the Bavarian city of Erlangen. Thirty-nine years old. Wasn't a particularly sociable pupil and left school without any exams. Took on a job in 2006 at a thermal power plant in Munich and moved here. Gave that up in 2015 and started getting unemployment benefits. Things start getting interesting two months later, when he's arrested for handling stolen commercial goods. Unlike the guy he was working with, Fürste got away with no charges. They were all dropped and nothing went on his record.'

'He must have snitched,' said Nik.

'Most probably. But there isn't anything about that in his file either.'

'And now he's dealing drugs on the side?'

'Not officially,' answered Jon. 'I can't find any entry about an arrest. But he hangs around the main station all the time and is on the CID's radar.'

'Any connections to the Somalians?'

'None.'

'Sounds like Clemens Grohnert: enough dodgy deals for someone to want to use the kid as a pawn. But is there enough here for any tangible lead?'

'Afraid not.'

Nik sighed loudly. 'Thanks anyway. Maybe Simon's mother will get me further.'

'Keep me informed,' said Jon before hanging up.

Not long after, the satnav announced that Nik had arrived at the Fürstes'. It was a clean, quiet neighbourhood. Not at all what he had expected from a small-time dealer. The block where they lived was lined with hip-high bushes. The street in front of the building was packed with cars and Nik could hear school children playing nearby. The block entrance was also clean, with only a tiny bit of painted-over graffiti, and an empty beer bottle near the rubbish bins marring the scene. Nik pressed the buzzer and waited for a moment.

Finally a voice sounded over the intercom. 'Hello?' She sounded tired.

'Anton Maier. City council,' said Nik. 'I need to speak to you about your son, Simon.'

'Do we have an appointment?'

'No. But Simon has been missing for a few days now so it's urgent.'

'I'm not dressed yet,' said the woman. 'Give me a couple of minutes and I'll buzz you in.'

Nik looked at the time. It was just before nine o'clock in the morning. The chances were high he had got Simon's foster mother out of bed. Two minutes later, the door buzzed and Nik went up to the second floor. A woman, who looked to be somewhere in her late thirties, opened the door. Her curly blonde hair, still fuzzy from sleeping, hung down to her shoulders and her eyes were red and puffy. She smelled of stale sweat. 'Come in,' she said, opening the door only just enough for Nik to squeeze into the flat, then bolting it shut behind them. The window was open and a chemical lemon smell was wafting through the air. Fürste had clearly used an air freshener to mask another smell. The kitchen counter was covered with sticky round marks, as if beer bottles had been standing there not long before and a line of smoke was escaping from a full ashtray.

At first glance the flat seemed tidy enough, but as Nik took a closer look, he began to notice dirty dishes that had been thrown in the sink, clothes that had been hastily stuffed under cushions and various pairs of shoes hiding under the sofa. A socket hung out of the wall behind an armchair and a broken curtain rail had been stuck back together with duct tape. With a bit more warning, Lisa Fürste could have easily cleaned the place up to give the appearance of a pleasant home, but the surprise visit had exposed the truth.

She sat on the couch, rubbing her hands together and looking nervously at Nik. 'Has something happened to Simon?'

'He's been missing for a number of days now. Have you seen him?'

'Not for a couple of weeks.' She looked down at the floor. 'He went back to the kids' home.'

'Do you know why?'

'Um, life at home got pretty bad over the last few months.' The woman was clearly ashamed. 'Simon was always fighting with my husband. He wanted to sort out a job for him but Simon always refused to take it.'

Nik listened, his anger starting to rise. He detested it when bastard drug dealers got children mixed up in their business. But he was there as a council employee today. He couldn't let Frau Fürste see his fury. 'What kind of job was it?'

'My husband gave up his job in a power plant a few years ago to go self-employed. He runs a courier service now. Delivers packages, moves larger items to and from companies . . . helps out with moves, you know?' The woman spoke with such conviction, Nik couldn't tell whether she was aware of her husband's drug dealing. 'Every time Timo brought up the subject, Simon would raise his voice and storm out the flat.'

'And where's your husband now?'

'He got a big job in Brandenburg,' answered the woman. 'He'll be away for another week.'

Nik sighed internally. It was clear Lisa Fürste didn't have the slightest idea that bloodthirsty Somalians were after her husband. He asked himself whether he should tell the woman the truth but decided against it. The lives of two children were at stake. As long as he wasn't entirely sure of Lisa Fürste's connection to the case, he would have to keep up his cover.

'Has your husband ever been in any trouble with the police?'

'Excuse me?'

'I'm referring to the possession of stolen goods.'

'He was let off that,' she said, defending her husband.

'Yes, that's true. But the others involved were sentenced.'

'Which department are you actually from?'

'Frau Fürste,' said Nik soothingly, 'I'm just trying to find your son. Maybe your husband's old . . . friends . . . feel betrayed somehow and are therefore looking for revenge.'

'And you think they've done something to Simon?' she asked, her words overflowing with anguish.

'Well, I don't know what these people are like. Do you think that's possible?'

'I've no idea. There are some really nasty people out there. I mean, just look at that girl who was kidnapped last week.'

'OK. Let me rephrase my question: is it possible that your husband's ex-colleagues have kidnapped Simon in order to blackmail him?'

Fürste clenched her fists to hide the shaking. She needed a cigarette, or a beer. Or both. 'After Simon went through puberty, he and my husband didn't get along at all. It was terrible,' she admitted. 'Timo worked a lot just to make ends meet and didn't . . . have much time for us.'

'So you're saying kidnapping Simon wouldn't be the way someone would go about blackmailing your husband then?'

Frau Fürste hung her head. 'No,' she said quietly. Then lifting her head, she looked Nik sternly in the eyes. 'Wherever Simon is, we've got nothing to do with it, OK?'

◆ ◆ ◆

Balthasar floated through the flat humming cheerfully, as if he had slept the whole night through like a well-fed baby. He sat down on the sofa and balanced a plate on his stomach. On top of the plate was a baguette filled with smoked salmon and a lick of remoulade. There was a glass of Prosecco on the table in front of him, along with a small bowl of sliced apple for Kara. She pecked at the slices gleefully. The pathologist was a cheery person in general but today his mood didn't seem natural. Undoubtedly his way of dealing with things.

'Salmon baguette?' he offered Nik with a smile.

'Had a kebab on my way back, thanks.'

Balthasar shrugged as Nik's phone began to ring. It was Jon. Nik put the call on speakerphone. 'We're both here,' called Nik as he stepped into the kitchen to grab a beer. 'Where should we start?'

'With the similarities between Greta and Simon,' said Jon.

'Are there any?' asked Balthasar.

'Both of them are fourteen years old and both were born in Munich. But that's pretty much where the similarities end. They never met during childhood. There are no parallels or links between Greta's parents and Simon's long-standing foster parents, and their schools are miles apart. Greta loves ballet, and Simon hangs around on street corners.'

'But then there's the tall stranger Simon was seen speaking to,' said Nik.

'Right, and by tall, we mean really tall,' added Jon. 'Around six foot eight, scrawny, with light blonde hair. He either has an injury or a deformity to his right foot or leg and drives a dark blue VW. It's a pretty vague description and I haven't found anyone that matches it,' Jon continued. 'No males of that height have a limp and all the men that limp are considerably shorter. Plus, none of the men I can find who are that tall have light blonde hair, nor are they scrawny. And none of them drive a dark blue VW. I'm stuck unless I get more information.'

'Anything on the gangsters from outside the Grohnerts'?' asked Nik, flashing a side glance at Balthasar.

'The police aren't looking for a group of that description and without an official search, it's going to be hard to find them. But I'm keeping your detailed description of the ringleader in mind. As soon as anyone similar shows up, I'll be in touch.'

'And what about your theory that the children have been kidnapped to put pressure on the parents?' asked Balthasar.

'It could be true in Greta's case,' said Nik. 'But with Simon, we don't even know if he's been kidnapped. There are no witnesses to any crimes, no demands have been made and his foster dad doesn't give a shit about him.'

'Right. Well, there's been nothing new in Greta's case,' added Jon. 'The police are still looking for her but she's losing priority. The public's already more interested in other stories.'

'Timo Fürste has disappeared and Simon's nowhere to be found.' Nik took a sip of beer. 'We've got no leads to follow up.'

'I might actually have something,' said Jon. 'Last year there was a police raid on the graffiti scene. They picked up one gang who'd been terrorising residents in Giesing. The complaints were so serious that the police and the CID carried out surveillance for days. They finally caught some of them red-handed. The youngest in the group was thirteen and wasn't charged but they did put his name in the system. It was our friend Simon.'

'Did you get the names of the others as well?'

'Yeah. I'll send you everything, including photos. They're actually pro graffiti artists who work legally but apparently got bored.'

'Are you going to visit them at home?' Balthasar asked, his mouth full of baguette.

'No, I've got a better place,' Nik answered.

◆ ◆ ◆

Sprayers had caused Nik a lot of grief during his CID days. But now, as he was walking alongside Munich's stockyard, he couldn't help feeling impressed with the work he saw. There were psychedelic mushrooms, characters out of a German cartoon from the 70s and a proud fist, held high in defiance against the development of a well-known, swanky club. Between the images were phrases such as 'Hipsters OUT!' and 'NO TO GENTRIFICATION!' The crumbling wall beside the train tracks made the area feel run-down but there were no homeless or drug dealers to be seen. Nik caught a glimpse of two teenagers standing underneath a large oak tree drinking energy drinks. He assumed the bags on the ground beside them were filled with paint. It was a mild afternoon but the boys had their hoods pulled over their heads. Nik kept driving, acting as if he hadn't seen them, and parked his car in a side street. Keeping close to the trees, he crept over towards them.

'Inspector Pohl, CID.' He lifted his hands to show he wasn't armed. 'I'm not here to cause any problems. I just have a couple of questions.'

The boys spun around, startled by the sudden arrival. 'You can ask as many questions as you want but you're not gonna get any answers,' said one of the youngsters gruffly. His long dreadlocks were swelling out from underneath his hood. Nik knew the boy would never give his real name so he decided to call him 'Marley'.

'I'm looking for a sprayer called Simon Fahl.'

'Try Google, mate,' said the second boy. Nik reckoned he was around sixteen years old. His near translucent skin was covered in freckles.

'Look, if you tell me you've seen Simon in the last couple of hours, then my work's done and I'll leave immediately. But if that's not the case, then we should be worried because a week ago a teenage girl was kidnapped, and Simon has also disappeared. I've got reason to believe there is a link between the two. Not only are there similarities, but Simon went missing not long after the girl did. Only difference is . . . while everybody and their granny knows about the girl, nobody has a clue about Simon. D'you understand what I'm saying here? I'm the only person out there looking for him.' Nik paused and looked at the boys. 'So, if you'd rather not hear about Simon getting fished out of the Isar because some sick paedophile got bored of him, then you should probably be a bit more helpful.' Nik knew a sentimental story wasn't going to work on these boys so he'd have to resort to a bit of exaggeration. Marley lifted his head and looked at his friend. He finally let go of the stubborn act.

'We haven't seen him in ages,' he said.

'How long exactly?'

'Five days.'

'Is that normal?'

'Simon's home life is a pile of shit. His foster mum's mental and his old man sells drugs. So obviously he spends most of his time with us.'

'How d'you know about the drugs?'

'Simon told us,' answered Marley. 'Wanted to get him selling too.'

'Anything strange happen last time you saw him?'

'Nothing, man. He was the same as always.'

'Did he tell you about any new acquaintances of his?'

Marley shook his head. 'Simon didn't make friends easily. That kids' home he lived in hardened him up.'

'A child care worker saw Simon speaking to a very tall, scrawny man on two occasions. He had a bad limp.'

Marley glanced at his friend again before speaking, as if looking for permission. 'Yeah, we saw that guy once.'

'We were picking Simon up from the home,' continued the boy with the freckles. 'He was speaking to that lanky dude when we got there. I noticed he was tall but other than that he seemed normal. Apart from the limp . . . That stood out.'

'And how did the conversation look? Did Simon seem nervous or threatened?'

'No idea. But they definitely waved goodbye. Didn't notice anything strange.'

'Did Simon ever mention the man?'

'Nope,' answered Marley.

'And we never saw him after that,' added the other boy.

Nik sighed. This man was the connection between the two missing teenagers but he wasn't going to get any further without a better description or a name. Simon was the only one who could help.

'D'you reckon Simon might be hiding somewhere? Has he got somewhere he goes to get away?' asked Nik.

'Simon likes being on his own, yeah. But he's not a complete loner. He doesn't just hide out for days on his own without telling anyone. So, if you're CID . . . isn't it about time you got on the phone to your buddies in blue and tried to find him?'

Chapter 6

Nik was woken by a sharp pain in the nose. He blinked quickly, opened his eyes and noticed a faint pressure on his chest. Kara was standing stock still on his solar plexus, not moving a feather, and glaring at him threateningly, as though weighing up the potential success of an attack to the nose. Nik was relieved that she was a grey parrot and not an Andean condor.

As he lay considering the best way out of the predicament, Balthasar's voice rang through the flat. 'Ni-i-k! Breakfast's ready-y-y!'

The parrot squawked, raised its wings and flew out of the bedroom. Just as Nik turned on to his side to go back to sleep, music started blasting from the living room. 'Fucking ABBA. Of all things, why ABBA?' He pushed himself up and turned to sit on the edge of the bed. Sinking his forehead into the palms of his hands, he focused his attention on his breathing. In and out. 'No violence, Pohl,' he mumbled to himself. 'Leave the gun in the drawer. And calm . . . down.' There was no room for aggression when it came to Balthasar at the moment. Even if he was sleeping better, he still needed time. Nik forced a smile on to his face, stood up and slumped his way into the kitchen. On the table was a small bowl of cornflakes that had been drowned in watery yogurt. Kara's head was dunked deep into the white mush, and Nik wondered how on earth the parrot was able to breath.

'Is that appropriate food for a parrot?' asked Nik.

'My Kara might be a sweetie pie, but she is also a real grouch in the morning. And you do *not* want to see her when she doesn't get her breakfast.'

'Hmm, probably best,' grumbled Nik. Kara lifted her head, took a deep breath and dived down for more.

'Did you sleep well?' Balthasar asked with a smile.

'I was fine after I stuck earplugs up my nose. Would have been suffocated by lavender otherwise.'

'You'll get used to it and then . . . you won't be able to do without it.'

'I wonder what it smells like when you throw petrol over it and put a match to it.'

'Like burned lavender, of course.'

'Balthasar, were you decorating the kitchen in the middle of the night?' Nik looked over at a colourful painting above the washing machine.

'Ah yes! That's a replica of one of Jackson Pollock's master-pieces,' answered Balthasar enthusiastically. 'Fabulous, isn't it?'

'Looks like a three-year-old ate their paint set and threw it back up on the wall.'

Balthasar turned off the hi-fi with the remote control and folded his arms across his chest. 'Nik Pohl. You are an utter philistine.'

'Been called worse names,' Nik responded, sipping his coffee. He picked up a slice of toast and shuffled into the bathroom, while Balthasar gazed at the abstract expressionism on the wall and Kara continued with her yogurt-diving ritual. Nik turned the tap to cold and let the water run over his head. After a minute, he dried off his hair with a lavender-scented towel. He yawned his way back to the living room, slumped on to the couch and called Jon.

'Morning, Nik. How's the flat-share going?'

'Well, the place smells like a brothel, the tables are covered in weird vases filled with just as weird-looking flowers and Balthasar's hung up the world's ugliest painting in the kitchen. Oh, and then there's the parrot with a psychopathic serial-killer vibe that likes to bathe its head in yogurt for breakfast.'

'Sounds like a match made in heaven,' said Jon. 'Anyway, it's good you called; something's happening with Greta's case. Turn on the local news.'

A special broadcast was underway. Clemens and Vanessa Grohnert were sitting at a table. Clemens was wearing a navy suit, while his wife wore a subtle grey dress. Her hair was tied back in a plait and she was wearing next to no make-up. Clemens was reading from a sheet of paper in a monotone voice.

'I would like to take this opportunity to make a confession: I was one of the people responsible for the northern Munich bypass embezzlement scandal. I will be working with the public prosecutor to help clarify this matter and I will meet the demands made by the kidnapper. You will get your money. By this evening, I will have set up a fund for the parties that were harmed by the construction scandal.' Clemens looked up. *'I'm begging you: please let Greta go unharmed so we can finally hold her in our arms again.'*

Clemens stood up and left the room with his wife, who had started to cry. Cameras flashed and flickered wildly. Reporters bawled out questions and a security guard stopped one overzealous journalist from following the Grohnerts. The shot returned to the news reporter in the studio and Nik turned off the TV.

'Looks like something's finally happening,' said Nik.

'Oh, that's only half the story,' explained Jon. 'Something happened last night as well.' Nik heard Jon typing in the background. 'At one a.m. the Grohnerts received a message from an anonymous email address giving Clemens twelve more hours to confess and to set up the account. If he didn't comply, the blackmailer would send Greta home in a body bag. A photo of Greta holding yesterday's newspaper was attached to the email.'

'Was it possible to trace it?'

'Not a chance,' replied Jon. 'It's easy to send an anonymous email these days. And the photo gives no clues to Greta's location. The CID forensics reckon it's real.'

'Well, at least Greta's still alive, I suppose.'

'Yes, but the kidnapper increased the sum. He now wants five million and an extra hundred thousand just for himself that should be handed over to him personally.'

'Now I understand why Clemens said "You will get your money."'

'Yeah, the CID aren't releasing that bit of information to the public,' said Jon. 'But I think all this just disproved your smoke-screen theory.'

'Not necessarily. I'm still not convinced. There are too many things that just don't fit a classic abduction. Not to mention a ransom handover will use up valuable resources that would've otherwise been put into the search for him and the girl. Did the kidnapper set down a time and a place?'

'The Old North Cemetery in the Maxvorstadt borough. At eleven p.m.'

'Not a good choice,' said Nik. 'It's very central but it's large and flat. It only has four exits and the high walls are hard to get over. The trees will make an aerial surveillance difficult and the gravestones offer great hiding places, but even with the thick vegetation, it's still not dense enough for someone to hide securely. And the park will be empty at that time so the kidnapper's got no chance of vanishing into a group.'

'True. And it'll be dark.'

'Oh, that's not an issue. Night-vision glasses aren't expensive these days and if the kidnapper memorises the way, the dark's not a problem anyway. Of course, the police'll have glasses too,' Nik remarked.

'The kidnapper's never gonna get away with the money. The police are planning to deploy more officers than there are residents in the neighbourhood.'

'Has an exact point of exchange been arranged?'

'The kidnapper's getting in touch just before eleven p.m.,' explained Jon. 'The money should be put into a bag and Clemens Grohnert has to pass it over himself.'

'And did the person make any more specific demands? Like the money needs to be in small notes or if the police are anywhere nearby the girl dies?'

'Nothing of the sort.'

Nik groaned sullenly.

'You don't think the kidnapper will turn up?'

'It's not important,' replied Nik. 'If they pick him up, fine. If he gets the money and lets Greta go, even better. But as long as the girl isn't back home, I'm going to keep looking.' Nik got up off the couch. 'Can we follow what happens without having to be right at the scene?'

'I can hook us up to the police radios but not their cameras,' Jon said. 'But I've got an alternative.'

'OK?'

'Airbnb.' Nik could hear Jon's proud smile over the phone. 'I'll send you the address in a minute.'

'And the CID's deployment plans as soon as they're available,' added Nik. 'Let's hope this whole thing is over by tonight . . . Or we at least get some kind of lead.'

◆ ◆ ◆

Nik walked over to the fridge and took out a beer. The attic flat was musty and the bed was uninviting to say the least. But the view of the Old North Cemetery was remarkable. 'How did you manage to book this place at such short notice?' Nik asked Jon over a headset.

'The guy who lives here rents it out on Airbnb,' replied Jon.

'And it was available tonight?'

'Actually, no. But I made him an offer nobody in their right mind would have refused,' said Jon. 'So now, he gets to spend a couple of nights in a five-star hotel and enjoy a bit of extra cash in his account.'

Nik bent down to look through a telescope. Hidden from the outside world by a curtain, Nik could aim it downwards to monitor Adalbertstraße. Jon had installed high-quality cameras on Arcisstraße, at the park entrance on Zieblandstraße and in front of the play park at Tengstraße. All the images were now visible on the three monitors that Jon had set up on a table beside the telescope.

'You not scared someone will find the cameras?'

'Don't worry. They're no bigger than lighters and very well hidden. Plus, the signal's encrypted and runs directly to me via an open Wi-Fi network. So even if the police do find the cameras, they won't be able to trace them to you or me.'

Nik looked at his watch. 'It's almost eleven p.m. The street's awfully quiet considering a team of more than twenty officers is out and about.'

'The police decided not to close any roads or set up control points. A flat in Adalbertstraße is being used as a central look-out post. Plus, four SEK officers are undercover in a bus parked in Tengstraße.' SEK was Germany's special operations unit that dealt with high-risk settings such as hostages, raids and kidnappings. 'Two CID officers are in an old building directly at the main entrance on Arcisstraße and four others are lying somewhere in the cemetery.'

Nik looked at a printed plan of the area. 'Depending on where the four from the SEK are situated, the chances of getting away with the money are slim. But who knows? Maybe we're in for a surprise. Maybe the kidnapper has a trick that nobody's been expecting.'

'So, the exact exchange location was just confirmed,' said Jon. 'The CID are saying another email came in from the kidnapper two minutes ago. The money is to be left behind Wagmüller's tombstone. The one with the angel of death and a child on top.'

The monitor suddenly grabbed Nik's attention. Somebody was leaving the building by the main entrance with a torch in his hand.

'Is that really Clemens Grohnert?' asked Nik.

'No, just a police officer with a similar figure,' Jon explained. 'And a wig and make-up. Since it's dark, the CID decided to take a risk and fake that demand.'

Nik watched the action for as long as the camera could follow the man. Then, four minutes later, the same man appeared on another monitor.

'Everything looks fine,' said Jon.

Nik sat down on the couch, his eyes never leaving the monitors. Every so often a car would drive past and at one point he saw an old man walking his dogs, but other than that, the area surrounding the cemetery stayed quiet.

He looked at the map and imagined all the ways he would have tried to get into the cemetery, take the money and disappear without being seen. But it was useless. He always ended up getting picked up by the police.

'I'm keen to know how the kidnapper plans on getting that bag,' mumbled Nik.

'We're about to find out,' said Jon. 'A person dressed in black just climbed on to some rubbish bins and over the wall. They're moving in your direction.' Nik ran to the telescope and looked through it but thanks to the trees, he could only see a thermal signature every so often.

'He's going straight to the tombstone,' said Nik. 'No hiding, no creeping.'

'And he's not limping,' said Jon.

'And he's too short,' added Nik as he moved the telescope so he could keep an eye on the tombstone. The man picked up the bag and as he did, two figures stormed out from their hiding places and threw him to the ground.

'They've got him,' said Jon.

Nik puffed out his cheeks and exhaled. He hadn't heard any shots but the man was lying on the ground. He was annoyed he couldn't be at the interrogation and for the first time, felt some regret at no longer working for the CID. He would just have to wait until the report had been uploaded.

'I'll wait here until all divisions have moved on and then head home,' said Nik. 'There's nothing else we can do now.'

'OK. I'll get in touch as soon as anything new turns up,' said Jon. 'Let's hope whoever they got is our kidnapper.'

Naumann looked through the mirrored glass at the man they had arrested. He looked to be in his thirties; his messy hair was wet with sweat and his worn-out T-shirt clung to his body, despite the coolness of the interrogation room. He sat rubbing his beard nervously, his eyes fixed on the floor and his shoulders hunched, as if afraid someone was going to throttle him at any second.

'That's not the kidnapper,' said Naumann to a colleague sitting beside him. 'He doesn't have the same figure or the limp.'

'Might be an accomplice though.'

'It's not. He was too surprised when we picked him up,' replied Naumann. 'He practically fainted when the SEK stormed him. And he didn't resist.' Naumann shook his head. 'Maybe we should have let him get away with a bug in the bag.' Naumann went out the door and entered the interrogation room. The man lifted his head with a start.

'Why am I here?' His voice was fearful.

'I'll get to that shortly,' replied Naumann, sitting down in the seat opposite him. 'First we need to go over the formalities.' He opened a folder with notes inside. 'Are you Dennis Erler, from Steinhausen in Munich?'

'Yes,' said the man impatiently.

'You were picked up in possession of drugs on two occasions last year by public officials in the park area at Isartorplatz,' read Naumann out loud. 'The large quantity led police to believe you had been selling the drugs.' He raised his head. 'Was dealing not paying the bills so you decided to get into the kidnapping business?'

'What are you talking about? I don't have anything to do with kidnapping,' replied the man. 'Why are you asking that?'

'OK. Let's start at the beginning. Last night at 11.07 p.m. you were caught red-handed by SEK officers picking up the ransom money for a kidnapping.'

'I swear to God I haven't kidnapped anybody.'

'You climbed over the wall of the Old North Cemetery in Maxvorstadt with a torch. You went directly to the Wagmüller tombstone, where you picked up a hidden bag. Was all of that just a coincidence?'

'I was paid to do it.'

'To pick up the bag?'

Erler nodded.

'By who?'

'By a girl.'

110

'A girl?' repeated Naumann, shocked. 'Not by a tall man with a limp?'

'No. It was a girl. Maybe fourteen . . . fifteen years old. Curly brown hair. About five five.'

Naumann took a picture of Greta from the file. 'This girl?'

Erler nodded.

'What did she say to you?'

'That I should go to that park at eleven p.m. and pick up a bag that would be lying in that spot. Then I was supposed to take the U-Bahn to Marienplatz, walk to the Frauenkirche and throw the bag in a bin without ever opening it.'

Naumann said nothing. This wasn't the conversation he'd been expecting. 'OK. Let's start with the girl,' he continued. 'How did she seem? Was she shy, scared? Was she constantly looking over her shoulder?'

'She seemed normal.'

'OK. So how did she *look*? Like she'd been wearing the same clothes for a long time? Did she smell like she hadn't washed in a while?'

'She just seemed like a normal girl from a good home. That's why I was surprised when she approached me.'

'And what did she say when she approached you?'

'That she had an errand for me and asked if I was interested.'

'An errand?'

'Yeah. Since getting picked up on Isartorplatz, I'm not allowed to sell anymore but sometimes people book me to take things from A to B. The code word's "errand".'

'So you thought you would be transporting drugs?'

Erler nodded.

'And what did you get for it?'

'The usual. A hundred up front and two hundred if the delivery was successful.'

'And you didn't wonder why a young girl was hiring you?'

'Minors ask me to do jobs quite a lot. Nothing happens to them if they're picked up.'

'Do you still have the banknote?'

Erler shook his head. 'I bought a drink with it. But I can show you the supermarket I went to.'

Naumann leaned back in his chair. He didn't know whether he should be happy that Greta was still alive, or angry because the kidnapper was a step ahead of them yet again. Without saying another word, he picked up his paperwork and left the room. It was going to be a long night.

◆　◆　◆

Going by the police officer's matter-of-fact voice, Danilo assumed nothing more could be done to help the man lying on the street. It was five in the morning and he'd been hoping for a quiet shift. But then, a body was found in Trudering so he and his partner had set off instantly to the crime scene.

As much as he had detested Nik's manners, Danilo now missed his ex-colleague's calm manner and the fact he had never jabbered on about his private life. He had always worked diligently and meticulously. He didn't need every last detail explained to him, and his ability to instinctively understand how a crime had unfolded was remarkable. His replacement – some newbie with next to no experience – didn't come close to matching him. He was a man so lacking in confidence he wouldn't even get himself a coffee without asking permission. Working with him frequently felt like babysitting an oversized toddler.

Desperate for a moment of peace, he had sent his colleague to ask for a statement from the police officers who had first arrived at the scene. The newbie was taking far too long to question them and going by the exasperated looks on the officers' faces, he was probing too deeply. Danilo noticed that all correct procedures had been taken: the area behind the supermarket had been sectioned off, the CID had been informed, and curious bystanders had been prevented from taking photos of the body.

The dead man, lying on his side, appeared to have been around fifty, Danilo guessed. He looked well groomed and smartly dressed in an expensive tailored suit. One shot had ripped a jacket pocket and the shirt underneath to shreds, while a second shot had driven through the shoulder to the jacket collar. Blood had coagulated around what looked like a further bullet hole at heart height. There was no question it had been murder. The prosecutor would now have the body removed and initiate the preliminary investigations into the death. The stiffening of the man's jaw indicated he had been lying on the street for around five hours. The killer would be long gone.

Danilo looked inquisitively at the bump underneath the man's jacket. Forensics were on their way and he wanted to leave the crime scene as untouched as possible, but his curiosity got the better of him. Carefully he lifted the fabric to reveal a gun in a holster. 'OK then,' he mumbled to himself. 'Might be a pretty interesting case after all.' He stood up and made his way over to the uniformed police.

Chapter 7

Nik sat in front of the large projector screen, coffee in hand, watching a discussion about yesterday's football match. Kara was sitting on the coffee table in front of him, pecking at the newspaper and scattering the frayed results over the floor, squawking with joy as she dropped each shred. The only time she was quiet was when a slow-motion replay showed on the screen, at which point she would take a break to watch, tipping her head to the side as if wondering why the men on the wall were moving so slowly.

As Nik sipped his coffee, his phone began to ring. The best thing about having a limited social circle was the small address book: only Jon and Balthasar had his number. Balthasar's rendition of 'Singing in the Rain' had come to an end but he was still in the bathroom. Chances were slim he would be calling from there. So that only left one option.

'Morning, Jon.'

'Morning,' Jon replied with a yawn.

'Someone's been busy.'

'Yeah, the night saw some interesting developments.'

'And what came from the interrogation?'

'The suspect was hired to pick up the money and take it to Frauenkirche. He thought he was moving drugs.'

'Any connection between him and the Grohnerts?'

'Nothing in his file but he says it was Greta that gave him the job.'

'Greta hired him to fetch the bag?' asked Nik.

'Yep.'

'OK, now I'm completely lost.' He muted the TV.

'Wait. It gets better,' Jon went on. 'According to the courier's statement, Greta seemed relaxed and in no way scared.'

'If it wasn't for the fact she's fourteen, we could have assumed she'd arranged the kidnapping herself.'

'I'm thinking it's maybe a case of Stockholm syndrome.'

'Nah, I'm not sure,' said Nik doubtfully. 'Yeah, it's possible the kidnapper's manipulated the girl into growing fond of him and being scared of the police. But that still doesn't tell us why. Greta Grohnert's no Patty Hearst; her grandfather isn't one of the richest men in the world. Hearst's kidnappers were left-wing radicals who encouraged her to fight the system. What cause would Greta stand for if she was to rebel against her parents or society?'

'True. And why would Greta not run away when she had the chance? According to the man they picked up, there was no tall man with a limp anywhere to be seen. Why would he send Greta out like that?'

'Well, now I'm positive the money exchange was merely a distraction to keep the police busy. For some reason the kidnapper is trying to buy time . . . I just can't think what the reason might be. And unless I or the special commission are enlightened somehow, we're not going to get any further.'

'I've emailed you the interrogation report. But I actually wanted to talk to you about another case.' Nik's mobile vibrated. 'Look at the photo.'

Nik looked at his phone. 'That's the bastard who beat up Balthasar!' He would have spotted his face in a crowd of thousands. 'Do you have his name?' asked Nik, jumping off the sofa.

'Vincent Masannek. But it's no good to you now. He was shot.'

'Where? Who by?'

'His body was found between two bins behind a supermarket in Trudering. He'd taken a bullet to the chest and neck.'

'Any witnesses? Evidence?' asked Nik, brimming with curiosity. 'What did the post-mortem say?'

'A paper boy found the body around four thirty this morning and called the police. According to the paramedics, rigor mortis was well underway so Masannek must have been lying there for a good while. Enquiries have only just started and there still hasn't been an autopsy yet.'

'Did they make any connection to Greta's kidnapping?'

'No. Apparently, you and Balthasar are the only ones Masannek threatened. There's nothing about him in the records, or about anyone interfering with the case for that matter.'

'OK, let's go back to the beginning.' Nik sat back down on the couch. 'Who was Vincent Masannek?'

'A man in his early fifties. Born in Lower Saxony but had lived in Munich for seventeen years. Consultant at a security company since 2009. That's why he was permitted to carry a weapon outside of business premises. Nothing in his record about any offences.'

'Any connection to Clemens?'

'Not that I can see,' replied Jon. 'I'm just in the middle of getting into the security company's database. Maybe I'll find something there.'

'Did he have a weapon on him?'

'Yeah, in his holster. And it wasn't a HK P30 like the one used on Greta's driver . . . in case that was your next question.'

'Any indication of what the motive for murder was? Was his wallet gone? Were his trousers down?'

'His wallet was still inside his jacket. That's why it was so easy to identify him. And his trousers were up on the crime scene photos at least. Trudering's not exactly known for its prostitution scene.'

'Something doesn't add up here. What's somebody like Masannek doing in a residential area late at night beside some supermarket bins?'

'That's what the investigators are asking too.'

'And he worked in security. It's not easy to just trap someone like that, and if you do, chances are high he's going to have his gun in his hand. The murderer must have surprised him.'

'He maybe wasn't as proficient as you'd expect: the report says a GPS transmitter was found in his suit.'

'A transmitter?' repeated Nik, confused.

'The shot to his neck had ripped open his jacket collar and a mini radio and antenna were found inside,' explained Jon. 'You can buy the things online if you know where to look . . . but I wouldn't say they're child's play to use. Weighs just a couple of grams, battery lasts a few days and it has a precise quartz resonator; the signal will reach up to a kilometre out on open land.'

'And Masannek hadn't noticed it?'

'This thing's tiny and it had been sewn into his collar.'

'Sewn in? So nobody just slipped it on to him while passing. It must have been someone he'd known who'd had enough time to cut open the suit.'

'The CID have it now and they're trying to use the serial number to locate the seller. But I'm not too optimistic.'

'Did they find anything else on him?'

'A scrunched-up map of Trudering-Riem and a pair of night vision glasses. Photos have been uploaded, so I'll send you a picture of the map. It's covered in scribbles and streets have been crossed out.'

'So he was looking for something or someone.'

'Or observing something or someone.'

'No, if he'd known the destination beforehand he wouldn't have needed a map,' Nik said.

'OK. So what good's all this to us?' asked Jon. 'Masannek's death is turning out to be more confusing than insightful.'

Nik picked up his coffee cup and took a gulp. 'Masannek was a ruthless bastard who wanted me and Balthasar to stop investigating Greta's kidnapping. We don't know why. There are no connections between him and Clemens Grohnert. Whatever he was doing in Trudering is a mystery because there's no link to Greta's kidnapping or Simon's disappearance. And finally, it's unclear who sewed the tracker into his jacket and why.'

'Probably his murderer, whoever that was and for whatever motive,' added Jon.

'We need to find out more about Masannek,' decided Nik.

'I kept up my search on him but couldn't find any new entries.'

'No, official channels are no use anymore,' said Nik. 'I need information from someone who regularly deals with security guards like Masannek. And I think I know who might be able to help.'

Cafes weren't really Nik's thing. He preferred sports bars with large screens, simple menus and cold beer. But nevertheless, he was impressed with the interior of the place. The elegant white pillars perfectly complemented the brown parquet flooring, which reflected a warm glow from the halogen lamps. And it was all tied in seamlessly by heavy wooden tables and chairs, while soft music played in the background. Nik noticed a young woman celebrating her birthday with her girlfriends. Helium balloons had been tied to an armrest and a cake sat on top of a dresser. On the other side of the room was a window through which you could watch a tall blonde florist at work. He had tied a bunch of autumn flowers together and was arranging them on to a long twig that had been painted white. A group of older men in Bavarian dress had made themselves comfortable at the tables near the front door. Had Nik ventured further into the cafe, he would have come to a magnificent conservatory with a domed glass roof, but the person Nik was looking for was sitting in the front area, away from the long bar and the stairway to the toilets in the basement. Engrossed in a newspaper article, the woman simultaneously poked at a slice of chocolate cake with a fork in her right hand. A large cup of coffee and a glass of orange juice were also on the table in front of her. Her handbag, adorned with rhinestones, sat beside her on the black leather bench next to a pair of cream-coloured sunglasses.

It was difficult to say how old she was. Her hair was shining white – the colour too even to be natural. A long pearl necklace hung delicately over her black jumper down to her waist, while at the neckline sat a sparkling choker with a butterfly pendant. Despite the warmth of the cafe, she was still wearing her fur jacket. The white gloves and diamond bracelet on her right wrist completed the look perfectly and left no doubt as to the extent of this woman's wealth.

In contrast to his usual attire, Nik had chosen to wear a tailored suit with a freshly pressed shirt and leather shoes. The outfit might not have been comfortable, but he was relieved not to look out of place among the other customers.

Nik hovered over the woman's table. Her eyes ran over him, starting at his feet and moving slowly up to his face. 'Herr Pohl,' she said, before calmly bringing her concentration back to the newspaper. 'Apparently self-employment is working for you. Last time we met, you were wearing ripped jeans, an odd-smelling leather jacket and those grotesque boots with the laces undone.'

Nik smiled. This woman had an amazing memory and never missed a beat. 'May I join you?' he asked, gesturing with an open hand towards a chair opposite her. She sighed and closed the newspaper abruptly before giving a nod of permission.

'Since you are no longer working for the CID, I can safely assume your visit is for personal reasons, yes?'

'Not entirely,' answered Nik. 'I need some information on a man who might be involved in the Greta Grohnert kidnapping.'

Her brow furrowed. 'As you are aware, I provide affluent people with men and women who can satisfy their particular, if not entirely savoury, needs. I do not, however, abduct people and neither do I have contact with people who do.'

'Frau Jablonski,' said Nik, the smile still on his lips, 'you are a keeper of secrets; a woman who could force members of the city council and German government to resign.' He leaned back in his chair. 'I didn't have an awful lot to do with your work during my time at the CID, but I certainly had the chance to see how powerful you are. And I also know that despite the garish façade, you're far more intelligent than you like to let on . . . if you don't mind me saying.'

She looked up to the ceiling, as if trying to decide whether she felt flattered or insulted. Her gaze lowered again and she sliced off a chunk of cake with her fork.

'You and your colleagues didn't make it easy for me,' she said, chewing on the creamy sponge. 'That raid four years ago cost me a lot of money and even more of my reputation. I lost important clients and had to make great efforts winning them back. Why should I help you?'

'Because of fourteen-year-old Greta.'

'Ha!' She pointed her fork at Nik. 'I see worse than that every day. You know, Herr Pohl, just being seen speaking to you will cause problems for me. Discretion is vital in my line of work. How do you think my clients will react when they see a former CID agent sitting at my table?'

'Help me and I'll be out of your hair immediately.'

'Listen. I'm a businesswoman,' said Jablonski. 'If you were still at the CID, we might have been able to come to a useful arrangement. But what good are you to me as a private investigator?' She took another forkful of cake.

'I can get you a name from an investigation file.'

Jablonski stopped chewing for moment and set her fork down on the plate. She looked at Nik. 'Go on.' She reached for her cup and took a sip of coffee, not breaking eye contact.

'You and your lawyer have tried for years to find out who gave us the crucial tip that got proceedings against you rolling. You were never successful.'

'And now you want to give me this name?'

Nik shrugged.

She placed down her cup. 'Don't get me wrong, Herr Pohl, but I actually know one of your previous bosses . . .'

'I wonder who that might be . . . ?' Nik mumbled.

'. . . And this particular boss assured me that even *he* didn't have access to that information. How is a former employee supposed to have such access?' She picked up her fork again.

'Someone I know has access to all CID records.'

'Such a someone doesn't exist. Unless of course you know the chief of police.'

'My someone is a rather savvy hacker who even has access to frozen files.'

Jablonski tapped her fork on the table before setting it down on her plate again. 'How do I know you aren't lying to me?'

'I wouldn't take that risk,' replied Nik. 'I know you're not just intelligent. You're powerful . . . and vindictive.'

She paused for a moment before finally nodding. 'OK. The files on my snitch for information on your man.'

'You can only get the name of the informant,' Nik replied. 'The files stay where they are.'

She pressed her lips together and held her breath while wrestling with the decision.

Nik went on. 'You'll get the file extract this evening, and I get the information on my man here and now.'

She finally made up her mind. 'OK.' She picked up her fork and polished off the rest of her cake. 'Who's the man?'

'Vincent Masannek.'

'Heard he wasn't feeling too good.' She giggled. An evil giggle that exposed her opinion on the man's fate.

'Could say that,' replied Nik, raising his eyebrow and curling the corners of his lips. 'What do you know about him? And do you have any idea who might have murdered him?'

Jablonski signalled a waitress and tipped her head towards the chocolate cake. 'This could take a while,' she said, taking a sip of coffee. 'The first time I met Masannek, he was working as a bodyguard for a prominent drug dealer. That was back in 2005. Never liked him from the start. Just your typical brutish gunman who enjoyed his work too much. Where Masannek differed, however, was that he was clever, calculating and reflective. It was no wonder he progressed so quickly in the job. Officially, he moved into the security field to become a consultant. But that was obviously just a front while he kept on working in the underworld. Doing the dirty work. Only difference was, he had more men.'

'And what exactly was his work?'

'Collecting money from the big boys who weren't easily intimidated. He'd break the bones of anyone who tried to misbehave and end any territorial conflicts.'

'So Masannek had a lot of enemies then?'

'Likely. But he had a network of very loyal employees ready to do whatever was needed. So nobody ever dared start anything with him. The vast underworld needed his services over and over again, and since he remained as neutral as possible, he had a good standing in Munich. Nobody had to worry about him wanting to steal business. He was the king of a niche market.'

'So what happened? Did he do something wrong in one of his jobs?'

'I don't know,' answered Jablonski.

'Do you know who he last worked for?'

She shook her head.

'But somebody was clearly angry with him,' Nik remarked. 'Otherwise he wouldn't have been shot.'

'Well, whoever it was must either be crazy or very confused. Masannek's men will be looking for revenge now. Whoever murdered him won't be alive for much longer.'

◆ ◆ ◆

'You want to pass on a top-secret file to Jablonski?' asked Jon incredulously. He was speaking over the hands-free in Nik's car.

'Just the page with the name of the informant.'

'You know you might be sentencing him to death if we do that, yeah?'

'Murder isn't Jablonski's style,' Nik said defensively. 'He'll just have to deal with a serious thrashing and then leave Munich for good.'

'I thought you once worked for the CID . . . Isn't protection of your informants of paramount importance?'

'Not in his case.'

'OK. D'you want to fill me in here?' said Jon.

'The man we're talking about is Bertram Laake.'

'Never heard of him.'

'Laake is a filthy, unprincipled bastard, who for a long time was suspected of working with a paedophile ring. He would pick up young homeless people, get them hooked on heroin and then prostitute them to sick punters.'

'And Jablonski worked with someone like that?'

'She chucked him out as soon as the rumours started. And then the very next day he was standing on the CID's doorstep offering his services as an informant.'

'That's top-secret information. Barely any agents had access to it. How do you know about it?'

'My former buddy, Tilo Hübner, told me once over a beer,' said Nik.

'And why wasn't he charged instantly?'

'Because there wasn't any evidence linking him to the paedophile ring. Only thing we had was a vague statement from a victim who was sitting in custody for robbery and battling with severe withdrawal symptoms.'

'So you want to punish Laake by basically sending him to Jablonski's slaughterhouse?'

'You could say that.'

'Definitely a unique way of seeking justice . . .'

'Don't go all fucking moral on me here, Jon,' Nik retaliated. 'You never saw the kids, did you? Twelve-year-olds with severe heroin addictions, traumatised by countless rapes. Two of them threw themselves into the Isar because they couldn't take it anymore.' Nik hit the steering wheel with his palm. 'Lives destroyed because a sack of shit like Laake runs a business hooking up sick paedo bastards with kids. The prosecutor never got enough to put an end to it so it's only fair someone else gets the job done.'

'It's OK, Nik. I get it,' said Jon. And of course he did. 'You'll have the file by this evening.'

'Thank you,' said Nik, still upset.

'But listen, I need to talk to you about something else as well,' said Jon, changing the subject. 'I might have found a new lead in the Masannek case.' Nik heard computer keys tapping. 'I looked at all the incidents in Trudering and the surrounding area on the day of his murder. There wasn't anything particularly interesting, but I did come across an entry about a towed car that belonged to Tina Vohl. She'd parked illegally in front of a school's emergency vehicle access. About a hundred metres away from the crime scene.'

'OK, and who's Tina Vohl? And what does she have to do with the case?'

'After closer inspection, it turns out that she works for the same security company as Masannek.'

'And you think she might be the murderer?'

'Unlikely,' Jon replied. 'I called the company today pretending to be a client who wanted to employ Tina. But the woman on the phone kindly explained that Tina has been in Brandenburg for the last two weeks and will only be available again at the end of the month.'

'Brandenburg isn't that far away.'

'No, but there's no way Tina drove from Brandenburg to Munich, shot Masannek and walked back to Brandenburg again.'

'True.' Nik ran through the events in his head.

'Masannek must have used Tina's car to drive to Trudering.'

'Didn't he have his own?'

'Can't find any record of it.'

'Does the CID know about any of this?'

'Not yet. But it's only a matter of time before they put two and two together.'

'Well, we need to take advantage of that then, don't we, and take a look at the evidence before they do,' said Nik. 'Where's the car now?'

'In police storage.'

'Then I know the perfect place for an evening stroll. And you're coming with me.'

◆ ◆ ◆

They waited until the train had passed before making a move. While Nik sprang across the tracks in two nimble steps, Jon was still heaving himself out of their hiding spot. 'This is exactly why I prefer to sit in front of a screen,' he muttered, stumbling after Nik.

'Shhh. Be quiet,' whispered Nik. It was a cloudy night, making it almost impossible to see him in his dark clothes and ski mask.

'Remind me why I gave up my job as a successful app programmer . . .' Jon continued. He finally caught up with Nik, who was waiting beside a bulky oak tree.

'Just one more time to make sure you've got it,' Nik said quietly. 'The vehicle yard is manned twenty-four hours a day. That means today as well. Someone could come and collect their vehicle at any time. And what do you do then?'

'I crawl along behind the cars, back to the trees. When I'm there I hide behind a tree trunk and wait until you give me a sign to say everything's clear again.' Jon was repeating the instructions Nik had hammered into him on the drive there.

'Can any of your equipment be traced back to you?' asked Nik.

'What do you take me for?'

'OK, good. Then we don't need to worry if anything gets left behind.'

Nik took a small ladder off his back and leaned it against the fence that surrounded the vehicle yard.

'Are there watchdogs?' asked Jon.

'No.' Nik shook his head.

'Cameras?'

'Not where we'll be.'

'This place has no CCTV?'

'Only on the barrier at the exit,' Nik explained. 'Normally if someone breaks in here, then it's to steal a car and not to get a satnav reading.'

While Jon stood debating whether he should have brought some pepper spray with him, Nik had already climbed up the ladder and stopped at the top of the fence. He listened to see if he could hear anything. After a moment, he waved to Jon and jumped down on to the other side of the fence. Jon made his way up the ladder somewhat less elegantly, very nearly lost his balance at the top, and broke a thick branch off the tree behind him when he jumped backwards off the fence. All the while, he could feel the laptop in his bag digging into his back.

'Be quiet!' Nik said.

Jon huffily wiped the sweat from his forehead. 'Could you not have just done this on your own?'

'What, read a satnav's history?' asked Nik. 'You clearly overestimate my computing capabilities.'

'And you clearly overestimate my burglary capabilities,' said Jon, straightening up his rucksack.

A car park with around fifty cars sprawled out in front of them. It was hard to see the make of the cars in the dark so Nik got down on his knees and started crawling from car to car until he found Tina Vohl's navy BMW. He then stood up and signalled to Jon with a flash of his torch.

'How do you plan on getting to the satnav?' asked Nik as Jon arrived at the car.

'It's a BMW with a keyless function,' answered Jon, as if that should answer Nik's question.

'Yes, and?' The information had meant nothing to Nik.

'All keyless cars can be hacked,' explained Jon, reaching into his rucksack for his laptop. 'Since I don't have the key here to tap into, it's a little more complicated.' Jon placed a radio scanner on top of the BMW's bonnet and started to run a program. After a few seconds he had found the frequency. He activated an opening signal and the car unlocked.

'That was fast,' Nik remarked approvingly.

Jon shrugged and opened the door on the driver's side. He located a socket underneath the bonnet lever, removed its plastic cap and connected it to a thick cable.

Nik took a thin black blanket from his rucksack and laid it over the windscreen. That way, no one would be able to see the light from the dashboard or the laptop. He then bent down to speak to Jon.

'What's that?' asked Nik.

'A diagnosis interface with an adapter for all models from the last twenty years,' explained Jon, starting up the software. 'Gives me access to all the car's functions.' A couple of clicks later, and he was in the satnav's memory, scrolling through recent entries.

'Masannek was in Trudering a lot,' said Nik as he looked at the data.

'Yeah, but why?' asked Jon. 'Our victim doesn't live there, nor does anyone else who has anything to do with the case.'

'Going by this, Masannek went about his visits very strategically. First, he went to the Riem Cemetery, then the industrial area and finally, he went to Neutrudering and Gronsdorf. The only thing not mentioned on the satnav is this vehicle depository.'

'So he was looking for something.'

'Now all those scribbles on the map make sense,' whispered Nik. 'The streets that have been crossed out are the areas of Trudering-Riem where Masannek had been but hadn't found anything.'

'So what was he looking for?'

'Someone, or someone's hiding place.'

'None of this is any help to us,' said Jon.

'Yes, it is. It means I can continue Masannek's search tomorrow morning,' Nik explained.

'Nik, it was that search that got Masannek shot. And he was in no way an amateur,' warned Jon. 'And there's not been a single trace of the murderer, which means they're still running around out there.'

'I'll be careful,' said Nik. 'I know what to expect.'

It was early afternoon and the lunchtime traffic had calmed. Nik drove through the areas of Trudering-Riem that still hadn't been crossed out on Masannek's map. He had spent a long time focusing on the street where Masannek had been murdered but nothing seemed suspicious. There were some terraced houses, a block of flats, a bar, a doctor's surgery and, of course, the supermarket where his body had been found. In the end, Nik stepped back into his car, drove for another two hundred metres and parked. Driving slowly around a neighbourhood attracted too much attention, so he decided to walk instead, taking in the houses and the residents.

He bought a chocolate croissant from a bakery that was just about to close, put on a headset and called Jon.

'Anything new?' Nik asked without saying hello.

'Nothing since our little trip to the depository,' said Jon. 'And with you?'

'I've been driving around Trudering for hours and haven't noticed a thing.' Nik scrunched up the paper bag from his croissant in frustration. He was getting fed up. 'Sussing out a criminal's motives isn't normally a problem for me, but my skills are failing me with Masannek. I know he was looking for something or someone he thought he would find in this area. And what or whoever it was must have been important to him, otherwise he would have just got someone else to take care of it.' Nik threw the paper bag into a bin at a bus stop. 'There's nothing to suggest Masannek was with a colleague, which makes me think he was trying to be as discreet as possible. With the amount of power he enjoyed, he could have had someone on look-out on every street corner. The fact he personally beat up Balthasar I take as another sign he wanted to deal with this on his own. But whatever it is, it must have something to do with the Grohnerts – and therefore with Greta's kidnapping. Why else would he have caught us in front of their property?'

'Let's go through all the possibilities,' said Jon, 'regardless of how ridiculous they might seem.'

'OK. You go first.' Nik was walking back to his car.

'Masannek was trying to find Greta's kidnapper or even Greta herself.'

'And who'd hired him to do it?'

'Greta's biological father perhaps?'

'Who we know nothing about.'

'Could even be Masannek himself,' suggested Jon.

'According to Jablonski, Masannek was the top dog in his field in Munich's underworld. And he was expensive. If we take Vittoria Monti's aunt's word to be true, then her niece wasn't involved with powerful people like that.'

'And Masannek himself?'

'He was already working in Munich the year Greta was conceived but if he'd cared about Greta's well-being, he would've got on board with my investigation and not tried to put an end to it by thrashing Balthasar.'

Nik got into his car and started the engine.

'OK. Then maybe the cases aren't linked,' said Jon. 'The search in Trudering has nothing to do with Greta's kidnapping or with your involvement in the case.'

'Possible,' Nik admitted. He was driving along a main street. 'But then, men like Masannek would only rarely take on two large jobs at the same time.'

'Well, that's where my ideas stop,' said Jon.

As Nik continued to drive down the street, he saw a remarkably tall man out of the corner of his eye. He slowed down and drove on to the pavement outside a telephone shop.

'I must be hallucinating,' he said. 'I just saw Greta's kidnapper.' He started turning the car.

'On the street?' asked Jon.

'Yes! It might've just been my imagination playing tricks, but I'm going back to check and then I'll be in touch.' He ended the call before Jon had a chance to reply.

The man had turned down a narrow one-way street. As long as Nik wasn't sure it was the kidnapper, he thought it best to avoid any illegal driving manoeuvres. So he took another street and let the car roll in first gear as he reached a narrow dead end. On the right-hand side was a plot of ground with no buildings and behind that, he could make out some train tracks. He let the car roll to the side of the street and turned off the engine. There was nobody out walking and his was the only car driving around. Nik smacked his palms down on the steering wheel in frustration. Suddenly, the man sprang up from between two parked cars. He was holding a gun with a silencer, and before Nik could react, he had fired off two bullets. The muffled bang of the gun was drowned out by the shattering of Nik's windscreen. The headrest on the passenger seat exploded. Nik threw himself down over both seats. More shots. The back window shattered, two shots hit the bonnet and a tyre burst. Nik protected his eyes from the shards of flying glass while reaching for his gun in the glove-box. He released the safety catch and opened the passenger door. The shooting had stopped. Too exposed inside the small car, he jumped out and rolled over to another car that was parked at the edge of the street. In the few seconds he had needed to reach his new cover, he hadn't seen anybody. The shooter must have either disappeared or was staying well hidden. Nik pushed himself up tight against the cars and crept alongside them until he had a better view of the street. He threw himself down on to the ground, gun grasped in front of him at the ready, but there was no sign of the man. He stood up and went to the other side of the street, but there was no one there either. As he started walking back to his car, he heard the police sirens. The gunshots hadn't been loud, but a vigilant neighbour had apparently watched the scene unfold and called the police.

Nik reapplied the safety catch and placed the gun on the passenger seat. It would be better if he didn't have it in his hand when the police arrived.

He leaned on his steering wheel and sighed, thinking up some story to tell the police.

The small dead-end street had been sealed off with police tape. Behind it, countless inquisitive neighbours were squirming to see what had happened, taking photos of Nik's car with their mobiles. While the CID forensics team were securing evidence and looking for more bullets, police officers questioned residents and tried to build an image of the attacker. It was a quiet neighbourhood, where illegal parking or piles of dog poo typically constituted the worst crimes. Nothing close to the scene they had just witnessed.

Nik sat at the side of the street in front of a detached house with a balcony. It had apparently turned into a meeting place for early pubescent kids, thrilled with the current neighbourhood commotion. He looked down at the broken glass with a vacant expression on his face, and played absentmindedly with a shard. That was until the exasperated groans of his ex-colleague ripped him from his thoughts.

'OK. I'll quickly run through it all once more,' said Danilo, pushing a hand through his curly black hair. He always did that when he hit a block or lacked enough information to build a picture of the situation. 'You were here in Trudering because a local pub does a good pork knuckle. On the way home, you got distracted, mistakenly turned into this side street where the assailant opened fire on you. Without any warning. After you got over the initial shock at what was happening, you took your gun from the glove compartment and crept out of the car. You wanted to corner the shooter but he had already disappeared. You didn't recognise the man. You can't describe him for me. And you also don't know where he ran off to.'

'My doctor told me pork would be the ruin of me,' said Nik, shaking his head. 'Now I know what he was talking about.'

Danilo clapped his notebook together. 'Do you really think I'm that fucking stupid?'

'Is that a trick question?'

'We might not have caught you yet. But it's no secret you've started mixing yourself up in CID cases. The lonely avenger, eh! And then today you just happen to be in Trudering, not even two days after a man was shot here. A split hair away from getting shot yourself. And it's all just a coincidence, is it?'

'If the body had been found on this street, I could understand your scepticism. But it wasn't. And, as I'm sure you're aware, I didn't exactly make many friends during my time at the CID. And Giesing Prison is full of guys who want to put a bullet in me.'

'I still don't believe you.'

'And you're fully within your rights not to, but it doesn't mean I'm going to change my statement.'

'It's not going to work, Nik.'

'Let's see, shall we.' He threw his car keys over to Danilo. 'In case you need it. And you've already got my number.' He waved goodbye and turned around. 'The old one that isn't in service anymore,' he mumbled under his breath as he made his way to the U-Bahn. He stuck his earphones in his ears and called Jon. 'Did you get all that?'

'Most of it. D'you really think it was a good idea not telling him the truth? I mean, Greta's kidnapper did try to kill you.'

'No, he didn't,' Nik replied. 'It was impossible for him to miss from that distance. My car looks like a hail of bullets hit it, but I don't have a scratch? It was a warning.'

'What kind of warning?'

'To stop sticking my nose in.'

'Well, that's obvious. Of course Greta's kidnapper doesn't want you to find her.'

'Yes, but the reason why hasn't been obvious: he's *protecting* Greta.'

'From who?' asked Jon. 'Definitely not from her parents.'

'From people like Masannek.'

'You think your new friend shot Masannek?'

'The gun from today was the same calibre as the one used to shoot him,' explained Nik. 'As soon as forensics inspect the bullets, the technicians will make the connection. I'm convinced of it.'

'And the shooter considered Masannek to be dangerous but thinks you're harmless, or what?'

'Exactly. That's why I'm still alive,' Nik agreed. 'If we can just find out what Masannek's motive was, we'll know why Greta was abducted.'

'I'll get searching again,' said Jon. 'Maybe there's something new on his murder.'

'Keep me informed,' said Nik.

'Will do,' answered Jon before hanging up.

Chapter 8

It was half past one in the morning when Balthasar's mobile rang. Still half asleep he picked up the phone and looked at the display. It was a Munich landline number.

'Hello?' he said, groggily.

'Yes, hello. This is Officer Rechmann from Munich Police Unit 14,' answered the man on the line. 'Are you a friend of Nik Pohl's?'

'Yes.' Balthasar sat up. 'Why? Did something happen to him?'

'I'm afraid so. Would you be able to come down to the station?' asked the man. 'You can see for yourself.'

After giving his details, Balthasar was taken down to the cells by a police officer.

'I'm sorry for having to get you out of bed,' said Rechmann. 'We couldn't locate any of Herr Pohl's relatives, so we had to call you.'

Balthasar guessed the officer was in his early twenties. He had very little beard growth and bright ginger hair. His beard didn't quite cover his acne scars, but he had a strong build and striking blue eyes.

'How did you get my number?'

'We found a mobile in Herr Pohl's pocket and unlocked it with his fingerprint.' He turned to look at Balthasar somewhat sheepishly. 'I'd appreciate it if you kept that to yourself. I realise it was a gross breach of staff regulations and data protection but . . . well . . . Herr Pohl worked at the CID for a long time and we needed to do something.'

'You know him?'

'Every police officer in Munich knows who Pohl is since he beat up a public prosecutor. And I hadn't even finished my training at the time.'

As Rechmann opened the door, both men were hit with the sour smell of vomit. The police officer took a step back and held his hand over his nose, but Balthasar kept walking, entirely unaffected. Being a pathologist, he'd smelled far worse.

Nik was lying on a mattress in the corner of the room. His shirt was covered in vomit and his trousers were wet with urine. His hair was dripping with sweat and the whites of his eyes were bright red. Noticing the light in the cell, he looked towards the door. 'Fffinally,' he slurred, trying to stand up. Only on his third attempt, and with the help of the wall, did he eventually manage to lever himself to his feet. He then staggered over to the cell door, propping himself up the whole way.

'Must have been a great party,' Balthasar remarked while Nik tottered past him.

'Ssshhut your mouth.'

They all moved slowly along the corridor until they reached the station entrance. As Officer Rechmann held the door open for them to leave, Nik stepped out the door and turned to him. 'And you're all a bunch of *dicks*!' he shouted. 'The whole fucking lot of you!' And with an enthusiastic swing, he attempted to turn around but, failing pathetically, he tripped down the three steps at the station entrance and smashed hard on to the pavement.

'Don't worry, he's pretty durable,' Balthasar told the officer with a smile, shaking his hand. 'Thank you for being so understanding, Herr Rechmann. And please do excuse my friend's terrible manners. He doesn't mean anything by it.'

The policeman looked at Nik regretfully before nodding at Balthasar and closing the station door.

'Offff *course* I mean it!' mumbled Nik as he tried to stand up. 'Every . . . sssingle . . . word.' He stuck his middle finger up aggressively at the police station. 'And *you* can stop sticking your *nose* in! . . . Smart-arse.'

Balthasar straightened himself up, took two steps towards Nik and shoved him hard in the stomach. Nik fell to the ground again. 'Being drunk is one thing. But getting me out here in the middle of the night to listen to your insults is another. I won't have it!'

'Look at you.' Nik glanced up. 'Are you not tired of life?' He was trying to lift himself off the ground. 'I could eat you for breakfast. Five times.' He lifted a swaying fist.

'Under normal circumstances, yes,' replied Balthasar, using his foot to push him back down. 'But definitely not after the amount of alcohol you've consumed tonight.'

While Nik lay cursing on the pavement, Balthasar opened the car boot and took out a cool box. He moved over to Nik, took off the lid and poured the entire contents over his head. 'Fresh tap water for you . . . with extra ice,' said Balthasar, chortling loudly.

Nik screamed from the pain, his eyes wide in shock. 'I'll *kill* you!' he shouted.

'So invigorating and refreshing, don't you think?' As Nik continued to flail around on the ground, Balthasar bent down and grabbed him by the shirt collar, pulling him on to his feet and over to the car. 'Plus, you smell slightly better now too.' He shoved Nik into the passenger seat and slammed the door shut. A minute later, they were driving back to the flat. Balthasar picked up a plastic cup from the drinks holder and passed it to Nik. 'Extra strong,' he said. Nik rubbed his head quickly to get the cold water out of his hair and ripped the cup from Balthasar's hand. Sceptically, he took a sip.

'D'you want to talk about it?'

'What's there to talk about?' answered Nik. 'I had one too many. Was a big day yesterday.'

'You mean the shooting?' asked the pathologist. 'That would have thrown someone like me, but you've experienced much worse.' By his standards, Balthasar was driving calmly through the night traffic. 'It's not a problem if you don't want to talk,' continued Balthasar, 'but please, don't lie to me.'

'What d'you mean lie to you?'

'The policeman had a few interesting things to tell me when he was taking my details.'

'Oh, really?' Nik mumbled into the cup.

'Yes. Said they got a call at around half twelve from a sports bar. Apparently you were acting like a complete savage because the staff wouldn't serve you any more drink. You were just about to throw your stool at a TV screen when the police arrived and managed to stop you.'

'What the fuck has it got to do with the barman how much I drink?'

'Nik, you'd consumed so much alcohol, your health was in danger. A little bit more, and you probably wouldn't ever have stood up again.'

'So?' said Nik quietly.

The men were silent for a moment.

'I would have expected a comment like that earlier this year, Nik. But you've changed since then. And you're right in the middle of a case!' Balthasar continued. 'Here you are, doing everything possible to save Greta – Jesus, you were even willing to take a shot for the girl. I had no idea *what* was going on. Until I got to the station, that is.'

'Oh, really? And what made you see the light?' asked Nik facetiously.

'That you were just as drunk at exactly the same time last year. You were picked up outside a pub because you'd destroyed the flower pots at the front door when they wouldn't let you in.'

Nik hung his head.

'The policeman thought it might have something to do with the fact that it's your birthday today. But I've never heard of anybody who likes to get completely wasted by themselves, the night *before* their birthday. Maybe on the big day itself . . . or with friends. But not like this.'

Nik sighed and opened the window, letting the cold air rush on to his face. The two of them sat in silence for a while, driving through Munich's empty, lamp-lit streets, where the shop lights and illuminated billboards promised a life of wealth in an ideal world, even on a bleak night like tonight.

'Was four years ago,' Nik began. He spoke quietly but clearly. 'I had the late shift on my birthday so I invited Mira around the day before. We wanted to see in my birthday at a restaurant with good food and good drinks, and views over the city. She worked in a gallery and it was hard finding times that suited so we didn't see each other very much. On that particular day I was exhausted; totally worn out from work. I'd had to break up a fight between two warring families and had taken some hard blows. And then, I don't know what started it . . . We'd barely even finished our starters before we began fighting ourselves. We did that a lot. My sister was always lecturing me and I would always get angry with her. So then, in the end, Mira had enough. She stood up without saying another word and left. I didn't try to stop her. I just stayed there, ate the main course and left to drive home.' He closed his eyes and played with the cup in his hand. 'When I was driving . . . not far from the restaurant . . . I came across an accident. The police had sealed off the road. The fire brigade was there and an emergency helicopter was landing. There was this massive lorry lying on its side. It had been transporting glass water bottles and there was broken glass everywhere. The blue light from the police car was reflecting in the shards. I was about to drive around the accident when I saw her car. Her old VW with its worn-out tyres and rusty rims. Smashed together like a tin can. Nobody was getting out of there alive. I stopped the car, ducked under the police tape and ran past the overturned lorry and over the sea of glass. The shards were piercing my boots and cutting the soles of my feet right to the bone. But I just kept running, leaving bloody footprints everywhere, until I got to her car. Then I saw her.' Nik lowered his head and wiped his eyes with the palm of his hand. 'It took them two hours to get her body out of the car.' He took a drink of coffee and looked out the open window. 'So all in all, if I hadn't been such a grumpy fucking bastard, Mira would still be alive today. The lorry driver might have hit a tree, or his truck might have just come off the road, or he might have hit somebody else . . . somebody whose car would've withstood the crash better.' He pushed his palm against his forehead, trying hard to force back the tears.

Nik didn't say another word for the rest of the journey and Balthasar didn't ask any more questions. Nik's intense state of intoxication had thankfully subsided, but he still needed Balthasar's help to make it up the stairs to the flat; help which he now no longer resisted.

When they were inside, Nik released himself calmly from Balthasar's grip and started walking slowly towards his bedroom. After three steps, he stood still. 'Thank you,' he said quietly, not turning around.

'It's OK. You're not the first friend I've had to save from the drunk tank,' Balthasar said, doing his best to make light of the situation.

'Not for that,' replied Nik before walking off. He reached his bedroom and closed the door.

◆ ◆ ◆

Hannes sat at the kitchen table and took a bite from the slice of tomato he was holding. He chewed it slowly and attentively. As always, he kept his eyes fixed on the grey fridge in front of him. It was as if the door guarded the entrance to another world; a world that only existed in his mind. On the table in front of him stood a small glass of water and a plate with two more slices of tomato.

Nina stopped tidying away the dishes for a moment and looked at her son. His face was still childlike and his short black hair had been combed to one side. Just like every other day, he was wearing a white T-shirt under a dark grey jumper with dark blue jeans. She would have loved more than anything to get a glimpse at his world; to understand what moved him, what worried him and why he barely talked. Life wasn't always easy with an autistic child, but it was full of beautiful moments as well. Quiet moments, like when he sat next to her on the couch, watching cartoons that would make the corners of his lips curl up, albeit only faintly.

The kitchen clock said 7.55 a.m. Hannes jumped up abruptly, as if reacting to a silent alarm, put on his jacket and went outside with his mother. She beeped the car open while pulling on her coat, and closed the front door, locking it behind her. As she turned around, a tall man with a scar across his right cheek was standing directly in front of her. His right eye was rheumy and the right-hand side of his mouth drooped. The woman was transfixed for a moment by the disfigured features. The man took out a plastic yellow gun from his jacket pocket and pointed it at Nina.

'I-I-I'm sorry,' stammered the man remorsefully. And then came the pain.

◆　◆　◆

The vibrations from Nik's mobile seemed to stab him in the temples. He opened his eyes and the room started spinning around him as if he was on a carousel. He could taste vomit in his mouth and last night's alcohol lay precariously on his stomach. He closed his eyes and felt around the mattress for his phone.

'Hello?' he croaked.

'Did I wake you?' asked Jon, sounding confused. 'It's half ten.'

'Was a long night.'

'Another kid's been kidnapped.'

'Shit.' Nik forced himself up and out of bed. 'OK. I'm listening.'

'His name's Hannes Lepper. Lives in Trudering. Barely two hundred metres from the place where they sifted through your car yesterday.'

'Right. No coincidence there then.' Nik staggered into the kitchen and turned on the coffee machine. 'How did it happen?'

'At 7.56 a.m., Hannes and his mum were leaving to go to his therapy. That's when the kidnapper pounced.'

'Therapy?'

'Hannes was diagnosed with autism as a young child. I've only skimmed over his medical history but it appears he has problems with social interaction and doesn't talk. The only way he can communicate is with a word processor.'

'Jesus,' mumbled Nik. The coffee machine reverberated in the background. 'Anyone hurt? Killed?'

'Not all reports are online yet,' explained Jon. 'But going by the first entries, the whole thing was pretty tame.' Nik could hear Jon's keyboard clicking in the background. 'As I mentioned, Hannes and his mother, Nina, were about to leave for therapy when our tall friend with a limp jumped out of his car and stunned the mother with a taser.'

'Painful . . . but efficient,' Nik remarked. 'At least he didn't shoot her like he shot Greta's driver.'

'According to Nina's statement, the man even apologised before he did it,' said Jon. 'After that, he shoved the screaming child into his car and drove away. The CID have reasonable cause to believe it's the same man who kidnapped Greta. Firstly, there was the description given by the mother, which matched the man. Secondly, his car was flashed only thirty metres down the road by a speed camera which got a razor-sharp image of him. And thirdly, the abduction location was a pretty stupid choice: the Lepper family live in a terraced house on a built-up estate so there were five other eyewitnesses.'

Nik drank some coffee. It was going to take a while for the effects of yesterday's escapades to diminish.

'Look at your tablet,' Jon continued. 'I've sent you the picture from the traffic camera.'

Nik picked up the tablet from the table and looked at the photo. The man seemed to be in his late thirties. He had short, shaved ginger hair and a slightly crooked nose. A flaky scar ran from his right ear down his cheek. His right eye was bloodshot and half shut. The right corner of his mouth hung downwards and he had slightly protruding lips. 'Looks like a character from a horror film,' Nik remarked.

'As soon as the search is announced, people will be seeing him on every street corner.'

'This was a sloppy abduction. Not at all like Greta's,' remarked Nik. 'If he'd been properly prepared, he would've never got caught speeding. And he would have chosen another place and another time. Not the middle of a housing estate when people are leaving for work.'

'So what changed?'

'Maybe it's because of me,' suggested Nik. 'Maybe the kidnapper was afraid I was on to him so he pounced in a hurry.'

'That's one possibility.'

'And what about Hannes' social circle? What's that like?'

'I've only got the basics at the moment,' replied Jon. 'His father is a teacher at a high school and his mother's a social worker. But she hasn't worked since Hannes was adopted.'

'Adopted?'

'Yep. That's our first similarity: Hannes was adopted, Greta too – in some way or another, and Simon lived with various foster parents.'

'OK. That puts a new spin on things.'

'Oh, it gets better,' said Jon. 'Greta and Hannes were born on 6 June 2003; and Simon on 7 June 2003. Hannes was born at 8.45 p.m. and Greta at 11.52 p.m. I don't have any information on the time of day Simon was born. But I wouldn't be surprised if it turns out it was early in the morning.'

'So only a few hours between them then . . .'

'And all three in the women's clinic on Maistraße.'

'Right. Well, the children are obviously connected in some way,' said Nik. 'We need to get the CID to include Simon in their search. Can you contact them anonymously and tell them about the birth date connections and the fact that all three children were born in the same hospital? And that Simon was seen talking to a man matching the kidnapper's description. That should make them take an interest.'

'Good point. I'll do that next.'

'Something strange must've happened around the time they were born.'

'I'd love to be able to tell you what, but the hospital files aren't on the server. Now, that might be because of the legal obligation to destroy information after ten years or . . . it might be because the files from 2003 were not fully digitalised. Whatever the case, I can't get any information on births from 2003. But I might know how we can,' said Jon enthusiastically.

'Should I be scared?' asked Nik, taking a sip of coffee.

'There's an archive in the hospital. There might still be paper-work in there.'

'Uh-huh.' Nik knew what was coming. 'And since they're not open to the public . . . ?'

'. . . One of us will have to get in and have a look,' Jon said matter-of-factly.

'And when you say "one of us", you don't mean yourself or Balthasar, do you?'

'Not if we actually want the plan to work.'

Nik sighed. 'I'll need the staff rotas; shift changes are the best time to get in there without being noticed.'

'Not a problem.'

'I'll also need scrubs and a name badge with the name of a fake doctor. I can't afford any embarrassing moments so it has to be someone who doesn't work in the clinic.'

'OK. I know someone who manufactures work clothes. He'll be able to help.'

'Good. But before anything, I need a cold shower and a proper breakfast,' said Nik. 'After that, I'll get my burglary gear together. With a bit of luck, we'll find something on those kids. But I have to admit, I've got a horrible feeling about the whole thing.'

◆ ◆ ◆

Nik was wearing a white shirt, light blue jeans and his custom-made leather shoes. He walked into the hospital holding a bunch of flowers and a small plastic bag containing his scrubs. He smiled and waved to the porter as he entered. Once he was inside, he went upstairs to the first floor and walked along the long corridor looking for a toilet. As he'd expected, there weren't many visitors in the hospital at this time of day. The day patients had all gone home, and the shift change meant that employees had gone back into their offices and staff rooms. Nik put the flowers on a table and went into the men's toilet, where he slipped the doctor's coat on over his clothes, then he hastily left the bathroom and, finding a staff stairway, hurried down to the basement.

The rooms upstairs had been flooded with light but down in the basement it was dark and forbidding. Thanks to the building plan that Jon had downloaded, Nik was quickly able to locate the archive room. The lock quality was mediocre and Nik only needed a few minutes to pick it.

Once inside, he paused for a moment, closing his eyes and focusing all attention on his ears. He couldn't hear a sound and the light was off, so he assumed nobody else was in the archive. He took out his phone, attached the headset and called Jon. The reception was bad but it was enough to stay connected.

'I'm inside.' Nik took a small headlamp out of his trouser pocket and looked around. There were ten rows of shelves in front of him, each eight metres long and three metres high. 'If we can't narrow down the search somehow, I'll be here for the week.'

'OK. We could narrow it down to the prenatal centre but even then, the files could be in a number of areas.'

Nik wiped the dust from the labels on the shelves, pushed some boxes around and tried to get to grips with the storage system. 'Everything's covered in dust,' said Nik, rubbing his nose frustratedly. 'I doubt anyone's even been in here for ten years.'

'Let's hope not,' said Jon. 'That would be an advantage for us.'

'I've found the birth registrations,' said Nik after a while. 'Starting in the 80s.'

'We're looking for June 2003.'

Nik walked up the aisle until he came to 2003. 'You're fucking joking,' he blurted out. A box was missing. 'They only go up to April 2003. And then start again in September.' He rubbed his finger along the empty space. 'Hasn't been gone long. There's no dust in the space.'

'Why are we always one step behind?' said Jon, beginning to feel the frustration himself now.

Nik leaned against the shelving and closed his eyes. 'So, what do we do now?'

'We could ask the clinic employees . . . ?'

'About a case from fourteen years ago?' Nik asked. 'Ten children are born here every day. No doctor or nurse is going to remember that night.'

'Yeah, but even if we don't know why or how, we *do* know that night was different.'

'That's true . . . Might be a good starting point,' said Nik pensively.

'What is? To find out how it was different?'

'Yeah . . . to find out what was so special about that night,' Nik replied. 'Did you look to see if anything out of the ordinary happened in or around the women's clinic on 6 or 7 June?'

'No, it didn't occur to me to look,' Jon admitted. 'I'll get on it straight away.'

Nik took off the doctor's coat and left the archive. 'But before you start, give me the details on Hannes' family.'

'Not much to report, really. As I said, Rene Lepper is a teacher and his wife, Nina, is a social worker. It was a conscious decision to adopt a child with autism. And if you go by the reports from social services, the boy is really happy there. Of course, I tried to find links to the other cases but I didn't get anything. No links to the Grohnerts, or to Simon. They even live too far away from one another to have just randomly become friends.'

'So the only similarity is the time of birth.'

'Right. So all in all, we're looking at three deaths at least here and possibly three abductions. Then there's Balthasar's attack and the fact that someone broke into the hospital archive,' said Jon. 'What kind of birth causes such chaos? And not only that, causes it fourteen years later?'

'Somebody wanted to get more information about that night. Why else would they steal the files?'

'Maybe they wanted to prevent other people from getting the information?'

'But why the abductions then? It would've been enough to just get rid of the files from 2003.'

'Wait a second.' Nik heard Jon tapping at his keyboard. 'I don't believe it. I've found something.'

'What does it say?'

'A nurse on night duty called the police at four in the morning because two men were making her give them information on a patient.'

'Which patient?'

'Doesn't say, but by the time the police got there, the men were already gone.'

'Any names?'

'The call was made by an Ingrid Gassen. I don't know if she still works in the hospital. But that doesn't matter; if she's still alive, you'll have an address shortly.'

'I'm going back to the car,' said Nik. 'Hopefully the woman can remember that night. I'll pay her a visit tomorrow morning.'

Chapter 9

Ingrid Gassen stood by her vegetable patch, using a hoe to loosen the weeds. Her hair was tied back in a ponytail and she was wearing old jeans, a faded T-shirt and a green apron. She looked younger than her sixty-three years: she had very few wrinkles and wielded the hoe with ease. Even her stooped stance didn't seem to bother her.

Nik stood at the fence of her small garden and waved over to her with a friendly smile. Gassen straightened and leaned on the hoe. She took a pair of glasses out of her apron pocket and looked more closely at him.

'Can I help you?' she asked politely.

Nik held up his fake badge. 'My name is Nik Pohl. I work for the Munich CID. Do you perhaps have a couple of minutes for me?'

'Did something happen?' asked Gassen, the concern on her face growing as she walked over to the fence.

'It's about a case from 2003,' Nik explained, shaking her hand. There was a layer of toughened skin on her fingers and she had a firm handshake.

'I think you might be overestimating my memory, young man.'

'Well, it was actually a case which you reported personally to the police.'

Gassen frowned.

'You were on the night shift and two men came into the maternity ward. They pressurised you into giving them the name of a patient.'

'Yes. I remember.' Gassen laid down her hoe at the side of the vegetable patch.

'Would you be able to tell me what happened?'

'OK. Well . . . it was early in the morning,' she began. 'It had been a busy night and I was using the lull to update some records when two men stormed into the ward. The first one grabbed me by the arm and showed me a photo of a young woman. They wanted to know if she was a patient. Then the second man took my file off me and flicked through the admissions.'

'Did you know the woman in the photo?'

'She'd given birth that night.'

'Did you tell the men that?'

'Of course not,' she said, offended. 'Brutes like them were forever coming into the clinic. Overeager dads who wanted to see their child and couldn't understand that the mother wanted to be alone at such a difficult time.'

'So what did you do?'

'After I got over the initial shock, I told the men to go to the other end of the corridor. It was actually just a storage room down there. I used that minute to go into the staff room and call the police. I locked the door and waited. Thankfully there was a police car nearby and they were there in a matter of minutes.'

'And the two men?'

'When I came out of the staff room, they'd both disappeared. I gave the police a description, but never saw them again.'

'Did one of the men happen to have a limp?'

'No.'

Nik took two photos out of his pocket. One was of Masannek and the other was the man with the scar. 'Was it by any chance one of these men?' Gassen looked at the photos closely. 'I'm sorry. I can't be entirely sure.'

'What do you know about the woman they were looking for?' Nik put the photos back in his pocket.

'Not very much. She'd staggered into the ward that evening with contractions. No suitcase, no sleeping bag, just the clothes she had on. She didn't even have any ID on her or a health insurance card.'

'And you took her in anyway?'

'Of course! What do you take me for? I would never turn down a woman in need, even at full capacity.'

Nik raised his palms to the woman. 'Sorry, I didn't mean to insinuate anything.'

'You know, all kinds of women get pregnant. Homeless women . . . refugees without papers. Didn't happen all that often, but they needed our help too sometimes,' added Gassen.

'Did the woman give a name?'

'Yes,' she continued, 'but it's always a fake in those kinds of cases.'

'And how did the woman seem to you?'

'Anxious . . . like she was in a hurry . . . but also confident. She had boundless strength, that girl. It was clear how much pain she was in; she was drowning in sweat. But she never screamed once during the labour.'

'And why did you think she was in a rush?'

'While we were pushing her into the delivery room, she looked at the door with this terrified look on her face.' Gassen sighed. 'Hours later, I understood why.'

'Were you at the birth?'

She shook her head. 'One of my colleagues was assisting.'

'And what happened afterwards?' asked Nik. 'Did you ask her why the men were looking for her?'

'I was planning to, but she'd already gone. Child and all.'

'So quickly after giving birth?'

'Most mothers can't even get out of bed without assistance. As I said: this woman was a fighter. When you've been bringing children into the world as long as I have, you know that when you see it.'

'Can you tell me what the woman looked like?'

She closed her eyes, as if transporting herself back to that night.

'Early twenties, long blonde hair . . . dark brown eyes. Had a southern European accent. Spanish or Italian perhaps.'

'Did you ever see the woman again?'

'Never.'

'Do you know if the baby was a boy or a girl, or the time of birth perhaps?'

'I'm afraid not. That's all I can remember.'

'Well, thank you very much for your time.' Nik shook the woman's hand and turned to leave.

'Herr Pohl,' she called out. 'Is the woman OK?'

'I'm afraid I don't know,' replied Nik.

'I thought about her a lot after that night and hoped she and the child had managed to get away,' said the woman pensively. 'They were not good men.'

'As soon as I find out anything, I'll be in touch,' said Nik. 'But unfortunately, I don't think you should get your hopes up too much.'

◆ ◆ ◆

Nik had laid out all the photos he had for the case on the coffee table: photos of the children, of the places they were kidnapped, and a photo of the murdered man, Vincent Masannek. There were also photos of the parents and their homes, as well as reports on the money exchange and the messenger's interrogation. He leaned back on the sofa, his hands interlocked on the back of his head, glancing from photo to photo. Kara was perched on the edge of the table and seemed to show a particular interest in Nik's bullet-battered car. It looked as if she was trying to understand all the chaos. Every now and then she would look up from the photo and give Nik a suspicious side glance. But Nik didn't even notice she was there.

'No new leads?' asked Balthasar. He was standing in the doorway with a cup of tea in his hand, looking over at the photos.

'Everything links back to the birth of a child in June 2003. But what the hell was so special about the child?'

Balthasar came closer to the table and pointed to the photo of the man with the scar on his face. 'Is that the kidnapper?'

Nik nodded.

'And who is he?'

'We can't find anything on him anywhere. We thought that with such obvious facial features, we'd be able to find a record of him in seconds. So apparently he's managed to stay under the radar until now.'

Balthasar picked up the photo. 'That scar is at least two years old and the injury could be the reason for the facial palsy.'

'Facial palsy?'

'Facial paralysis,' explained Balthasar.

'What do you mean by that?'

'I mean, it might be a mistake to concentrate on the obvious external characteristics.'

'How so?'

'OK. Let's say he was injured two years ago,' Balthasar began. 'As well as the obvious scar, the injury also caused the facial paralysis and the eye clouding. But if we go back to before those two years . . .'

'. . . Our kidnapper would have looked different.' Nik caught on to Balthasar's logic.

'You need to build a photo that undoes his injuries.'

'Is that possible?'

'Facial plastic reconstruction is a science all of its own,' Balthasar explained. 'A former fellow student of mine earns a fortune in Munich doing nose corrections and covering up defects after accidents. Still owes me a round of beers as it happens.' Balthasar laid the photo back down on the table. 'With his knowledge and Jon's computer skills, we should be able to generate a photo of the kidnapper before his injuries.' He smiled at Nik. 'I might not be an investigator, but I bet the man that turns up in the photo is a criminal.'

'It was unbelievable!' said Jon enthusiastically. 'Balthasar's friend from uni is a plastic surgeon, and after his degree he did a course on forensic facial reconstruction in the USA, where he learned how to give skulls a face again. His knowledge of bone and soft tissue is perfectly suited for the process.' Nik could feel Jon's fascination permeating down the phone. 'Him and Balthasar gave me exact instructions on how to build up the paralysed side of the face and to see how the cheek would have looked without a scar.'

The man in the photo now had symmetrical features and he certainly looked far less forbidding. 'Ismail Buchwald,' Nik said slowly under his breath, as if locking it firmly in his brain.

'After I had the reconstructed face, I managed to find his file in minutes,' explained Jon. 'He was once arrested for bodily harm after breaking a rowdy drunk man's arm and nose. But he got off with a one-year suspended sentence and never got into any trouble again.'

'It's a pretty big step from bodily harm to murder.'

'You won't find it in his records, but it turns out Buchwald worked for Vincent Masannek's security company.'

'How d'you find that out?'

'After Masannek was murdered, I hacked into the company server and downloaded the employee list. It took a good while because the server was so well secured and I barely got around to it because I was so busy with the investigations. But it was worth the effort.'

'The fact that Buchwald and Masannek worked together changes things drastically. Especially if we assume Buchwald shot his former boss.'

'The scribbles on Masannek's map make even more sense,' said Jon. 'He'd written "IB?" at two points.'

'Ismail Buchwald,' Nik realised.

'So Masannek was looking for Buchwald . . .'

'. . . But Buchwald found him first and shot him.'

'Which brings us back, once again, to our original questions,' continued Jon. 'Why did Buchwald kidnap the kids and how was Masannek involved in the case?'

'Well, we can't ask Masannek, can we? So we'll need to get hold of Buchwald. You got an address?'

'There was one in the employee database. But the house there was ripped down two years ago because it was so dilapidated and they wanted to put a supermarket in its place.'

'And what about the police? What are they doing?'

'The search for him is running full steam ahead. Every civil servant knows Buchwald's face, which means he won't be able to leave his hiding place. It's not looking good.'

'Then we'll just need to pull the snare tighter,' said Nik. 'Can you get hold of cameras that are so discreet we can install them on the street, but strong enough to still give us a sharp picture in the dark?'

'No problem. What you planning?'

'I'm going to make George Orwell's nightmares a reality and put the residents in Trudering-Riem under constant surveillance.'

'You'll need a lot of cameras for that,' said Jon.

'We'll only need them at the spots Masannek marked on the map. It's just a few streets and junctions.'

'OK. So you're talking around thirty to forty cameras.'

'When can you get them by?'

'Tomorrow morning,' answered Jon. 'But how d'you plan on rigging them up?'

'I'll need a cherry picker and clothes that a street light electrician would typically wear.'

'Bit short notice, but I'll manage.'

'Get a set of clothes for you too. You're coming with me.'

'Oh, come on. You know how much I hate outdoor operations. And I'm scared of heights.'

'Stop moaning. The cameras have to be installed correctly and we don't have much time.'

Jon groaned loudly.

'So when should we meet?' asked Nik.

'Nine o'clock tomorrow morning in front of your flat,' replied Jon. 'By the time we get to Trudering, the morning rush hour will be over. Then we can work without being disturbed.'

'Let's hope Buchwald doesn't get caught in the meantime.'

◆ ◆ ◆

Nik pretended to tinker with the street lamps while Jon hooked up the cameras. The device was the size of a table tennis ball, just as round, and had a small lens on the front. Jon attached it to the light with grey duct tape that matched the lamppost's colour almost perfectly. Nobody would notice it from the street.

'And you can monitor the street with that tiny thing?'

'It's the latest model from China,' explained Jon. 'It's got an impressive wireless coverage, HD resolution, really good battery life and great software that lets you control the lens. Moving cars would be a problem, but if Buchwald's on a bike or walking, we'll get a good picture of him.'

'How did you get that sent over from China so quickly?'

'I've got a dealer here in Munich for that kind of thing,' Jon explained. 'He was a bit surprised when I said how many I needed but thankfully he's got a good warehouse in the Czech Republic, not far from the border.'

'So this is all illegal stuff we're hanging up here?'

'Well, the entire device is banned on the German market but . . . the camera itself is allowed. It's just what we're doing with it that's illegal.' Jon pulled his tablet out of his bag and opened up an app. The street below them appeared on the screen. Jon zoomed down to two small children standing at the fence of their nursery school staring up at the cherry picker. Nik could make out their eye colour.

'Impressive.' Nik couldn't deny it. 'But how are you going to keep an eye on the footage from thirty of them?'

'That's only possible on an overhead projector,' explained Jon. 'The images would be too small on a single monitor.'

'Can you use facial recognition with them?'

'If only it was that easy,' replied Jon. 'You'd need special software and hardware to be able to identify moving figures. And they exceed even my budget. I'll just need to sit and watch the projector myself. The fact Buchwald's tall and has a limp will make things a bit easier. You can cover up a scar with make-up but you can't just stop limping.'

'And what about when it gets dark?'

'The cameras are sensitive enough to show a good picture in just the light from the street lamps,' said Jon. 'And when I go to sleep, I'll set the device to record and watch the footage when I wake up.'

Nik lowered the cherry picker's platform, to the immense excitement of the children below. 'Just eighteen to go and our network's ready,' said Nik.

◆ ◆ ◆

Jon rubbed his eyes. Continually watching the footage from thirty cameras on a large canvas on the wall wasn't an easy job and although the projector produced a clear picture, it was still too much to ask from one brain. He'd already taken two painkillers but the pressure in his head wouldn't shift. The fact it was getting dark outside also didn't help and the lack of light was causing outlines to become blurry. He attempted to ignore the faces and concentrate on any tall people who were walking slowly. The limp was included in the official search criteria so Buchwald would undoubtedly be trying to cover it as well as he could. Another reason to remain extra alert.

In a desperate attempt to stay awake – and hopefully for the whole night – Jon reluctantly drank an energy drink. Just as he was considering how awful the stuff tasted, he noticed a tall figure shuffling along the street carrying two shopping bags.

Jon picked up his tablet, switched the program to control the corresponding camera and zoomed in. The footage was of a side street near an industrial area not far from the main station. Despite the mild weather, the man was wearing a woollen hat. He also had on a pair of tinted glasses and was keeping his head down, as if afraid of being recognised. Jon looked at the man's gait. He was almost dragging himself along, concentrating on each step. A random passer-by on the street wouldn't have noticed a thing, but Jon saw it straight away: the man was limping.

◆　◆　◆

Nik stood in front of the couch and looked at the printouts he'd pinned to the wall. He'd spent the last hour rearranging everything he had on the case. He'd pinned Buchwald over by Masannek, and he'd grouped Greta, Simon and Hannes together. A long piece of string stretched upwards from Masannek to a large question mark.

'Still no breakthrough, eh?' asked Balthasar. The pathologist was wearing a dressing gown and smelled like sweet aftershave. He doused his face in the same stuff every day after he shaved. Kara was sitting on his shoulder, mesmerised by the pictures on the wall. The glint in her eye seemed to suggest she was considering the best way to rip every last one down.

'We're missing something,' said Nik, shaking his head. 'I still don't get what Buchwald and Masannek have to do with everything. Why did Buchwald kidnap the kids and why was Masannek going after him? What the hell happened that night in June 2003 that could justify all this insanity? Who was the woman who arrived at the hospital on her own with contractions and left just a couple of hours after giving birth? What happened to the baby? And could that be one of the three kidnapped teenagers?'

'Just a few questions then. Are the police making any progress?'

'They've managed to identify all the children who were born in Munich at that time with help from the city council and have notified their parents directly. The connection between the three abduction victims has not been made public yet. Police cars are patrolling high schools and doing stop-and-search operations on cars. They're using all available resources and *still* haven't had a breakthrough.'

'How's the surveillance operation going?'

Nik pointed to the screen behind him. It showed thirty tiny little windows. 'Jon's monitoring the live camera footage while I go through everything. He'll call me as soon as he notices anything and link the right camera up to our monitor.'

Just then, Nik's phone began to ring. Both he and Balthasar jumped at the noise while Kara flapped her wings frantically and squawked in shock. A close-up image of two legs appeared on the screen. Despite the attempt at covering up a limp, it was easy to see who they belonged to. Nik answered the call.

'D'you see who it is?' asked Jon eagerly.

'Well, whoever it is has difficulties walking,' answered Nik.

The image zoomed out. 'The figure matches Buchwald's.'

'Where's he heading?'

'Into an industrial estate.'

'We got cameras there?'

'Unfortunately not,' said Jon.

'Why didn't we notice him on the way to the supermarket?'

''Cause he took a street we're not watching,' said Jon. 'I've narrowed it down to possible routes and think I know which one he took.'

'Let's hope he didn't just park his car somewhere and that's where he's headed.'

'I doubt it. He wouldn't have parked that far away from the supermarket,' said Jon. 'He's covered his face well; scar and all. And his head's so low, I can't see much but the limp's the most important thing anyway; the police have emphasised that many times. Buchwald's hideout can't be far off.'

The man went down a narrow street and disappeared from the picture. Nik reached for his car key.

'He'll be gone by the time you get there, Nik,' said Balthasar.

'Yeah, but most of the properties over on the industrial estate will be locked up,' said Nik. 'That will limit the routes he can take. It'll only be a question of time before I find out where he's hiding.'

Chapter 10

Nik looked at the building from his hiding place behind a tree. It was an old box-like industrial warehouse, about twenty metres long, with a crumbling exterior. The building had a metal door and next to that were two windows made of frosted burglar-proof glass.

'Did Buchwald go in there?' asked Jon over the headphones.

'I've ruled out all other possibilities,' explained Nik. 'Only eight of the buildings here are non-residential, four of which are still in use and three of which are too big and too well monitored for somebody to be able to hide themselves and three children inside. And there's been no evidence that Buchwald's working with anybody.'

'If you're not sure, why not put up a camera at the entrance? Then we'll see Buchwald when he goes shopping again.'

'That'll take too long,' said Nik. 'Buchwald just bought loads of food and we have no idea what state the children are in.'

'Yeah, but remember we've only got one chance at this,' warned Jon. 'What if he really is hiding out in some residential building?'

'The houses are built too close together,' said Nik. 'Buchwald would never have been able to get three children inside without being noticed. But this warehouse has its own car park and a rear entrance they can drive right up to. The back end is surrounded by high beech trees and all the other warehouses on the way to it are closed at night, which makes it easier to go shopping. Plus, if you look a bit closer, you can see the place is falling apart. The concrete slabs around the building are all loose and there's moss growing over one of the walls. Not only that, an area of the wire-mesh fence at the back has been kicked down. The building's been abandoned.'

'So what are you planning?'

'I've spent the last half an hour going over the building inch by inch with my binoculars and only managed to find a small camera at the rear entrance. The front door will be barricaded and as I can't see through the frosted windows, I'll need to use another method to see if they're inside.' Nik took a small device out of his bag, no bigger than a packet of cigarettes. 'I brought my mini amplifier with me. It's got a directional microphone. I'll sneak along the side without any windows and hold the microphone up to the wall. As long as it isn't too thick, I should be able to hear sounds from inside the building.'

'And then, if you hear something . . . are you planning on storming the building?' asked Jon.

'God no. That'd be stupid and unprofessional,' answered Nik. 'I'm on my own and have no idea what's going on in there. And I don't have the necessary training for freeing hostages. I'll leave all that up to the pros from special operations.'

Nik crept up to the building, got down on his knees and turned on the amplifier. He moved the device along the wall until he could hear something. He stopped to listen and closed his eyes. Ten seconds later he put down the device and picked up his mobile again. 'Jon, get in touch anonymously with the CID and tell them everything we know. Especially the information about the warehouse and the camera at the back door,' said Nik. 'I was right.'

◆ ◆ ◆

Nik climbed on to the roof of an old car showroom a hundred metres away. It had a good view of the warehouse's side wall and rear entrance. He lay down to watch the SEK raid from underneath a dark blanket.

A large dark blue van sped up to the warehouse. The sliding doors opened and six heavily armed men stormed out. They were all wearing the same dark green uniform with bulletproof vests and helmets. With their weapons at the ready, four of them ran around the building to the back door, while the others moved into position at the front.

Meanwhile, police officers were blocking off the streets into the industrial estate, the blue lights on their patrol cars flashing brightly. The operation had been coordinated with top precision.

Typically, special forces would have rammed the entrance with a pile driver, but the back door was too stable for that, so they mounted something – it was too small for Nik to see – on to the hinges of the door and ran away quickly. Seconds later, there were three small explosions and the door fell inwards, crashing to the floor. The officers charged inside, the flashlights on their rifles shining blindingly.

Nik had done his best to hear the task-force leader's radio, but it had been useless. The only thing he could do was wait. No shots had been fired and there hadn't been any further explosions, which Nik took as a good sign. Two police cars and an ambulance drove up close to the building.

The men at the front door lowered their weapons and relaxed. A paramedic jumped out of the ambulance and ran towards the back entrance with a large bag.

'Anything happening?' Jon's voice rang over the headphones.

'The situation's under control,' said Nik. 'I didn't hear any shots so they must have subdued Buchwald and the paramedic has entered the building so hopefully the children will be fine.'

Jon sighed. 'Let's hope all this is over now.'

◆ ◆ ◆

Large headlights illuminated the warehouse from all sides, and while SEK officers started packing away their equipment, the forensics team arrived at the scene with bags and cameras, ready to examine every inch of the hideout. Naumann appeared. He was wearing a bulletproof vest over his shirt. The task-force leader from special operations was filling him in on everything that had happened.

'The kidnapper, Ismail Buchwald, and Simon Fahl were not inside the building, sir,' said the man. 'But there were four used beds in the warehouse, so we can assume the two of them had also been staying there.' He took off his helmet and balaclava and wiped the sweat off his forehead with a towel.

Naumann shook his head. 'And what happened to the girl?' Nik had seen two paramedics supporting Greta as she left the building, before lifting her carefully on to a stretcher.

'She and Hannes Lepper had hidden themselves behind a table when we entered. After getting over her initial shock, she positioned herself in front of the boy, as if she was trying to protect him from us. She threatened us with a kitchen knife. We were able to take it off her, but she still refused to come with us and defended herself forcefully. In the end we had to put her in handcuffs.'

'Did she say anything?'

'That we wouldn't understand and that she had to stay there.'

'And the boy?'

'He just sat hunched over on the floor, staring at his hands. He was unresponsive and didn't react to our questions. But he did let us take him out of the building without any resistance.'

'Hannes Lepper was diagnosed with autism at an early age. *His* behaviour can be explained but what the hell was Greta playing at? Trying to attack her rescuers with a knife?' Naumann wondered.

'Stockholm syndrome, sir?'

'Can't think of a better reason right now.' Naumann sighed loudly. 'But I'll leave it up to the experts to make that decision.' He patted the SEK officer encouragingly on the shoulder. 'I'm just pleased we at least manged to get two of the three kids. Everything else will be solved in good time.'

The man shivered as he took his mobile out of his pocket and called a saved number. He ran through the instructions in his head again: never mention any names or addresses, or obvious descriptions of places, and finally, be brief.

He listened to the phone ringing. One ring. A second ring. 'Hello?' answered a man in a solid, scratchy voice.

'We've found the girl,' said the man instantly.

'Do you have her?'

'Not right now. It's still not possible.'

'Why not?'

'I can't tell you on the phone, but if you just read the local paper, you'll have all the necessary details.'

'Did anyone notice anything?'

'Not as far as we know.'

Both men went silent. 'OK,' the powerful voice said finally. 'Don't lose her again and leave the mobile turned on. I'll be in touch.' He hung up.

The man nervously wiped away the sweat from his forehead and exhaled loudly. It had all gone well and he was still alive. To celebrate, he decided to treat himself to a nice breakfast in a cafe. Whatever he wanted. And a couple of half pints. Maybe then his hands would stop shaking.

◆ ◆ ◆

Nik had spent the whole day pinning up photos of the crime scene, reading reports and scanning every news article he could get hold of. He was now sitting on a chair with a cup of coffee, trying to build a picture of the SEK operation. Kara was on the coffee table working her way through a bowl of sunflower seeds. After retrieving the seed, she would use her beak to push the shells to the side of the table and over the edge. She watched with curiosity as the shells fell, as if expecting something spectacular to happen when they hit the ground. The telephone rang. Nik stood up and put the call on speakerphone. Balthasar appeared with a steaming cup of ginger tea and sat down on the sofa.

'I've read through all the reports and looked at the hideout features in detail,' began Nik. 'Together with the incidents over the last few days, I've come to a conclusion.' He picked up his cup of coffee. 'I don't have the faintest idea what's going on.'

As if acknowledging Nik's disappointing words, Kara squawked loudly and flew on to Balthasar's shoulder, managing to sweep the remaining shells off the table in the process.

Nik stood and looked at the photos of the hideout. 'The location was well chosen: it's possible to get on to the road unseen via the rear area of the premises; the few windows are made of frosted glass; and the two regular doors are just as solid as the rolling door on the right-hand side of the building. The front entrance was barricaded, and the rolling door's mechanism was broken. Until now everything seems to fit a kidnapper's hideout. But the first inconsistency comes with the rear door.'

'Why? It was bolted from the inside,' said Jon over the hands-free.

'Yes, with a firm but easily opened bolt,' added Nik. 'The children could have walked out at any time.'

'And so why didn't they?' asked Jon.

'I don't know,' said Nik. 'And that's exactly what doesn't make any sense.'

'Maybe Buchwald had sedated the kids before he left.'

'Neither drugs nor medication were found in their blood,' explained Nik. 'And no drugs were found at the premises. They also didn't find any chains or handcuffs, or any other kind of restraining device.'

'Maybe he'd scared them so much they didn't dare run away?'

'That conflicts with the state of the warehouse's interior,' said Nik, walking over to the photos. 'All four beds were comfortable and clean. The fridge was bursting with food and drink – albeit the majority of which was a nutritionist's worst nightmare: chips, chicken wings, cola, chocolate, crisps and gummy bears. For breakfast there was cornflakes, Coco Pops, muesli and milk. And there were even gluten-free products for Hannes, who has coeliac disease. There were takeaway boxes from a local restaurant in the bin and three empty cases of Coke. There was a TV on the wall and it had been hooked up to a games console. The bathroom was clean, every child had their own towel, and there was strawberry shower gel. Clothes had been hung up to dry in a side room – clothes which Buchwald must have bought himself so they'd have a change.'

'So, from what you're saying, we could assume Buchwald was actually trying to protect the children from something and was trying to make things as comfortable as possible,' remarked Balthasar.

'Yes. But who or what was he trying to protect them from?' asked Nik. 'The only dangerous man in the picture was Vincent Masannek. And he's lying in the morgue at forensics.'

'Until now, we've been thinking that Masannek was working for himself,' said Jon. 'But what if he had actually been hired?'

'By whom?' asked Nik. 'We haven't seen the slightest bit of evidence to suggest who that could be; neither in the security company's database nor at any point since the kidnapping.'

'We also don't have a link between Masannek and the births,' said Jon. 'We don't know who the men were that day in the hospital and we know just as little about the woman who gave birth – not her name nor why she fled right after giving birth.'

'Are there statements from the children?' asked Balthasar.

Nik shook his head. 'Greta's still under medical supervision and Hannes doesn't talk.'

'And what's with Simon?'

'Still no sign of him whatsoever,' said Jon. 'The four beds made it pretty easy to conclude he'd been in the warehouse too. He just managed to get away . . . like Buchwald.'

'And how did Buchwald manage to get away?' asked Balthasar. 'I thought you heard his and the children's voices.'

'I heard the voice of an adult who had difficulty speaking,' Nik explained. 'I thought because of his injuries that must've been Buchwald. And I also heard Greta's voice . . . which was why I got you to call special operations. And as soon as I did that, I left immediately so I wouldn't bump into the police when they arrived. There was enough time for Buchwald and Simon to disappear.'

'Maybe Buchwald saw you,' said Jon.

'I don't think so. Then he would've taken Greta and Hannes with him,' explained Nik. 'And Buchwald's cupboard was still full of clothes and a suitcase. There was nothing pointing to a hasty getaway. He was very lucky.' Nik took two steps back and stared at the wall of photos, longing to make sense of it all.

'So what happens now?' asked Jon, stealing Nik from his musings.

'Well, the entire Bavarian police force is looking for Buchwald, so we should concentrate on Simon,' said Nik.

'We already tried to find him before without any success,' said Jon. 'And now, after an SEK operation, he'll be hanging out even less at his usual spots.'

'I'm going to speak to someone who maybe didn't tell me the entire truth during our first chat. But I'll need a little pocket money for that.'

'How much?'

'Twenty thousand,' said Nik. 'I need to track down a guy who even the CID can't get hold of.'

◆ ◆ ◆

Nik ran along the hall towards the forensics department. It was hot and sticky. All the children's parents were there: the Grohnerts, the Fürstes and the Leppers. And beside them were Nik's former colleagues, Naumann and Danilo. He could also see Jon, Balthasar and the dead Vittoria Monti. They were all furious with him; hitting him, spitting on him and blaming him for everything. Their faces were grotesquely contorted and they were pointing towards a large room that was flooded with a glaring light. A room where the reeking stench of formaldehyde made Nik gag. He staggered on, covering his head with his hands to protect himself from the blows, until he had managed to leave the corridor. All at once, the screaming stopped, as if somebody had closed a heavy invisible door. The silence was blissful. Nik lowered his hands and went further into the room. The smell of formaldehyde was still suffocating and black smoke was wafting up from the floor. The light was so bright that he couldn't see the walls. But he could make out three chrome tables, on top of which lay the bodies of Greta, Simon and Hannes. Their eyes were wide open, as if death had seized them in a moment of horror. Their skin was pallid, and their fingers were still clawing agonisingly at the sides of the tables.

He heard approaching steps, quiet at first, then louder, until the floor started to vibrate. Vincent Masannek emerged from the light. He was wearing a dark suit, a white shirt and shiny polished shoes. His hair was perfectly styled. His fingernails were manicured and the smell of his aftershave even managed to cover the stench of formaldehyde. He stopped two steps in front of Nik and casually leaned on Greta's chrome table.

'You failed,' he said, folding his arms across his chest and looking at Nik. His grin became wider with each inhalation until a thundering laugh escaped his mouth and echoed throughout the room.

◆ ◆ ◆

Nik crossed the busy station forecourt and over the tram tracks to Schillerstraße. A headache had plagued him the whole morning. Even two cups of coffee and a cold shower couldn't shift the nightmare from the night before. Masannek's laugh was still bellowing in his head and the image of the dead children followed him with every step. Greta and Hannes might be safe for now, but nothing would feel resolved until he knew the reason for the abduction. Buchwald and Simon were still out there somewhere, and Masannek's motive was still a mystery. He only had half the story.

Walking along the narrow pavement, Nik took out his phone and called Jon.

'Did everything work?' asked Jon.

'I got the money,' answered Nik.

'And who is it you want to bribe?'

'A filthy dealer who'll take me to Timo Fürste.'

'That's going to be pretty difficult as long as the Somalians are trying to kill him.'

'In the Munich underworld everybody knows everybody, and everybody knows who to ask if they need something.'

'And this dealer's going to hand Fürste over to you just like that?'

'The Somalians aren't exactly a friendly bunch so nobody's just going to hand him over. But I don't present a danger, so I'll at least be able to get a conversation organised.' Nik stopped outside a grimy cafe beside a sex shop. There were plastic chairs on the pavement, and the stench of old fat smothered the smell of coffee, which was coming from a machine that looked as if it would fail every possible health and safety regulation. 'I'll be in touch later,' said Nik before hanging up.

The cafe was quiet. An old couple sat at one table complaining to one another about the lack of police in the area, while a long-haired man stood leaning against the door, absorbed in his mobile. There was a woman doing her best not to demolish the place in her attempts to catch a little boy. Next to them was a broad-shouldered man sweeping the floor, although looking at the broom's grimy bristles, it was possible the place would look worse by the time he'd finished. There were six television screens hanging on the walls, all broadcasting different sport events. The man Nik was looking for sat in the corner of the cafe, left of a display fridge that was stocked with rolls and croissants. He absentmindedly stirred his coffee while watching a boxing match on the TV. His woollen hat was concealing most of his shaven head and spider tattoo.

'Family's a wonderful thing, isn't it?' said Nik, planting himself down on the chair opposite Paddy. The man's left hand inched its way to his hip, where he normally kept his knife, while his right hand carried on stirring his coffee. 'If only you'd joined your brother here instead of dealing drugs, you would've had far fewer problems with the police.'

'It was a pretty stupid idea coming here if you know this place belongs to my brother,' retaliated Paddy with a smile. 'You still owe me after our last meeting.' He got up from his chair.

Nik didn't budge and pushed an envelope across the table towards him. 'Why not take that as an apology.'

Paddy froze, somewhat bewildered. He looked around him, as if expecting to see the SEK at the front door. He lowered his gaze and picked up the envelope with his right hand, his left not budging from his hip. His eyes doubled in size when he saw the money. He folded the envelope over again and sat back down on the chair.

'So where's the catch?' he asked, not taking his hand off the envelope.

'No catch,' said Nik. 'I just need to speak to Timo Fürste.'

'Fürste's gone underground,' replied Paddy. 'If he shows his face in public, the Somalians will chop him into pieces.'

'I don't plan on meeting him in front of the main station. I want to see him in his hideout.'

'And how am I supposed to organise that?'

'You know everybody on the scene. Make some calls.' Nik signalled to the money with a nod of the head and a raised eyebrow. 'That's twenty grand in there. I'm sure if you invest half of it in your contacts, an address will turn up. Ten thousand for making a couple of phone calls doesn't seem like a bad cut to me.' Nik shrugged.

Paddy tapped his finger nervously on the envelope before standing up and turning to the man with the broom. 'Make sure this prick stays put,' he said, pointing at Nik. 'And smack him if he so much as scratches his balls.'

The tall man nodded sedately, still sweeping the floor. Nik leaned back and closed his eyes for a moment. It was a welcome rest. With a bit of luck, the CID would soon get a breakthrough, but as long as they still hadn't got hold of Buchwald, he'd have to keep looking himself.

He was woken from his snooze by a firm shake on the shoulder.

'In five minutes, a friend of mine will take you to Aying,' said Paddy. 'If you start any shit, he'll put a bullet in your head. You get it?'

'Lovely. Was nice chatting with you, Paddy.' Nik stood up and waved goodbye, grabbing a croissant from the cabinet on his way out. He didn't have high expectations for the meeting with Timo Fürste, but for the time being, it was his best lead.

Chapter 11

The ride to Aying wasn't too disconcerting. Nik had been through much worse. Nobody pulled a hood over his head or tied his hands together, and the driver acted more like a businessman than one of Paddy's dealers. He was wearing a navy suit and a white shirt and didn't have any piercings or tattoos. The only garish thing about him was the bulky gold ring on his right hand. The man hadn't uttered a word since getting in the car. He was more than likely used to driving odd clients to odd places and Nik was well aware that in situations like this, it was better not to ask too many questions. He hadn't seen a gun on the man, but considering the car had reinforced doors and bulletproof tinted windows, it could be assumed the driver would know how to defend himself if necessary.

After a good half hour of driving, the car stopped in front of an old farmhouse with a large barn. The paint on the outside of the building was flaking and the only thing that was still in any reasonable state was the wooden balcony on the first floor. Two small Italian family cars were parked at the entrance and beside them were three piles of chopped wood and a battered old gas barbecue. The mound of manure at the side of the driveway was still steaming and there were countless potholes. The property was situated on a side street that trailed off to a small forest. The nearest neighbour was a hundred metres away and a large beech tree at the front entrance prevented anyone from seeing into the house. Nobody just randomly passed this place.

Nik's door unlocked. With a brief goodbye, he got out of the car and walked over to the farmhouse. An elderly man wearing a pair of dirty dungarees appeared from a small shed. He was holding a gardening fork over his shoulder. Without saying a word, he signalled over to a low batten-door that led into the barn. The door squeaked loudly as Nik entered and he saw a mouse rushing back into a hole in the wall. The barn was dilapidated and covered in a thick layer of dust; it looked as if the place had never been renovated. Clouds of dust wafted through the air and there was a strong stench of cow manure. A man was sitting on a narrow platform underneath one of the small windows. He was playing with a silver cigarette lighter and had a gun on his lap. It was a Taurus Millennium G2. Small, easy to handle, loaded and ready to shoot. Saying nothing, the man pointed to a grubby stool.

Nik knew Fürste from the photos but he'd lost a lot of weight since they'd been taken. He was gaunt, his hair hadn't been washed in a good while, he needed a shave and his T-shirt was filthy. He looked exhausted and Nik concluded that the hiding place probably wasn't conducive to getting a good night's sleep.

'So you're Paddy's . . . business partner?' the man asked in a tired voice.

'That's right,' said Nik, nodding.

'He promised me two thousand if I spoke to you,' continued Fürste. 'As you can probably see, I could do with the money.' He clicked the lighter. 'So, what do you want?'

'It's about your foster son, Simon,' Nik began.

'That little shit,' grumbled Fürste.

'You mean because he didn't want to help you with your business?'

Fürste spat on the floor. 'I wasn't earning much at the power plant so I had to make some money on the side. Would have been tight otherwise. And Simon never seemed to complain when I used the money to buy food. So he could have helped me out once in a while to push the stuff.'

'Not exactly the attitude you'd expect from a foster dad.'

'Simon doesn't give a shit about school. He just hangs around spraying walls all day with potheads,' replied Fürste. 'So nothing's coming from that either, is it?'

'Simon's not been seen in a long time.'

'Yeah, my woman mentioned that.'

'Do you think it's possible he's been kidnapped?'

'You mean by this child kidnapper who's driving the Munich pigs insane?'

'Yeah, or your Somalian friends. The ones who made you end up in this humble abode.'

Fürste laughed. 'I took Simon in so my woman would have something to do at night. Not because I love children. If the Somalians have got him, they can keep him. They won't get me with that.'

Nik took a photo of Ismail Buchwald out of his pocket and handed it to Fürste. 'Do you know him?'

Timo looked at the photo and nodded. 'Not exactly a face that's easy to forget, is it?' He handed the photo back to Nik.

'His name's Ismail Buchwald,' said Nik.

'I saw him once with Simon. The two of them were speaking at the front door when I got home. Just thought he'd brought him home from school.'

'And did you speak to him?'

'Nah. He limped away without saying a word when he saw me.'

'And did you ask Simon about him?'

'I don't give a shit who Simon hangs around with.'

'Did Buchwald seem like a friend or did Simon seem hostile towards him?'

'They both had their heads down, as if they were hatching some kind of plan.'

'And did you see them speaking before or after Greta Grohnert's abduction?'

'When was she abducted?'

'Twenty-ninth of September.'

'Was about two weeks before that.'

Nik put the photo of Buchwald back in his pocket. 'Do you think it's possible Simon could be involved in a kidnapping?'

Fürste opened and closed the lighter. 'He never wanted anything to do with my drug dealing so it's a bit hard to imagine him working with a kidnapper.'

'But you think he'd be able to?'

'Simon's the smartest fucker I've ever met,' answered Fürste. 'He could do anything he put his mind to . . . So yes, he'd be able to carry out a kidnapping.'

Nik sat on the couch and looked at the few pictures of Simon that he had. He wasn't smiling in a single photo. He looked like a teenage revolutionary with his long hair, a hoodie and ripped jeans. Although he was only fourteen years old, he appeared older; far too mature for someone who was still supposed to be a child.

Nik was so absorbed in his own thoughts he didn't notice Balthasar was in the room until he spoke.

'You assume Simon's in on it all?' asked the pathologist.

'It's been a long time since I've assumed anything,' Nik answered. 'I'm just trying to think in all possible directions, hoping I'll get some genius idea where everything links sensibly together.'

'Does Simon have a record?'

'Nothing to get too excited about.' Nik pointed at two pieces of paper. 'Breach of peace, damage to property and trespassing. Pretty harmless stuff for a kid with his background. No bodily harm or any other kind of serious crime. Not even shoplifting. Conversations with his care workers suggest he's a difficult kid but not one with criminal tendencies.'

'So why are you including him as one of the suspects then?'

'Because he wasn't at the police raid,' said Nik. 'Why were Greta and Hannes in the warehouse but not him?'

'Are you sure he'd been there at all?'

'The investigators found four traces of DNA there: two of them matched Greta and Hannes and the other two were male. One of them will be Buchwald's and the other could be Simon's.'

'Or it could belong to another male kidnapper.'

'Going by the clothing that was found, there has to have been a third teenager there,' said Nik. 'Plus, no other child has been kidnapped so there's a good chance it was Simon.'

'And what are the other two teenagers saying?'

'There still isn't anything on that,' answered Nik. 'It's possible they've already been questioned and the reports just haven't been uploaded yet. But I can't be sure. Whatever the case, both families are being protected from the public eye.'

The conversation was interrupted by Nik's phone.

'There's been a shooting in Grünwald,' said Jon instantly. 'Buchwald broke into a villa and killed two security guards.'

'Which villa?'

'I still don't know, but he didn't get far. He was still at the entrance when he got shot himself.'

◆　◆　◆

Nik knew a large section of the neighbourhood would be sealed off but he still wanted to try and get a picture of what had happened. He decided to park his car close by and go the rest of the way on foot. Police cars were blocking the street and barrier tape had been hung up to restrain the customary crowd of curious onlookers. Journalists were trying to get their first titbits of information, and cameras had been rigged up high in the hope of catching a lucky snapshot that would make the morning's front page. But the crime scene itself had been hidden with large tarpaulin sheets. Nik spotted his former colleagues from the CID and forensics. Two ambulances were parked on the pavement.

The villa in question must belong to a rich man. The price per square metre in Grünwald was obscene and all the villas enjoyed gardens the size of small parks. This particular man's house was light brown with dark shingles on the roof and a balcony that was supported by thick beams. The high grey wall surrounding the house made it impossible for anyone to see into the garden, as did the large gate at the driveway entrance, which was lined with magnificent oak trees.

Nik stood back from the gawking masses and called Jon.

'Anything new?' Nik asked.

'All your ex-colleagues are on site but barely anything's been uploaded on to the server.'

'Who does the place belong to?'

'Olaf van Berk.'

'Should I know him?'

'I'm still putting together some information on him. Ask me again tomorrow.'

'What was Buchwald doing here?'

'This is the first I've heard of van Berk,' said Jon. 'And I've got no idea how he's linked to Buchwald.'

'Maybe a deal went badly?'

'According to the reports, Buchwald tried to violently break into the house. After climbing over the gate, he was shot in the driveway. If this was a gangster film, I'd say it was an act of revenge.'

A siren started to sound and the air filled with blue flashing lights. Nik held a finger up to his free ear. 'There's nothing I can do here,' he said. 'I'll head home and wait for the first reports.'

'OK. I'll carry on looking into van Berk,' said Jon.

◆ ◆ ◆

Nik pinned a photo of the villa on the left-hand side of the wall, along with a map of the area and photos of the fatalities from the shooting. On the right, he'd hung a list of names of all the people involved. Each name was accompanied by a brief life summary. There was an empty packet of chocolate biscuits on the table and a large bag of crisps that had been ripped wide open. Beside that was a thermos flask and a white cup with the dry brown remains of his coffee. Nik stood in front of the wall and scanned back and forth across the pieces of information, unconsciously tapping a black felt-tip pen against his chin.

The home phone rang over the living room speakers and Nik blinked rapidly, bringing himself back from wherever it was he'd been. He looked at the time. Exactly 12 p.m. Jon had promised he'd call to discuss the case. Not a second later, Balthasar appeared wearing his white yoga trousers and a sand-coloured low-cut T-shirt. Kara was perched on his shoulder. As soon as she caught sight of the biscuit crumbs, she flapped down quickly to peck at them before ripping at the packet with her beak. Nik answered the phone and put it on loudspeaker, his gaze not budging from the wall.

'What a night!' said Jon, yawning. 'Couldn't murderers kill early in the morning for once? Then we could at least get a good night's sleep and be able to concentrate the next day.'

'It'll take more than a good night's sleep to help me figure out what the hell this case is all about,' said Nik. 'But anyway, let's take things one step at a time.' He went over to Ismail's photo. 'Our suspected kidnapper went to Olaf van Berk's villa yesterday at 7.27 p.m., climbed over the gate and shot the first security guard, who was standing in front of the house, in the head.' Nik pointed to an area on the map. 'A heavy crowbar was found in the suspect's equipment so it can be assumed he was planning to break in. A second security guard, who was also in the garden at this point, opened fire on Buchwald immediately. Buchwald managed to shoot the second guard dead, but in doing so, received a bullet to the left arm. This significantly broke his momentum.' Nik pointed to a picture of the house door. 'The moment of weakness gave the third security guard, who was inside the house, enough time to get to the entrance, open the door and start shooting at the intruder. Despite managing to shoot the third guard in the hip, Buchwald was shot fatally in the lungs. But somehow he still managed to climb over the gate and get back on to the street.'

Nik looked at the photo showing the deceased Ismail Buchwald. He was lying on his right-hand side with his fingers still closed around the gun. Blood was running from his mouth, forming a dark, sticky pool in front of him, and he was staring towards the villa gate. There was a large hole in his jacket at lung height, and blood-drenched feathers from the down lining were sticking to the navy fabric on his back.

'My God. Sounds more like an insane suicide attack you'd see in a film,' said Balthasar. 'Until this, Buchwald's actions have always been well planned.'

'Well, the attack wasn't actually that far from being successful,' said Nik. 'Word had it that van Berk's property was protected by *two* security guards. And he killed two. Had the third man not been on the premises, Buchwald would have got inside. He even managed to shoot the third one, albeit not fatally.'

'OK. And then what would he have done?' asked Jon. 'Gone inside and shot van Berk?'

'Most likely.'

'And what does that have to do with the kidnappings?'

'No idea,' said Nik, his confusion clearly grating on his nerves. 'Van Berk's name isn't mentioned in a single document.'

'Well, I actually might have some good news there,' said Jon. 'As soon as the names of the deceased were uploaded on to the CID system I did a search on them. I'll give you three guesses who they worked for.'

'Beate Uhse?' offered Balthasar.

'Nope. Second guess.'

'Vincent Masannek?' said Nik.

'Exactly.'

'OK. Now we might be getting somewhere. If Masannek was contracted by Olaf van Berk, then we might just have found the man behind all this.'

'True, but we still have no idea *why*,' said Balthasar.

'No, we don't,' Nik agreed. 'And to find out, we'll need to get more on van Berk.'

'Unfortunately, that's easier said than done,' said Jon. 'To the outside world, van Berk runs a financial consultancy company but his clientele is decidedly exclusive. When I tried to arrange a consultation, a secretary politely told me that van Berk was no longer taking on any new clients.'

'So the consultancy firm is just a front?'

'Looks like it. His financial assets are certainly impressive but until now I haven't been able to stir up any dirt on him. I'll need to dig a little deeper.'

'And what about his family? What's that like?'

185

'He has a son called Elias,' said Jon. 'I found some photos and entries on him up to 2009. But nothing after that. It's as if he disappeared into thin air overnight. There are no links to our kidnap victims and there's nothing on Elias at the Munich registry office. It's a dead end from where I'm sitting,' concluded Jon.

'The photos of the crime scene also show the crowd of onlookers. Most of them are playing with their phones but there's one woman standing at the barrier, crying.'

'That's pretty normal, isn't it?' said Balthasar. 'Most people get upset at the sight of a dead body or the scene of a violent crime.'

'Yes, but why is she there then?' asked Nik.

'Where are you heading with this?'

'The woman's wearing a headscarf and you can't fully see the front of her in any of the photos. But if you could join all the individual clips together . . .'

'. . . You'd be able to confirm her identity,' Jon concluded.

'How long would that take you to do?'

'Two minutes.'

'That fast?' asked Nik.

'You might not have heard, Nik, but I'm not too shabby with computers and in the days of Photoshop, it's really not that big a deal.' Nik heard Jon's keyboard tapping. 'The woman with the bright red headscarf, yeah?'

'That's the one.' Nik heard Jon hang up.

Nik picked up his coffee cup from the table and looked inside. Empty. After putting it back down, Kara hopped over to peep inside herself. Also disappointed with the outcome, she returned her attention to the chocolate biscuit crumbs. Balthasar was sitting casually on the couch, one leg crossed over the other, concentrating on the busy wall. A few minutes later, Jon was on the phone again. 'I've sent the photo to your mobile.'

Nik picked up his phone from the table. 'Bloody hell . . .' he mumbled. 'That's Daniela Haas. The care worker from Simon's home.'

'Maybe she was just there by chance,' suggested Balthasar.

'Neuhausen and Grünwald aren't exactly neighbouring districts,' said Nik.

'OK. So d'you think she's involved somehow?'

'Jesus! I'm beginning to think I've lost all my investigating instincts.' Nik was angry. 'I mean, it's completely feasible that Buchwald's a kidnapper. I can *almost* believe Simon's an accomplice in a kidnapping. But I would have *never* suspected Haas was involved.' He put his phone in his pocket and picked up the car keys from the top of a chest of drawers. 'All this sitting around speculating is beginning to piss me off. I'm going to visit Haas at her house and ask her what she was doing at van Berk's villa.'

'I'll send her address to your phone,' said Jon.

The door slammed shut. Startled, Kara flapped her wings madly and flew on to a shelf.

'I think he might be in a bit of a bad mood,' said Balthasar with a grin.

'Well, I hope for that woman's sake he calms down a bit on the ride over there,' said Jon. 'It'll be a pretty unpleasant conversation if he doesn't.'

◆ ◆ ◆

It was Sunday lunchtime and the rows of terraced houses felt like a ghost town. There were no children playing or parents washing their cars in the driveways. It was as if everybody had gone inside to eat lunch at exactly the same time. The only person to be seen was an old woman tottering along the pavement with her dachshund, her eyes squeezed almost shut as if she could barely see one step ahead of her.

Nik arrived at Daniela Haas's house and rang the doorbell three times. No answer. He knocked on the door but there was still nothing. In the end, he decided to go through the open gate to the side of the garage and into the small garden. But Daniela Haas was nowhere to be seen. The blinds on the patio doors were pulled down, preventing him from seeing inside. He considered breaking a glass pane but decided not to as it would attract too much attention. And anyway, he wasn't going to find any clues inside that would be of help. He needed to speak to her personally.

He took his mobile out of his pocket and called the children's home where he'd first met her. A woman's voice spoke after the third ring.

'Hello, Frau Eichert,' said Nik. 'It's Inspector Pohl here.'

'Oh, hello, Herr Pohl,' said the woman. 'Any news on Simon?'

'Unfortunately not,' said Nik. 'But I do have a question for Frau Haas and she's not at home. Is she maybe working today?'

'No, Daniela asked to use up some of her annual holiday yesterday. Said something about a family crisis.'

'How long will she be gone for?'

'A week.'

'Do you have a mobile number for her you can give me?'

'Just her landline,' replied Eichert.

'No, then don't worry. This is urgent,' said Nik sighing. 'Please can you call me if Frau Haas comes back to work earlier than expected?'

'Of course.'

'Thanks.' Nik hung up and called Jon.

'Does Daniela Haas have a car?' asked Nik. He was walking back through the side gate to the street.

'Just a minute,' said Jon. Nik heard him searching the web frantically in the background. 'Nope,' said Jon finally. 'Not getting a registration under her name or address.'

'Well, she's disappeared and I've got no idea how I'm supposed to find her.'

'I'm assuming she's not going to be a pro at going underground. She's bound to make a mistake.'

'We don't have time to wait for her to make a mistake,' said Nik. 'Why are we always one fucking step behind? We manage to make some kind of connection and then . . . someone gets shot or kidnapped . . . or a completely new suspect turns up out of nowhere!'

'So what d'you suggest?'

'I suggest we forget about Daniela Haas and concentrate on the man Buchwald wanted to shoot: Olaf van Berk.'

'Well, we can't connect him to the kids and we've got no idea why Buchwald would want to shoot him. The only thing that seems in any way suspicious is the fact he's out of the country so often. He's got a private jet which he's always using to fly abroad.'

'Any particular destinations he flies to most often?'

'It's hard to find out. I can only follow the routes between Munich and the subsequent airport. From there, he could be flying on to anywhere in the world without being tracked.'

'OK. Well, where was he last?'

'His last destination was Milan but that was a week ago,' said Jon. 'Came back Friday night.'

'And Buchwald tried to shoot him the next day. That's no coincidence,' said Nik. 'We need to speak to someone who can tell us more about van Berk.'

'OK. But please not this Paddy guy.'

'No, he's only useful for the drug stuff,' Nik explained. 'We need someone who's deep in the Munich underworld.'

'Your girlfriend, Jablonski?'

'She'll be too busy hunting the guy who gave her up,' said Nik. 'I need someone even the CID would kill for, just to get their hands on his knowledge.'

'That person exists?'

'Yes, but I'll need records from the CID server to get hold of him.'

'My back door into the system is still working.'

Nik got into his car, switching the call to speakerphone. 'I also need access to the Munich registration office and to a few security cameras in the city.'

'Also manageable.'

'The person we're looking for is a phantom but with the right documents and your hacking talents, we might get a bit closer to him than we did when I worked for the police.' Nik started the engine.

'Ahh . . . I love it when an ex-CID agent entices me into committing crimes,' said Jon, almost giggling.

With that, Nik started to explain the whole story behind their next source.

Chapter 12

The espresso bar was innocuous. Outside the front door were a number of dark grey wicker chairs and cheap chrome tables, most of which were in the shade being provided by two large sun umbrellas. The interior had been painted light brown and was furnished with dark bar stools, high tables and a kitsch ceiling lamp that didn't match anything; two mirrors on the side walls made the place feel slightly bigger. The focal point of the room was a large espresso machine, in front of which was a display fridge filled with cupcakes, paninis and focaccia.

The bar was almost empty and the owner was clearing away glasses into a wall cabinet. Nik noticed one customer who was fiddling with an espresso cup while deeply engrossed in an article in the *Gazzetta dello Sport*.

Nik went over to the counter, ordered a coffee and sat down at a free table. From there, he scoped the room, stood up, did a 360-degree turn and sat down at another table. He made a show of looking from the floor to the ceiling and then at his watch, before sliding over to the next stool, banging his briefcase on the table in the process. The man reading the newspaper pounded his fist on the table and forced a smile at Nik. 'Are you looking for something?'

Nik turned around swiftly and looked at the man as if noticing him for the first time. He had short black hair, a thin moustache and long sideburns. The sleeves of his grey shirt were rolled up and a heavy silver watch sparkled on his wrist.

'I'm actually looking for some*one*, not something,' replied Nik, sitting down opposite the man. 'Maybe you can help.'

'If it'll stop you from flailing around the place like a headless chicken . . . then gladly.'

Nik smiled and offered him his hand. 'My name's Nik,' he said in a friendly tone.

'Luca,' answered the man, taking Nik's hand.

'The person I'm looking for is actually a legend in Munich's criminal underworld,' said Nik. 'He goes by just "The Collector".'

'And what is it he collects?' asked Luca. 'Stamps?'

'Information,' replied Nik.

The bar owner brought Nik's coffee over to the table. 'I need to hunt down a man who's involved in a particularly nasty case,' Nik continued. 'And that's exactly where The Collector comes into play.'

'You should watch less Sunday night crime drama,' said Luca, turning his gaze back to his paper. 'But good luck with the search.'

'Oh, it's not luck I need. I just found him.' Nik smiled and took a sip of coffee.

Luca winced, irritated by the clumsy customer. 'Does it look like I'm here collecting information?'

'What else would you be doing here?'

'Drinking the best espresso in town,' replied Luca, tapping his cup.

'Oh, really?'

'By far. Did you know . . . there are three vital conditions for a good espresso,' Luca started to explain. 'First there's the *macchina*.' He pointed to the coffee machine. 'Anything other than a traditional portafilter is an offence. Second, it has to be the right coffee mixture. You could talk about that point alone for hours. And finally, the production has to be carried out perfectly. That means freshly ground coffee and ninety-degree chalk-free water, in a pre-warmed cup.' He folded his hands over his chest. 'Even in Munich, that's not an easy thing to come by but my friend behind the counter over there sticks to all the rules.'

'Fascinating stuff,' said Nik. 'But it's not the information I'm looking for. You see, I need . . .'

'Yes, yes . . . information about a man who's involved in a nasty case,' said Luca dismissively, looking back at the newspaper.

'I used to work for the Munich CID and while I was there, we tried to identify The Collector for four years. We never did, but we *did* manage to narrow it down to three people.'

'And let me guess: I'm one of the three?'

Nik pulled an envelope out of his briefcase and placed some photos on the table. 'Luca Marino, you run a successful company that imports Italian gastronomic products and you also provide catering for small parties.' The pictures showed Luca standing with numerous people, some of whom, Nik assumed, were his friends, while others looked more like business acquaintances. Luca glanced at the photos.

'And what are these supposed to prove? That I get along well with my clients?'

'Don't get me wrong, I'm sure most of the people in these photos are respectable law-abiding citizens, but there are a handful of men who are rumoured to have links with the Mafia.'

'That's pure speculation,' said Luca. 'If those accusations were true, the men would be sitting in jail and not having fun at parties, wouldn't they?'

'Oh, but these men are just as clever as you. They know who they can trust and would never involve themselves with the likes of a former CID officer.' Nik packed the photos away. 'And that was exactly the CID's problem. We had nothing in our power to catch The Collector, and nothing we could use to persuade him to work with us.'

'So why are you looking for him then?'

'Because I don't need to follow the rules anymore. I can play dirty without having to worry about criminal proceedings or being fired.' Nik smiled contentedly and took another sip of coffee, his gaze anchored to the man's eyes. 'I can tag along behind each of the three suspects and pop up at the most inconvenient of times – at receptions or meetings with clients. It would only be a matter of time before The Collector loses his reputation . . . because *nobody* wants a former CID officer sniffing around, especially one with my reputation.' Nik placed his cup back down on the table.

Luca closed the newspaper and pushed it to the side. 'But if The Collector is indeed working in such dangerous circles, it's more than just his reputation that would be in danger.'

Nik shrugged his shoulders. 'I couldn't care less. I'm an arsehole.'

'You're right, Herr Pohl. You are.'

Nik leaned back, watching the man closely. His eyes seemed to flicker. They had become sharper, more vigilant; nothing like the eyes Nik had seen reading the paper as he had arrived at the cafe. 'I can't quite put into words how satisfying it is when a gut feeling turns out to be right,' said Nik. 'You see, my ex-colleagues concentrated their efforts on a fence from the Borstei, but I put my bets on the most inconspicuous man in the group: you.'

'That's very touching. But if you know the men in the photos, then you'll also know how powerful I am.'

'You really think that's going to worry me?' said Nik.

'Your first years at the CID were impressive,' Luca continued. 'But then your sister Mira died, and there was that case of the missing Rachel Preuss. You know, the one where you beat up the prosecutor?' Luca shook his head disingenuously. 'It's a miracle they even let you back in.'

'Must have been down to my irresistible charm.'

'I actually thought you'd be back on Rachel's case again, now that you're a private snooper.'

'Who says I'm not?'

'I know back then you got a well-known Thai detective involved, which is strange 'cause I thought you were the kind of guy who did everything himself.'

'Nah, you see my Thai's a bit rusty. And over the years I've learned that if you want well-hidden information, you need to ask local people with local expertise.'

'People experienced in bribing the authorities, you mean?'

'Among other things.'

'And to achieve what exactly?'

'Proof that Rachel Preuss isn't in Thailand. That she never entered the country, and that she *didn't* leave her husband for a Thai lover.'

'Still believing the conspiracy theory then?'

'It has nothing to do with belief.' Nik caught the owner's attention and ordered a croissant. 'Can I get you something else?'

Luca shook his head.

'You sure? We've only just started.' Nik took another folder out of his bag and opened it to reveal a photo of Olaf van Berk.

Luca glanced at the photo for a split second, then looked out of the window, as if ensuring they were alone. He turned the photo over. 'That's a dangerous man.'

'Yeah, well, I wouldn't be sitting here if he was Santa Claus, would I?'

'Listen, I'll tell you something about van Berk and after that, you can decide if it might not be better to try to get what you want by some other means.'

'I'm intrigued.'

'But you'll owe me a favour.'

'OK. And what would that be?'

'I don't know at the moment. But, when I come back to you one day, you'll help me out with whatever it is I need.'

'A heavy demand, considering your situation.'

'My life's on the line here just as much as yours, and if van Berk ever gets hold of you, there's no doubt you'll spew out everything, including the bits about me. Then he'll want revenge and I can tell you now, that will not be pleasant.' Luca offered Nik his hand.

Nik swallowed and accepted. 'OK. But only if the information you give me actually gets me somewhere.'

The Collector leaned back in his chair. 'How much do you know about money laundering?'

'Only what I learned during my training,' Nik began. 'That illegally acquired money is brought into the legal business cycle via concealed transactions and without law enforcement noticing. The expression goes back to Al Capone, who put the money he made from gambling and prostitution into launderettes.'

'Well, a lot has changed since Al Capone,' explained Luca. 'And van Berk is someone who really understands the business.'

'He launders money?'

Luca nodded. 'From the big boys. People who'd be *really* unhappy if his service was no longer available to them.' He was fiddling with his empty espresso cup. 'You see, that's the most dangerous thing about van Berk: if he feels threatened, he calls up a business partner and gets them to sort it out without getting a single finger dirty.'

'Well, looking at his villa, it appears business is going well.'

'The Treasury believes around one hundred billion is washed every year in Germany. The methods the launderers use are limitless but van Berk specialises in a few.' Luca bent forward on to his elbows to be closer to Nik. 'The first method is almost as old as Capone's launderettes: money-laundering in restaurants. So, back in the day, somebody would take on some old, decrepit restaurant and declare ten times as much turnover as they had actually made. So then, even after paying taxes, there's enough illegally acquired money left over that it was all worth it. But at some point, the authorities started monitoring the cost of goods. So the industry moved over to counterfeiting, where they use cheap products but forge the bills for expensive ones. And if the restaurant has a catering service on the side, one that delivers food to large events, the profits are impressive. It's impossible to know if your tomato soup has been made with quality organic tomatoes or the mushy leftovers from Dutch greenhouses.'

'Sounds old-fashioned.'

'Maybe. But it was van Berk's first mainstay . . . even back before the internet was around,' explained Luca. 'And he plays that game better than anyone. But it's not the only method he uses. You see, the more money-laundering methods used, the more difficult it is to track them. His second mainstay is smurfing.'

'Like the Smurfs?'

'The phrase actually does come from them, yes,' said Luca. 'With smurfing, lots of bank accounts are opened up and money is regularly paid into them. The amount paid in is always under fifty thousand euros – any more, and people are obliged to declare it. The job requires a lot of employees and very good accounting so as not to lose an overview.'

'And what does that have to do with the Smurfs?'

'Lots of tiny blue people make up one large group. On their own, the result would be negligible, but when you add them all together . . . they generate an impressive sum. Lots and lots of payments, which are under the declarable threshold.'

'So what happens after the money's been paid in? Do the bad boys come along with a suitcase and clear the account?'

'It's not quite as easy as that. After depositing the money, we come to the concealment stage.' Luca pushed his empty espresso cup into the middle of the table. 'The money is sitting legally in a bank account but under a middleman's name. If that middleman was to transfer the money into the account of a Mafia boss, the authorities would catch wind and everything would've been for nothing. So, in the concealment phase, the money becomes anonymous by being transferred into another account abroad. And this stage happens as frequently as possible, and in as complicated a manner as possible.' He put his hand on top of the cup and pushed it to the side.

'And then someone uses the money in the foreign account to go shopping.'

'Exactly. A house on the Côte d'Azur, a private jet or a nice yacht,' said Luca, shrugging. 'And that's the third and final stage: the integration period. Money that was illegally acquired is washed and integrated into the legal cycle.'

Nik paused to consider what he had been told. 'So that's van Berk's business.'

Luca leaned back in his chair and nodded. 'Now you know his background. He's a dangerous man and as soon as you are on his radar, your life's at risk.'

'It's a risk I'm willing to take.'

'What are you prepared to do?' asked Luca, obviously quoting the film *The Untouchables*.

'Anything,' answered Nik, acknowledging the quote. 'Just like Eliot Ness.'

'Then I've got something for you,' replied The Collector with a smile.

'You know van Berk's weak spot, don't you?'

'I know everybody's weak spot.' Luca placed one hand over the other and rested them on the table. 'I'm a vindictive man and Olaf van Berk actually ruined an important business venture of mine a few years ago.'

'So, you want to see him fall?'

'God, you won't be able to bring down van Berk. But you do have the potential to hurt him at least. Even with all the risk involved, I don't want to lose this chance.'

'I only want to talk to him, but there's no way he'd give me an appointment,' said Nik. 'And . . . I need to be sure that when we talk, he tells me the truth. And for that I need some kind of leverage.'

'I can arrange that. But first I need another espresso.' Luca raised his hand. 'This could take a while.'

Nik sat on the couch in the living room, cleaning his picklock with a soft cloth. He lifted the small metal tool to the light and checked whether it was bent or not.

'What are you breaking into?' asked Balthasar from the door. Kara was sitting on his shoulder, pecking at a peanut.

'A council flat in a large tower block,' answered Nik, concentrating on his picklock. 'Shouldn't be a big deal.'

'I'll come with you,' said Balthasar. 'I'm an expert at picking locks.'

Nik laid the picklock down and turned to look at Balthasar. 'I don't know if that's a good idea. You've only just started to feel better in the last couple of days. I don't want you to get worse again if things get difficult.'

'I carried out a self-analysis and I believe I'm ready to work again.'

'You carried out a self-analysis?' asked Nik, bewildered.

'I had enough time during my degree to attend lectures in psychology and psychiatry.'

'OK. And what was the result of your self-analysis?'

'I'm now able to fall asleep without sleeping tablets and I'm no longer having nightmares,' said Balthasar. 'And I don't jump every time a van pulls up beside me. Over the last few days, I made myself imagine kidnapping situations while walking down the street. When I started the exercise, I winced each time – especially with black vans without any windows. But that stopped yesterday.'

'And what if there's trouble at the flat today? If they threaten us with weapons or try to beat us up?'

'Well, if that happens, then I'll turn into a desperate, crying baby, of course . . . flailing around on the floor, stuttering and drooling.'

'I don't know,' mumbled Nik.

'Let's have a competition.' Balthasar went into his room and returned with a large suitcase. 'We both have to pick three locks. If I'm faster than you, you'll let me come.'

'Picking locks is a hobby of mine,' said Nik proudly. 'It wouldn't be a fair competition.'

'Well, then you don't need to worry, do you?' Balthasar opened the suitcase. It was full of padlocks and door cylinders.

'Do you collect this shit or something?' Nik picked up a large padlock with a shackle that was about the width of his finger.

Balthasar ignored the question. 'Find us three each. Then we'll see who's better.'

'If I have to.' Nik frowned. He'd studied locking mechanisms during his police training and would regularly talk about them with the specialists from forensic technology. Only a pro burglar would be able to beat him. Definitely not some amateur. Nik chose two padlocks and one door lock with a double cylinder and anti-drilling protection. He gave three of the same kind to Balthasar as well.

Balthasar took out a pencil case full of picklocks and planted himself beside Nik on the couch.

Nik reached for the first padlock. It had five security pins. The key for the lock could turn these five pins to the side, allowing the shackle to click upwards. Picking a lock like this required very sensitive fingertips. Firstly, Nik put in the clamping tool: a piece of metal in the shape of a square S. He pulled the tool towards him, thus applying pressure to the locking mechanism, then reached for a picklock with a tip that was bent upwards, and put it in the lock. He closed his eyes and concentrated on the pins. Millimetre by millimetre, he pushed the pick further until he reached the next pin. Whenever he managed to push a pin upwards, there was a soft click. It was an exceptionally delicate task and one that demanded a calm hand and a lot of patience. And then, as the fifth pin was pushed upwards, the clamping tool turned and the shackle sprang out. He turned to look at Balthasar with a satisfied grin.

The pathologist, however, was leaning back on the couch, with not one, but three open locks sitting on his lap. He even had a chocolate biscuit in his hand. 'You've got a very interesting technique,' he said, munching on the biscuit. 'But you need to work on your speed. Furthermore, your clamp is too thick . . . and you apply too much pressure to it.'

Nik looked down at the three open locks. 'How is that possible?'

'Our nanny always used to hide the chocolate biscuits from me,' said Balthasar. 'And since she always kept the key on her, I had no choice but to learn how to pick locks. As you can see, I became very good at it.' Balthasar patted his tummy. 'Right, I'm off to feed Kara and then we can get going. What d'you say?' The pathologist stood up. 'I've got an idea for our disguise.'

'That's not possible,' mumbled Nik under his breath as Balthasar left the living room. Nik inspected the locks closely, but they seemed fine. He threw his picklock down on the table. 'And I do *not* apply too much pressure to the clamp!' he called out to Balthasar.

◆ ◆ ◆

Clemens Grohnert sat at Naumann's desk, with his arms crossed. He pursed his lips as he stared at the CID officer. It looked as if he was about to pounce on him at any second. Grohnert had arrived half an hour later than arranged, only to then park illegally in front of the station's main entrance. An offer of coffee had been turned down with a grunt.

'We understand your irritation,' said Naumann, trying to calm him down, 'but we've been waiting for your daughter to say something for four days now. Not only might she be able to give us important information about Ismail Buchwald's motive, she might also be able to tell us why he was on Olaf van Berk's property.'

'Have you seen what's happened to my daughter?' asked Grohnert, not actually looking for an answer. 'She barely speaks and sits staring out the window most of the time or just watching TV. She doesn't want to eat, drink or sleep, and nothing seems to give her any pleasure anymore. She's stopped reading and she ripped down her poster of Polina Seminova from the wall. I haven't seen her smile *once* since your officers found her.'

'I know children can be severely traumatised after an abduction . . .'

'You don't know anything!' Grohnert growled. 'If my daughter's well-being was in any way important to you, your team wouldn't have tied her hands together and dragged her violently out of that warehouse.'

'She was going to attack SEK with a knife.'

'You mean after they blew up the warehouse door and stormed the building with their weapons drawn?'

'We thought the kidnapper was in the warehouse,' said Naumann, defending his, and the team's, actions. 'We suspected he was armed and willing to use violence.'

'Do you know what my wife found underneath Greta's pillow yesterday when she made her bed? A massive kitchen knife!' said Grohnert. 'A knife! As if we were living in some fucking war zone!'

'Ismail Buchwald was shot,' Naumann explained. 'He doesn't pose a danger anymore. So I don't understand why . . .'

'It doesn't make any difference if you understand Greta's fears or not,' interrupted Grohnert. 'The fact is, she still can't sleep at night and doesn't dare leave the house. She doesn't even go into the garden!'

'Have you spoken to her about it?'

'I've tried hundreds of times,' answered Grohnert. 'But she avoids any conversation.'

'We've got a good psychologist who'd like to speak to Greta . . .'

'Not a chance! I won't let *anyone* bring up those horrifying memories.'

'We could organise a team of officers to monitor your property,' suggested Naumann.

Grohnert shook his head vigorously. 'I don't have enough faith in you or your men for that,' he said. 'I've hired a private security company to monitor the house.'

'As you wish.' Naumann lifted his hands to show his compliance.

Grohnert stood up abruptly and pointed to each of the CID officers in the room. '*Nobody* is allowed to question Greta before she gets better. And until then, I ask you *not* to bother us anymore.'

◆ ◆ ◆

Nik straightened his tie impatiently and smoothed down his jacket. He was sitting on a garden chair in front of a small table that was covered in an indeterminable sticky layer, stirring a coffee that had gone cold a long time ago. The high-rise flats in front of him were blocking out the evening light and casting a morose shadow over the busy streets below.

'What's wrong?' asked Balthasar. He looked abnormally conservative in his dark grey suit. As per usual, the pathologist was in a good mood and seemed unaffected by the depressing surroundings.

'What on earth is *that*?' Nik pointed to the small notepad in his hand. It had the word 'Enlightened!' on the front.

'We're Jehovah's Witnesses! It's perfect,' said Balthasar. 'Firstly, people avoid you, and secondly, they don't take you seriously.' He smiled at an elderly woman who walked past on the pavement. 'So, what do you want to do in the money launderer's flat?'

'I want to plant something.'

'Drugs?'

'Instructions for building a bomb.'

Balthasar let out a quiet whistle.

'Harsh, I know,' Nik continued. 'And I only feel OK doing it because the money launderer isn't exactly a saint. But if you want to get out now, I understand.'

'Listen, these abductions are the only thing I think about right now,' said Balthasar. 'So, if this is the only way to get to the bottom of them, then I'm fine with it.'

'Our man is one of van Berk's most important money launderers. We're never going to get to van Berk directly, so we're going to take down his business ventures, one by one.'

'By getting his money launderers sent to jail?'

'Oh, that's just an added bonus. You see, according to my sources, the guy who lives here received another large cash payment today. He'll now launder the money and invest it over the next few days in luxury goods. After that, he'll sell the goods on large auction platforms and in online forums throughout the whole of Europe, using various accounts. The money will then wander into foreign bank accounts which the German authorities have no access to.'

'So how much cash are we talking here?'

'A large seven-figure sum.'

'So why don't we just break in and steal the money?' asked Balthasar. 'I'm sure van Berk wouldn't like that either.'

'Because it's not enough,' Nik explained. 'The money will be in a safe, and that'll be much harder to pick than a flat door. Also, we have to make sure the money launderer gets put under so much pressure that he testifies. The money in the safe doesn't prove a thing. But if we frame him with bomb-making materials, he might admit to the laundering in order to escape a terrorism sentence.'

'And van Berk's name is supposed to appear in this statement, is it?'

'That's the plan.'

'That'll be why you're carting that around with you then?' Balthasar pointed to a tattered old brown leather bag that was sitting on a free chair.

'Just a couple of toys: cables, a soldering iron, two digital timers, a metal box and lots of nails.'

'And that's reason to call up the police?'

'I think you're forgetting I worked for the CID,' replied Nik. 'I know exactly where to call and what to say for SEK to storm the flat and rip the place apart, right down to the thinnest carpet fibre.'

'OK. So we're just going to wait here until our money launderer goes out shopping, right?'

'That's right. And according to my source, he's a late sleeper and doesn't leave the house before five in the afternoon.'

'It's almost six o'clock,' Balthasar remarked.

'Yes, I can see that,' said Nik. 'It's not like I'm waiting here for the soggy croissants.'

'What does the man look like?'

'About five seven, slim, with red hair and freckles. Apparently, he likes wearing flashy jackets and shoes.'

Balthasar lifted his cup to his mouth. 'I think he's awake.' He nodded towards the high-rise entrance. A man exactly matching Nik's description of him was standing in front of it. He was wearing a shiny blue jacket with a bright white skull-and-crossbones on the front and camouflage sleeves. On his bottom half he was wearing washed-out jeans and white trainers with thick soles that made him appear a foot taller than he was. He looked up at the dreary sky, as if letting the non-existent sunrays hit his face, and smiled. It was a smile that oozed a mixture of satisfaction and arrogance, demonstrating his assurance that he thought he was the king of the neighbourhood. He lifted his collar and set off towards the U-Bahn.

'Jesus. One day, I'd really like to meet a criminal who isn't a cliché,' mumbled Nik as he stood up from the chair. He grabbed his bag and crossed the road with Balthasar. When they reached the tower block, the pathologist pressed four buttons. After a moment the fragile voice of an elderly woman sounded through the intercom.

'Post!' said Balthasar with a friendly voice. A second later, the door buzzed open.

'Post? At six in the evening?' Nik said as they made their way inside.

'It's a reflex,' said Balthasar. 'Works every time.'

When they got up to the flat, Balthasar inspected the lock. 'No big deal.' He reached into his jacket pocket for his picklock. 'Let's just hope he doesn't have an alarm.'

'He does,' said Nik.

Balthasar turned to look at him. 'And how do you plan on turning it off?'

Nik pulled out a piece of plastic about the size his hand. It looked like a garage door opener.

'What's that? A universal alarm disabler or something?'

'Such a thing doesn't exist,' said Nik. 'But if the person buys their alarm system online and doesn't properly secure their account, then talented hackers can easily find out which model they bought and disable the alarm when necessary.'

'But it will still register the door opening.'

Nik took his gloves out of his pocket and put them on. 'Yes, it will, and by that time the SEK will also be on their way too. So no dilly-dallying, Herr Super Intruder. Get picking!'

Balthasar demonstrated his disapproval by raising one eyebrow, but then got to work and a few seconds later, the door was open.

Nik took his bag off his shoulder and went inside the flat. 'Time for some redecoration,' he said, grabbing a roll of thin cable.

Chapter 13

Nik sat on the couch with his feet up on the coffee table, sipping at a cold beer and holding a large packet of crisps under his arm.

'The press is being awfully quiet, considering the police just arrested a guy on suspicion of terrorism,' said Jon over the speakerphone.

'Officially, they're calling it a "drug crackdown",' explained Nik.

'Which is probably true if you think about where the dirty money actually came from,' Balthasar remarked. He was sprawled over an armchair wearing his baggy yoga trousers and a salmon pink T-shirt, and was feeding nuts to Kara, who had established herself firmly on his shoulder.

'The plan worked,' said Nik. 'The money launderer was arrested and won't be getting out for a long time.'

'How much money was in the safe?' asked Balthasar.

'Three hundred thousand euros,' said Jon. 'When they picked him up on his way home, he was wearing a Rolex and a two-carat diamond ring.'

Balthasar let out a long whistle, obviously impressed.

'Even van Berk's gonna feel the pinch after losing that kind of money. Not to mention the fact he lost one of his best money launderers in the process.'

'And he'll have no idea why his man was arrested on suspicion of terrorism,' added Nik. 'That'll make him nervous.' He took a gulp of beer with a satisfied expression on his face.

'I haven't managed to find an interrogation report,' said Jon.

'That can wait,' said Nik. 'I've already got the next target in my sights. And for this one I'll need fake IDs.'

'Am I allowed to tag along again?' asked Balthasar.

'As long as you dress up.'

'Dress up? You mean like for carnival? With a fake nose and a wig?'

'Just something that means you can't be identified.'

'What are you planning?' asked Jon.

'I'm going to a restaurant where van Berk does a fair share of his money laundering.'

'And why do I need to dress up?'

'Because the restaurant has CCTV and I want van Berk to concentrate only on me.'

'And who are you going to go as?' asked Jon.

'A food-safety inspector.'

'Perfidious,' said Balthasar with a grin.

'I've never faked any IDs from them before,' said Jon.

'It's the regional administrative office that's responsible for food safety in Munich,' said Nik. 'Can't be that hard to get to them.'

'And when are we going?' asked Balthasar.

'This evening.'

'You think you're going to be able to ruin one of van Berk's money-laundering sources by pretending to be a food-safety inspector?'

Nik laid the packet of crisps down to the side. 'I do. And I know exactly how we're going to do it.'

◆　◆　◆

Nik looked through the restaurant window. All the tables were occupied and two waiting staff were carrying large trays with drinks through the bar.

'Very posh,' said Balthasar, appreciating the interior. The place had been painted bright white, the floor was filled with chrome-rimmed tables and there was modern art hanging on the walls. The pathologist was wearing a blonde wig, frameless glasses and a fake moustache. He was also wearing a white doctor's coat and light blue jeans. 'What kind of restaurant is it?'

'A fusion steak house. Combines Middle Eastern and Asian cooking.'

'Sounds delicious. Don't we want to eat something before we begin with the assessment?'

'No. We need to hit fast and hard. And with the biggest audience possible.'

'And he launders money in *here*?' asked Balthasar. 'I was expecting some shitty little Italian place with a 1980s interior.'

'Apparently, not *all* clichés are true.' Nik pointed to a man of around forty with long, glossy black hair that fell over his shoulders. He was wearing a light beige suit and a thin tie with a silver pin. 'That's Roman Zehnke. The owner.'

'Doesn't look like your classic Mafia member.'

'And on paper he isn't,' added Nik. 'Clean record.'

'And we're definitely at the right address?'

'According to my source, the money is laundered through the catering. The Argentinian steaks are actually cheap cuts from China and the expensive whiskies are relabelled bottles of crap. But to the outside, all the sums add.'

'And nobody notices?'

'It's really hard to prove,' said Nik. 'It's not enough just to have a few suspicions.'

'And by closing it down, you hope to meet van Berk?'

'I've already taken one of his main players out of the game,' replied Nik. 'The restaurant isn't his biggest earner in the laundering business, but it's a well-loved meeting spot for van Berk's clients. If the restaurant gets closed down, they'll find out about it.'

'So how are you going to get it closed?'

'I dabbled with my thermometer set. And . . . in my left pocket I've got some mouldy tropical fruit, while in the right, I've got some dead cockroaches.'

Balthasar stood back, disgusted. 'That should do it. But how does it get us closer to van Berk?'

'I'll write him an email.'

'An email? Saying what? "I'm Nik and I'm going to destroy you if you don't speak to me"?'

'Pretty much.'

'OK . . . An interesting plan.'

'The launderer and the restaurant are just the start,' explained Nik. 'I'll keep going until van Berk buckles.'

'Or gets you shot.'

'I'm not leaving enough clues behind for that and the email won't be traceable. Van Berk's gonna have to meet up with me at least once and I won't be alone when we do.'

Balthasar looked into the restaurant again. 'So how d'you want to play out this food-inspector role?' he asked. 'Serious and professional? Strict and unrelenting?'

'All the inspectors I've ever met were very polite. They were precise and thorough, but they always tried to disturb business as little as possible. They'd never do an inspection when it's a full house like it is here tonight.' Nik pointed at the restaurant. 'But if we stuck to that, the owner would never fluster. We need to stir the place up, create a bit of chaos. But we need to do so without doing anything obviously illegal.'

'Oh, you mean like using fake food-inspector IDs?'

'We can forget about that for now, OK?'

'Well . . . creating a bit of chaos won't be a problem.' And with that, Balthasar pushed his fake glasses up the bridge of his nose, opened the door to the restaurant, went up the steps and tripped on a carpet. He stumbled forward, trying to hold himself up on a champagne cooler that was filled with ice. The cooler tipped, ice poured out on to a couple at a two-seater table, while the bottle spun around on the floor like a spinning top, spraying rounds of champagne over the other guests. The guests jumped up hectically, throwing their red wine and gin and tonics everywhere. Attempting to stand up, Balthasar slipped on an ice cube and tried to steady himself on a cutlery tray. Cutlery cascaded on to the floor deafeningly.

Nik had to grit his teeth to stop himself from laughing. With a concerted effort, he managed to maintain his serious expression and took a large step over the ice cubes. He walked over to the owner, who was standing paralysed and staring in disbelief at the commotion.

'Munich City Council, sir. Food inspection.' Nik showed him the fake ID. 'Do you have some time for us?'

'An inspection?' asked the man. 'What, now?'

'Yes, I'm sorry. Our last inspection at a bistro took longer than expected,' said Nik apologetically. 'But I can assure you we won't take up much of your time.'

'Is that your colleague?' asked the man, horrified.

'Gosh, I know. Please don't pay much attention to him,' said Nik with a quick glance at Balthasar, who was still lying on the floor. 'He's in training.'

◆ ◆ ◆

Olaf van Berk was sitting behind a large oak desk with his arms crossed. He wore a white shirt underneath a dark jacket and was sucking on a cough sweet. He was watching a large television screen on the opposite side of the office. It was showing CCTV footage of the restaurant. In the background, a fat, blonde man was lying on the floor, surrounded by exceedingly upset customers. Another man was walking over to the owner, ignoring the chaos. He showed the owner his ID. The footage was paused, and the picture zoomed in on the man's face.

'That's Nik Pohl,' said a tall man with a crew cut. Van Berk found the man's fat lips and crooked teeth repulsive but Hans Groppe had been Masannek's right-hand man and after his death, he'd been promoted to security manager. He might not be as clever or shrewd as his predecessor but until he found a new man for the position, van Berk would have to make do with Groppe.

'Pohl was at the CID for a number of years and left in early 2017,' Groppe continued. 'Rumour has it he's now a private investigator but he's never registered any company or got any kind of licence. We went to his house but he wasn't there. His neighbours haven't seen him in weeks so he must be hiding out somewhere else.'

'And who's the other man?'

'We weren't able to identify him.'

Van Berk tapped his index finger on the table. 'What's Pohl trying to achieve here?' he asked, looking at the monitor.

Groppe fiddled with the remote control in his hand. 'We . . . don't know,' he replied hesitantly.

'You don't know?' repeated van Berk. 'This Pohl character comes into my restaurant with a blatantly fake ID, scares my customers, gets the place closed, and you don't know why!' He slammed his fist down on the table. 'And then there's this . . .' He held up a printout of an email and showed it to Groppe. 'Two hours after his performance, he sends me an email, overtly threatening to ruin me, telling me about how he managed to get my buyer thrown in jail.' Van Berk ripped up the piece of paper and threw it on the floor. 'I've lost more money in the last few days than I have in the last ten years!' he continued. 'I've been able to keep that from my business partners so far, but they're going to start asking questions very soon. So I want to know where the hell Pohl got the information. And I want to know immediately!'

'We do have one idea,' said Groppe.

'Oh, an idea?' Van Berk mimicked the words. 'So, what's your *idea* then?'

'We were able to narrow down the possible informants,' said the man. 'We're convinced one of them is working with Nik Pohl. My men are currently interrogating the man in question.'

'Then you'll need to hurry up because I intend on taking Pohl up on his invitation –tomorrow evening!'

'For security reasons, sir, I would advise you to turn down the invitation. Only when—'

'No!' interrupted van Berk. 'Always know your enemy! A meeting's exactly what I need.'

'But while we still don't know whether Pohl has accomplices it would be very risky—'

'It's non-negotiable,' said van Berk, holding his index finger near the man's face. 'Find that source and bring him to me. Then we'll deal with Pohl.'

◆ ◆ ◆

Nik parked his car two streets away from the arranged meeting place, got out and started meandering along the pavement. Jon had carried out a check on the cafe and no links to van Berk had turned up. He'd also given Nik a building plan that clearly indicated three different emergency exits. Jon had been far more tense than normal and had repeatedly voiced his concern about the meeting, but in the end, he had realised there was no other option.

As a precaution, he'd hired the best bodyguard money could buy. A six-foot-six giant with wide shoulders and muscles that made even Nik nervous. Despite the brutish exterior, the man seemed focused and appeared to know exactly what he was doing – he didn't seem to be some dumb thug who would draw his weapon at the first sign of difficulty. Jon had clearly briefed him well, as he wasn't asking any questions and knew the way to the meeting point.

'Is van Berk already there?' asked Nik into the microphone under his lapel.

'Been there for ten minutes,' answered Jon. Nik had a small receiver in his ear.

'Any uninvited guests nearby?'

'Nobody's turned up on the camera footage. But that doesn't mean there isn't a raiding party sitting somewhere waiting to pounce.'

'You should have more faith,' said Nik. 'Everything's going according to plan.'

'It's too smooth for my liking,' said Jon. 'We write van Berk an email telling him you're responsible for the whole mess and force him to talk to you. A couple of hours later, we get an answer with a meeting location and time . . . for the following evening! No threats, no warnings. It was like organising a game of cards at a friend's house. He didn't even ask *why* you wanted to meet him.'

'You're underestimating the predicament he's in,' Nik responded. 'I got one of his money launderers locked up on suspicion of terrorism and robbed him of a second source of income by getting his restaurant closed down – he won't be too happy when he sees this morning's newspaper article about the dead cockroaches. And in the end, it's not just the restaurant clientele he's going to lose, he'll also lose all his catering jobs. And by now all his business partners will have noticed the chaos, so he *has* to meet with me to try to avoid any further losses.'

'And what if he shoots you in the head?'

'He won't. That's not van Berk's style. He's not some ghetto gangster with too much adrenaline,' said Nik. 'He has no idea if I'm just a lackey or the guy behind everything. And as long as he doesn't know why I'm doing all this or what I want from him, he'll be the perfect host. And anyway' – Nik looked at his bodyguard – 'you organised someone to look out for my safety.'

'Stéphane's the best man I could get at such short notice,' explained Jon. 'He worked in the French Foreign Legion for ten years and collected an impressive number of medals. He practises more forms of martial arts than I even knew existed.'

'Well, thank you for your efforts, Jon. It's touching,' said Nik. 'Anyway, what's our bug up to?'

'I've got it here,' said Balthasar, wheezing. 'I'm lying underneath van Berk's car trying not to burn myself on the exhaust. I sincerely hope my efforts will be worth it. I look like a street sweeper who's been dancing in warm tar.'

'Time to turn the radios off,' said Nik. 'I'm going into the cafe.' Stéphane went one step ahead of Nik and opened the door. He went inside first, looked around in all directions and gave a nod.

The cafe was painted light grey, with white tables and Caspar David Friedrich paintings hanging on the walls. The display fridge near the cash register was stacked full of various cakes and tarts and the air smelled of freshly ground coffee. An old man with well-groomed grey hair and lightly tanned skin sat at one of the tables, his hands clasped in front of him. He had a flat and exceptionally large nose, which, thanks to his long face, wasn't too distracting. He was wearing a black tailored suit with fine grey pinstripes, a white shirt and a tie the colour of red wine. Behind him stood a tall man with dark brown hair and a figure which was almost the double of Stéphane's. He was wearing a dark grey suit.

Taking his time, Nik made his way over to the table. As he got nearer, he realised the older man's slightly brown skin tone was the result of a thin layer of make-up. Van Berk watched Nik's every step until he had sat down in front of him. He then pushed his small espresso cup to the side and began to talk. 'So, you're the one who's been causing me so much hassle,' he said in a self-assured voice. His tone was calm, free of anger.

'My name's Nik.'

'I know who you are, Herr Pohl,' replied van Berk. 'Hopefully you're well aware that you've made some powerful enemies with your latest moves . . . because it wasn't *my* money you gave up to the police.'

'I'm aware of that,' answered Nik. 'But I doubt the real owners have found out about what happened. That would make you look pretty stupid. Not only would you have to admit to losing their illegally acquired money, you'd also be obliged to explain that your top launderer is being held on suspicion of terrorism. It's a stroke of bad luck for you that investigations into terrorism are much more intense than those into money laundering.'

Van Berk smiled.

'I don't want to waste our time,' Nik continued. 'I realise you were abroad recently but I'm sure you heard about the kidnappings of Greta Grohnert and Hannes Lepper?'

'It's possible to read the newspapers abroad, Herr Pohl.'

'So, what do you have to do with the abductions?'

'You know my field of activity,' replied van Berk. 'Abduction isn't my thing.'

'Tell me what Ismail Buchwald and Vincent Masannek have to do with the case?'

'And how am I supposed to know that? Shortly after I returned home, Buchwald tried to kill me. And Masannek was murdered while I was out of the country.'

'Why did Buchwald try to kill you?'

'Enemies are easily acquired in my line of work and every one of mine has enough money to set a henchman on my back.'

'But this particular henchman used to work for you.'

'Which makes for a very clever strategy, doesn't it?' said van Berk. 'The more a hitman knows about his target, the higher their chances of being successful.'

'Why did you employ Buchwald?'

'He was a competent man.'

'And why did you fire him?'

'Because he was no longer of any use to me.'

'Could you maybe be a bit more detailed?'

'At the start of last year, I only just managed to evade an attack,' explained van Berk. 'There was a shooting and Buchwald was severely injured. So while he was in hospital, I had to employ other people.'

'And why didn't you hire him again after he'd recovered?'

'Because he blamed Masannek and myself for his injuries and the subsequent deformities.'

'Which is true to some extent, isn't it?' remarked Nik.

'Buchwald was my *bodyguard*. It was his *job* to protect me. And he knew the risks.' Van Berk's anger was rising. He clenched his fist in the air and was about to pound it against the table when he was consumed by a coughing fit. It was a dry, wheezing cough. Van Berk took a sip of coffee and exhaled loudly, bringing himself under control again. 'In my position, I need to be able to rely on my security guards.' He picked out a cough sweet from the bag and put it in his mouth. 'Trust is of the utmost importance.'

'And that's why he wanted to shoot you?'

'That's what it looks like.'

'You can't think of any other possible reason?'

'For example?'

'Like the kidnapping of children?'

'If I understand the papers correctly, it's Ismail Buchwald who's the main suspect.'

'Which just leaves the question of who he was working for.'

Van Berk sighed. 'Why would I incite Buchwald into abducting children? My other business ventures are significantly more lucrative.'

'Look, I'm here because of the kidnappings.'

'In which case this meeting is a waste of time, isn't it? I was abroad at the time of the kidnappings. And . . . if I wanted to abduct someone, I would have found someone far more capable than Buchwald.'

'Like Vincent Masannek?'

'Perhaps. Until not that long ago, I would have considered him the best in the business. But . . . looking at the way he died, there was apparently someone even better.'

'We're going in circles,' said Nik. 'If I don't get the information I'm looking for, I'll keep going with our little game. Your money laundering won't be the last thing I put out of business.'

'Oh, yes it will,' said van Berk. 'Do you honestly think I wouldn't find out who gave you the information?' He reached for his espresso cup and drained the contents, eyes fixed on Nik's. 'There are very few people in Munich who know about my business. It took a lot of effort to put all the pieces together, but in the end, only one person was left.' Van Berk smiled – a chilling, satisfied smile. 'The only thing The Collector will be collecting from now on are the maggots crawling through his head.' He spoke quietly. 'And . . . all the people he had any knowledge of have now been replaced. Which means you have nothing you can use against me.' Van Berk picked up a leather glove from the chair and put it on. 'I kept you a little souvenir from The Collector. I'm sure if you ask your hacker friend nicely, he'll be able to get into the federal police fingerprint database and prove I'm telling the truth.' He pulled a small wooden box out of his jacket pocket and placed it on the table in front of Nik. 'And if you stick your nose in my business one more time, there will be even less left over of the hacker or your pal, Balthasar.'

◆　◆　◆

'Well, that didn't exactly go as planned,' said Jon over the phone's loudspeaker. He was still as nervous as he had been before the meeting. 'It normally takes a lot to faze me, but that number he pulled with the finger and the threat against Balthasar really got to me.'

'At least he didn't shoot me.' Nik took a sip of beer.

'Yeah, and that's where the good news ends,' said Jon. 'Now we've got The Collector on our conscience.'

'Luca,' said Nik quietly. 'His name was Luca Marino.' He sunk his head in regret. 'I never intended any harm to come to Luca. But he paid us a last service and now we know for sure van Berk's involved.'

'And how can you be so sure?' called Balthasar from the kitchen doorway.

'*Nobody* knows I work with Jon,' explained Nik. 'When I met with Luca, I told him I wouldn't leave him alone and that a hacker would help me make his life hell.'

'OK. The only thing that proves is that van Berk interrogated The Collector before cutting him up into tiny pieces,' said Jon.

'But van Berk only said "a hacker". He didn't say Jon or Jonathan Kirchhof. So, he knows I work with a hacker but he doesn't know who you are or where you live,' said Nik.

'OK,' Jon replied, 'but if you consider how quickly he managed to get *your* name, I'm not so convinced my cover's bulletproof anymore.'

'I still don't understand why you're convinced of van Berk's involvement in the case,' said Balthasar.

'Because he knew about *you*.' Nik turned to Balthasar. 'And I never mentioned you to The Collector. There's only one other way he could have known we're working together.'

'From Masannek. When he and his men caught me on my way to the Grohnerts',' said Balthasar.

'Exactly,' said Nik. 'Van Berk must have hired them. Or in other words, Masannek was working on his behalf.'

The pathologist nodded. 'A logical conclusion.'

'Then let's start monitoring van Berk thoroughly,' suggested Jon.

'That would be useless,' Nik responded. 'Van Berk was out of the country during the kidnappings. If Masannek hadn't been shot, he wouldn't have come back.'

'He's looking for a new henchman,' Balthasar realised.

'There's enough of them around if you've got the money,' remarked Jon. 'And someone like van Berk won't even have to leave the house to find one.'

'Can't we use the finger to pin something on him?' asked Balthasar.

'I did a check on the box,' said Jon. 'No prints, and traces of bleach, which means they won't find any of van Berk's DNA on it.'

'And the finger?'

'Luca Marino's,' confirmed Jon. 'The print was identified in the system. I sent it anonymously to the CID, so who knows . . . maybe they'll find something I couldn't.'

'Another dead end then,' said Balthasar. 'What the hell should we do now?'

'We need to understand what van Berk wants with these kids,' said Nik. 'The fact they were born on the same night, in the same hospital, and that one of their mothers disappeared is strange enough as it is.'

'We've been looking for the connection for weeks and haven't got a single step closer to finding one,' said Jon.

'I need to speak to the parents again,' said Nik. 'Maybe the incidents over the last couple of days will help them remember something. Or one of the teenagers might have seen something.'

'All the commotion has calmed down,' said Jon. 'Police aren't monitoring the premises as thoroughly anymore and the press have got new stories. Plus, the suspected kidnapper is dead.'

Nik looked at his watch. '12.30. It's too late to pay the Grohnerts a visit right now, but I'll head over there early in the morning.' He leaned back on the couch. 'Unless we get another lead, we'll never solve this case.'

◆ ◆ ◆

The police cordon began thirty metres away from the front of the Grohnerts' house. Two police cars with blinking blue lights were blocking the street, and the entrance to the driveway had been covered with fencing. The pavement was sealed off with a long stretch of tape and four police officers were guarding the area, despite the fact the streets were always dead at that time in the morning. There were no photographers, and no broadcast vans or camera crews, so whatever it was that had happened had yet to be reported.

Casting his eye over the sealed-off area, Nik spotted his former boss walking along the length of the barrier. He was wearing dark trousers and a creased blazer. His black hair hadn't been combed and he looked as if he'd jumped straight out of bed.

'Naumann!' called Nik. Naumann turned to Nik and rolled his eyes.

'I really don't have time for any hassle right now, Pohl,' he said, walking over to Nik.

'I come in peace.' Nik raised his hands facetiously. 'What happened?'

'You know I'm not allowed to talk to civilians.'

'Oh, come on, Naumann. It's not like you don't have me to thank for the last breakthrough.'

'What the hell are you talking about?'

'That lead on Buchwald's hideout . . . that came from me.'

'That was *you*?'

'If you don't believe me, I'll happily tell you the details.'

'Why are you getting mixed up in this case, Pohl?' asked Naumann. 'You don't work for the CID anymore.'

'Oh, please. Enough of the authority bullshit,' replied Nik. 'The lives of three children are at stake here. If it hadn't been for me, they'd all still be camping out with Buchwald in the warehouse.'

Naumann clenched his fist, close to losing it. But then he sighed loudly and his tension dissolved. He took a step closer to Nik and spoke quietly. 'Greta Grohnert's gone missing again.'

'Shit.'

'So that's why this lot are here.' Naumann tipped his head towards the police officers.

'I heard she tried to defend herself when she was being rescued from Buchwald's hideout,' said Nik. 'Maybe she just ran away.'

'The security guard was shot,' said Naumann, shaking his head. 'Greta was definitely kidnapped again.'

'How could that happen?'

'I don't know,' replied Naumann. 'All the windows and doors were secured. We'd replaced all the locks and installed new movement sensors. Then there was the security team hired by Grohnert and the police officers in front of the house.' He shook his head. 'Forensics are inspecting the crime scene right now, but if you ask me, it's completely incomprehensible how the kidnapper managed to get inside the house without being seen. Her parents only noticed Greta was missing an hour ago; they wanted to let her sleep in.'

'So it's possible she was kidnapped yesterday?'

'If we use rigor mortis on the security guard as a point of reference, then it must have been around midnight,' said Naumann. 'When the press get wind of this, the phones at police headquarters are going to explode. We're getting every uniformed officer in Munich out of bed so we can put everyone on the search. Problem is, the kidnapper's got a massive head start and—' Naumann lifted his hand to the bud in his ear and turned away from Nik. He listened carefully to someone speaking. 'Jesus Christ,' he said, his voice shaking, as he lifted his hand across his mouth.

A woman's scream came from somewhere behind the wall surrounding the Grohnerts' villa. The scream – loud and long – pierced the air with despair.

Chapter 14

Greta had been beautiful. Alert eyes and a magical smile. But the dead body lying on the bank didn't resemble that girl in any way. Her dark, wet hair clung to her forehead, her skin was bereft of colour and her eyes stared lifelessly up at the sky. Her beige pyjama bottoms were ripped and her white T-shirt was covered in encrusted blood. There was a gaping wound in the middle of her chest, the edges of which were ragged, indicating the shot had been fired at close range.

Naumann sat on a rock near to where her body had been found and closed his eyes. In what kind of world does someone kidnap a young girl, shoot her and throw her dead body into a lake like a bag of rubbish? He thought about his own daughter. She was only two years older than Greta. Naumann didn't even want to consider what it would be like if something like this happened to her; how meaningless his life would become without her – how hollow the days and how quiet his flat.

He heard steps approaching. A CID officer was walking towards him. 'We've searched the area but haven't yet found a weapon or any evidence that could point to a possible offender,' he began.

'Were there any witnesses?'

'A walker found the body at 8.24 a.m. and called the police immediately. According to his statement, he didn't see another person or any vehicles. It was, however, misty at the time so visibility would have been limited.'

'Do we know anything about the man?'

'Going by initial information, he's a sixty-seven-year-old pensioner who is neither linked to the case nor to the people involved in any way. He's got a clean record and walks his dog along the bank three times a week.'

Two men lifted Greta into a black body bag and zipped it up. Naumann looked away.

'I'll drive back to the station and inform the chief of police.' He stood up. There was nothing else he could do there. 'Keep me up to date.'

On his way back to his car, he took out his phone. 'Hi, honey, it's Dad,' he said when his daughter picked up the phone. 'Yes, everything's fine, darling. I just wanted to see how you were doing . . .'

Naumann listened as his daughter talked. 'Hey, that's great.' He smiled. 'Listen, I'm afraid I'm going to have to work late again today, OK? But I'll take some time off at the weekend and we can head over to the stables so you can finally show me your new horse. How's that?' He opened his car door. 'No, really. Everything's fine,' he repeated, wiping his eyes.

Nik balanced himself on the edge of the roof with a cigarette in one hand and a bottle of vodka in the other. He was wearing an old pair of jeans and a dirty T-shirt, and his feet were bare. It was a cloudy, drizzly night and the city was quiet. Only a couple of cars were to be seen on the streets.

He stood still and looked down; the brightly lit street was only six floors away.

'So, you want to kill yourself?' he heard Mira ask.

'Still not sure,' he answered without turning around. He swayed slightly and his left foot slipped a little over the edge. He waved his arms and almost lost his balance but finally managed to throw himself backwards. He giggled and took a swig from the bottle, as if it was all just a silly game.

'It wasn't your fault, Nik,' said Mira.

'Do you know how many times I've heard that in the last couple of hours?'

'Words can't describe such a tragedy, but . . .'

'Stop!' Nik screamed. 'Stop being so compassionate, and understanding, and fucking thoughtful!' He smashed the bottle on the ground. 'Greta is *dead*! Luca is *dead*! And no amount of consolation can change that.'

'And neither would your suicide.'

'Yeah, but nothing changes if I live either.' He turned to look at Mira. She was wearing a pair of lightweight trousers, a white blouse with a frilled collar and a thick jumper, as if she was preparing for the winter to arrive. 'I've been on this case for weeks now and I haven't understood a single thing. I still don't even know *why* Greta was murdered.'

'Then come down and find out who killed her. Van Berk is a suspect. You understand that, don't you?'

'I don't want to get van Berk convicted,' said Nik. 'I want to go to his house with a baseball bat and break every bone in his body. I want to hear him screaming . . . feel his desperation and watch him die! I want to see blood!' Nik yelled over the city.

'I'm surprised you've not done any of that already.'

'Only because I still don't have a solid way of getting to him, but as soon as I do, you'll know where to find me.'

'And what if you don't find a way?'

Nik stretched his arms out in front of him like a cliff diver. 'Then I'll dive on to the yellow Mustang that's parked down there – you know, the one that wakes us all up every morning with its thundering engine? Consider it a last good deed for my neighbours.'

'So that's it? You're just giving up all hope?'

'Hope, in reality, is the worst of all evils because it prolongs the torments of man.'

'Nietzsche doesn't suit you, Nik.'

'Today it does.'

'And what about the two other kids?'

'They'll be better off without me.'

'Don't forget you still managed to get Hannes and Greta rescued from the warehouse.'

'If I'm honest, I'm not sure whether I got them rescued or just signed their death warrants,' said Nik. He was walking along the building's edge with his arms stretched out to the sides. 'If they were in Buchwald's hideout, Greta would still be alive.'

'And what if Greta's death wasn't the end of all this?' asked Mira. 'What if Hannes and Simon are still in danger?'

'I just don't fucking get it!' Nik's thoughts were going in circles. 'I've got no idea what makes these three teenagers so special or why someone wants them dead. I could go through my files a hundred times and I *still* wouldn't get any further. The investigations into Greta's case haven't thrown even a glint of light on to the case.' He turned to Mira. 'I'm just not good enough. Maybe there's a better investigator at the CID, because this case is beyond me.' Nik turned back to look at the drop in front of him. He closed his eyes and breathed in deeply, trying to absorb the moment.

'Then don't help the two of them as an investigator. Help them as a bodyguard,' said Mira.

Nik opened his eyes and blinked.

'You might have no idea who's behind all this or why they want the kids, but you do know they might be in a position to get hold of Hannes and Simon.'

'Nobody has a clue where Simon is.'

'No. But Hannes is with his parents at their house.'

'I know . . . It's unbelievable,' said Nik. 'They should be leaving the city as quickly as possible and going underground.'

'Not with an autistic kid, they shouldn't,' said Mira. 'I can't begin to imagine how Hannes must have suffered during the kidnapping. He needs to be in a familiar environment now. Somewhere he feels safe.'

'Well, Greta showed us just how safe home is right now.'

'Then get your gun and stand at his front door.'

'The flat will be under police surveillance. They won't let me anywhere near the place.'

'That's a terrible excuse,' remarked Mira. 'You'll find a way to protect Hannes and hide from the police.'

'I don't even know if he's in danger.'

'Have you got anything better to do, Nik?' She signalled with her head and eyes towards the broken glass bottle.

Nik bent forward until he could see the yellow Mustang, then squatted down and screamed as loudly as he could. It would have been so easy to jump. He closed his eyes and waited as his racing heart slowed down.

◆　◆　◆

Nik had parked the hire car across the street from the Leppers' home. The car had tinted rear and side windows and he had mounted a barely visible camera lens on to the bonnet. He now sat on the back seat watching the Lepper household on a small screen that was attached to his rear-view mirror. The lens was light-sensitive and he was able to zoom in on the target if he needed. The terraced house looked exactly like all the others on the street: narrowly built, with stone steps leading up to the entrance and a bin shelter to the side. There was one large and one small window on either side of the front door, two windows on the first floor and a sloping skylight at attic level. The family kept the light at the front door on all night, while a police car with two patrolling officers was constantly parked on the other side of the street across from the house.

By using an aerial photo of the house and surrounding properties, Nik had managed to think up possible attack situations that a kidnapper might use. In addition to that, the CID had surveyed the building and Jon had downloaded all the information for him.

'Why don't they realise how stupid it is to stay in the house?' Nik asked Jon over the phone. He was looking at a photo of the rear of the house with a small torch. 'Both sides of the garden connect to properties that are easy to enter. The windows are made of standard glass and the doors aren't properly secured.'

'Right, but that's why the blinds are down. And the patio door and basement windows have all been bolted shut,' said Jon. 'You'd need brute force to get into that house and the police across the street would hear that.'

'One police car isn't enough.'

'A second car is patrolling the estate, keeping an eye on cars and people out walking. They'd be there in a minute.'

'The Leppers should be sent to a safe house until Greta's murderer has been found.'

'And the police suggested that, but the parents said no.'

'Idiots,' mumbled Nik.

Jon decided to change the subject. 'Did you notice anything new when you went through the files?'

'Nope. Not drunk or sober.' Nik took sip of coffee. 'Did Balthasar get the autopsy report back?'

'I did,' said the pathologist over the phone. 'And I came across a couple of interesting things.'

'OK, well, let's go through it all from the start and you can add what you found.' Nik placed his cup back in the holder and reached for the printouts from his bag. 'Maybe you two will think of something.'

'Greta's disappearance was reported to the police at 7.46 a.m.,' Jon began. 'When exactly she was kidnapped cannot be determined because there were no witnesses. Even the parents didn't notice anything.'

'Rigor mortis on the security guard was fully developed when the police arrived,' said Balthasar. 'That means he'd been killed between midnight and two o'clock in the morning.'

'His body was lying in the back garden,' said Jon. 'He'd received a shot to the front of the forehead. No gunshots were heard, so it is assumed that the perpetrator used a silencer on the gun.'

'And that's how he managed to get in,' added Nik. 'Splashes of blood were found on the door and small amounts were also found on the carpet in the house.'

'The intruder shot the security guard the minute he came out the door.'

'How did he get on to the property?' asked Balthasar.

'Across the back garden.'

'But that area was covered by CCTV.'

'The camera was intact when the police inspected it,' said Jon. 'It's possible someone had programmed it to play an endless footage loop, but the investigators are still racking their brains about that one.'

'So, who was this person who broke in?' asked Balthasar. 'Batman?'

'You'd think,' said Nik. 'But it was definitely two people because two sets of footprints were found in the garden.'

'And the ones that led away from the house were deeper than the ones that led to the house because they were carrying Greta,' added Jon.

'This is unbelievable,' said Balthasar, perplexed. 'Somebody takes the Grohnerts' daughter from her bed, throws her over their shoulder, marches out of the house with her, carries her through the garden with an accomplice and then climbs over a wall with her. And the parents don't notice a thing!'

'No footprints or mud were found inside the house so the kidnappers must have taken their shoes off,' said Nik. 'The house has no laminate or floorboards so there won't have been any creaking and the carpet would have cushioned their footsteps. The doors are too new to squeak and the parents' room is separated from Greta's by a large bathroom and walk-in closet.'

'Greta was drugged and carried out of the house,' Jon continued. 'Getting her over that wall would have been a struggle but she was a slim girl so it's definitely possible.'

'There must have been someone else monitoring the property who told the two kidnappers the whereabouts of nearby patrol officers,' said Nik. 'They would've got Greta on to the other side of the wall and put her straight into a car.'

'And then, at 8.24 a.m. a man out walking his dog found her body at the edge of Lake Feringa, not far from the A99.'

The photo of the dead Greta was burned into Nik's memory. The colourless face, framed with wet, straw-like hair, and her staring eyes, lifeless and glassy. The large hole in her T-shirt and the dry blood enveloping her chest. A young girl who had been so beautiful, left floating on the bank of the lake like an old piece of driftwood. Disposed of like worthless rubbish.

'I think it's best I spare you both the autopsy details,' said Balthasar. 'But we know, at least, she was neither tortured nor raped. All investigators agree that the lake wasn't the murder location: she had lost a lot of blood from the gunshot wound to the chest and there wasn't much blood found at the scene. She was just thrown into the water there. Estimated time of death is 7 a.m.'

'So where was she in the hours between the time she was kidnapped and when she was murdered?' asked Jon.

'There's no evidence to suggest where she was,' said Nik. 'The bank is still being searched. And considering the size of Lake Feringa, that will take a good while.'

'Throwing a body into the water to destroy evidence is nothing new, but why were the wounds washed out with bleach?' asked Jon.

'Because they took the bullet out of her chest,' explained the pathologist. 'Her murderers wanted to be sure they left no clues behind.'

'And what kind of gun was it?' asked Nik.

'Hard to tell under the circumstances,' answered Balthasar. 'But investigators believe it was a nine mil.'

'I understand the bit about removing traces from the gunshot wound,' said Jon. 'But why had her hands also been washed with bleach?'

'Because Greta had defended herself,' said Nik. 'So it would have been possible to find DNA from the murderer under her nails.'

'And why didn't they just shoot her in the house?'

'I've asked myself that question a hundred times,' said Nik. 'And the only plausible explanation is that the murderer wanted information from Greta.'

'Information from a fourteen-year-old?' asked Jon. 'What kind of secret could a young girl be keeping that would justify so much violence?'

'No idea,' said Nik.

'And if we take information as a motive for the kidnappings, the whole thing gets even more absurd if we consider Hannes a victim,' said Balthasar. 'He won't be able to say a thing! And even the most brutal of methods wouldn't change that!'

Jon sighed. 'So, all of that, and we still have nothing new. We still have no idea what's going on.'

'What was van Berk doing last night?' asked Nik.

'According to his tracking device, he was in his villa. His car was there all night until nine o'clock this morning. Greta had been dead for at least a couple of hours by then.'

'It's possible he took another car,' suggested Balthasar.

'Van Berk definitely wasn't actively involved in Greta's kidnapping or murder,' said Nik. 'He's not that stupid.'

'So the only thing left to do is wait,' concluded Jon.

'Wait and hope that Greta's murder will be the end of all this insanity,' added Balthasar.

'I'll keep an eye on the CID server,' said Jon. 'I'll be in touch as soon there's anything new with the investigations.'

'I'll stay here and keep an eye on Hannes,' said Nik, putting the files back into his bag. 'I won't let them get their hands on him.'

At precisely 7.55 a.m., Hannes and his mother left the house and got into their car. Nik let out a sigh of relief, the tension in his body easing instantly. He put his gun in the glove compartment, turned off the camera and waited until the car had driven away with the police escort. He started his engine and set off home. Not long after, he got a call from Jon.

'Everything's fine,' said Nik, rubbing his eyes from exhaustion.

'Glad to hear it but I'm calling for another reason. Olaf van Berk was taken into hospital last night.'

'OK. What happened?'

'I can't see,' said Jon. 'I carried out the routine checks on the bugs that Balthasar had attached to his car and saw that he drove to Harlaching hospital at around two o'clock in the morning and stayed there for a long time. When I hacked the hospital server, I managed to find his name on the patient admissions list but his medical complaint was described merely as "some vague discomfort".'

'Does he have a record there?'

'I searched everything but couldn't find any entries. He normally goes to a private hospital.'

'Is he still there?'

'I don't know. The car drove back to van Berk's forty minutes ago. Either with or without him.'

Nik scratched at his unshaven chin. 'So what does this mean?' he mumbled.

'Not sure. I'll keep an eye on the hospital database.'

'OK. I'm going home to get some sleep so I'm well rested for the next watch duty,' said Nik.

Nik wished it had been a sunny day for Greta's funeral but instead, there was a solid barrier of grey clouds in the sky, waiting for an opportune moment to release their rain on to the crowd of mourners. There were a lot of people at the cemetery: friends and family, but mostly lots of teenagers who had come with their parents. Most of them had tears in their eyes, while others looked apathetically at the floor, as if realising for the first time what had happened to their friend.

Nik stood at the edge of the large crowd that had gathered around the grave. He couldn't hear the minister's committal, but he didn't care. He didn't want to hear it. And neither did he want to read any of the messages on the countless wreaths. He was so engrossed in his own thoughts, he didn't even notice Naumann was there.

Nik should have been feeling sad, or angry. Angry with himself, and the CID's failures, or with the whole world, which was still consumed by things it deemed more important than the death of a young girl. But instead, he felt nothing: as if he were an uninvolved bystander. Now was the time when he should have gone over to Greta's parents to offer them his condolences. But that too seemed pointless. The young, pretty, lively girl was dead and he hadn't been able to save her. Nothing was going to bring her back. He couldn't even say *who* had murdered her or *why* she'd had to die. Had God made him the offer, he would have taken her place in that coffin. But instead, fate had decided he would carry on living, constantly aware of his failings. For the rest of his life.

The minister came to the end of his speech and shook hands with the Grohnerts. Party by party, the mourners started to move away from the grave.

Nik made the sign of the cross. He hadn't done that for many years but today it somehow felt right. As he started to leave the cemetery, it began to rain so he lifted his jacket collar. Arriving at his car, he turned around to look at Greta's grave one more time. Then he stepped into his car and made his way to Hannes' house.

By the fourth night of his self-imposed surveillance duty outside the Leppers' house, Nik had developed a routine. He would park in front of the entrance to a paint shop that was closed at night. To the side of the shop was a large bush which he could conveniently use in case of any toilet emergencies. Every night, Balthasar supplied him with a flask of coffee and a home-made panini, which – thanks to the lashings of garlic Balthasar would plough on to the bread – made Nik's eyes stream. Nevertheless, the sandwiches tasted so good they were always gone by midnight. Thanks to a digital radio, he was able to listen to his favourite rock station – albeit turned down very low. He'd had much worse surveillance jobs.

Each night, he had pointed his camera towards the house and watched intently. Over the last few nights, however, the most interesting thing he had seen had been a pine marten. No roaming figures, no large cars with tinted windows – in fact, not a single person who seemed interested in the house or the people living there.

Nik flipped unenthusiastically through the most recent police files on Greta's death but there was still no trace of her murderer. It would have been unfair to say the special commission weren't doing everything in their power, but despite all their efforts, neither the investigation of the crime scene nor the questioning of possible witnesses had provided any useful evidence. There had been no DNA on the dead body, no fingerprints, and not a single clue as to how the body could have got to Lake Feringa.

A blue light snatched Nik from his thoughts. A police car was driving at high speed out of the residential area along the road parallel to the one he was parked on. Not long after, he heard sirens coming from another direction. The sounds wailed distressingly through the silent night.

Nik looked at the time. It was just before four. He turned off the radio and called Jon, who picked up after the first ring. 'Apparently I didn't wake you?' said Nik.

'Unfortunately not. Someone's being held hostage in Sendling,' said Jon. 'Somewhere in the wholesale market.'

'The market's massive and there'll be loads going on this close to opening time. A hostage situation there could escalate really quickly.'

'That's why the police have called out all available units. To block off all the roads.'

'Why would anyone hold someone hostage there?' asked Nik. 'I'm assuming it's not because they're pissed off after being sold rotten fruit.'

'The situation's unclear and police are getting contradictory information. Some people are reporting a robbery, while others are saying someone's being held hostage. One caller was rambling on about some Islamic fanatic, but the market hall manager can't confirm anything of the sort.'

Nik was taking a sip of coffee when he got cut off. 'What the hell?' He put his cup back in the holder and looked at his phone. No service. 'Piece of shit!' He went to call Jon again, but just before he could, someone started shouting loudly, startling him.

'Stay where you are!' cried one of the police officers. The young man had stepped out of his car but Nik couldn't see who he was shouting at from where he was sitting. Just as Nik laid his hand on his gun, there was a tremendous bang followed by a glaring explosion.

Nik covered his head. He knew that noise. Stun grenades. An efficient weapon and nobody stood a chance against them, not even if they squeezed their eyes closed and pressed their hands up to their ears. The noise reaches 170 dB and is louder than a lightning strike. The strain on the inner ear is immense and the flash caused by the magnesium causes temporary disorientation. The police officers would be of no use to Hannes anymore but Nik had thankfully been far enough away. He grabbed his gun and jumped out of the car. Crouched down with his gun stretched out in front of him, he ran down the street towards the house. A hefty man in dark clothes and a ski mask was running towards the Leppers' front door. The man had a sledgehammer in his hand. When he arrived at the front door, he started slamming down the tool on to the door lock. Nik stopped running, aimed and fired. The bullet hit the man in his right thigh. He cried out, dropping the sledgehammer and falling to his knees on to the stone steps.

Nik started running again. When he got to the man on the steps, he kicked him as hard as he could in the face. His head was thrown back, and he rolled down the stairs unconscious. Nik immediately rammed his shoulder into the door and ran into the house. He came across Hannes' parents in the hallway. They were wearing their pyjamas and looked deeply confused, staring around nervously with no clue as to what was happening. Nik pushed the father to the side and ran up the stairs to Hannes' room. The teen-ager was sitting on the floor in front of his bed, pressing his hands against his ears and crying out. His whole body was shaking and his pyjamas were wet with urine.

'I'm sorry, buddy.' Nik tucked his gun into his waistband and heaved Hannes over his right shoulder. The boy screamed even louder and drummed his fists on Nik's back. But Nik ignored him and hurried down the stairs. 'We need to get out of here!' shouted Nik to his parents but the parents just stared at him, frozen with terror.

There was no chance the man with the sledgehammer would have come alone, thought Nik. With a bit of luck, his accomplices would try to come in the front door. The unconscious, bleeding man at the front door would make them nervous and hopefully stall them. They had, after all, only expected the two police officers and not a third man. Nik had to make use of the time to get away. The attackers would have studied the house plans meticulously and would know who slept where, how many rooms were in the house and where each piece of furniture was. If the accomplices con-fronted him and the Leppers inside the house, they'd be trapped. He had to move things to another location; a location where the terrain would be unknown. Hannes' mother tried to hold Nik still

239

and grab on to her son, but he hit her hands away, ran through the house, slid open the left patio door and went outside.

The surrounding gardens were separated from one another by low fences. They wouldn't present a challenge to Nik, even with someone on his shoulder. If the two of them managed to get a head start, they would be able to hide in a nearby garage or summerhouse until the police arrived. Hannes' constant screaming, however, was going to make escaping difficult.

Nik had only moved two steps forward when he heard a bang and felt a piercing pain in his left calf. His leg collapsed and he couldn't keep his balance. He used all his strength to reduce the fall and prevent Hannes from hitting the ground. He pushed him into a corner of the patio, crawled behind a large terracotta pot that had been planted with a palm and took out his gun. Nik hadn't seen exactly where the attacker was, but the muzzle flash had briefly illuminated a silhouette. Whatever the case, the shooter was far too close. Not even enough time had passed for the accomplices to have checked the entire house. This suggested they must have got here at the same time as the man with the sledgehammer, coming through the surrounding properties to arrive at the Leppers' garden. Blood ran from the wound in Nik's calf and the pain made him groan. As he looked out into the garden, he saw a shadow in the corner of his eye. Hannes was still lying in the corner of the patio, now silent from the shock, and his parents were presumably still in the house. With this in mind, Nik pointed his gun to where he'd seen the shadow and fired two shots. The muzzle flash illuminated the setting and he saw the second bullet hit a masked man in the forehead. The head was thrown backwards and the man fell to the ground.

Nik crouched down again behind the pot. He was well hidden, but the downside was he could barely see anything. Hannes had started to scream again, making it impossible to hear any noises coming from the attackers. He counted to three and carefully raised his head. The light from the opponent's gun and the pain in his shoulder came simultaneously. He'd been hit by a second bullet. He fell back and his gun rolled out of his hand. He hollered, trying to grab the weapon, but the patio began to spin around him. His vision blurred and glittered. 'Stay awake,' he mumbled, biting down on his lip. Two black boots were stepping towards him and he felt a hard blow to the head. He fell unconscious.

Chapter 15

The incessant beeping followed Nik into his dreams. It was a synthetic, unnatural noise, like a radio alarm clock calling him to get up for work. Then the dream ended and he opened his eyes to a blinding light. He turned his face to the side and the beeping stopped. Somebody was standing beside the bed. They were hanging a bag filled with clear liquid on to a metal stand and fumbling around with a thin plastic tube which led to a catheter in the back of Nik's hand. The figure stepped out of Nik's field of vision and he heard a door close.

He was aware he was lying in a hospital bed. His head thumped dully and his legs felt as if they had been buried in concrete. His throat was dry and his lips were stuck together with gluey saliva. As his eyes became accustomed to the light, he noticed a man sitting at the end of his bed, his face consumed by worry, as though unsure Nik was going to survive the next few hours.

'Didn't expect to see you here,' whispered Nik. His former boss smiled back at him gently. His white shirt was crumpled and he wasn't wearing a jacket. An unusual sight for the CID agent who was normally so well groomed.

'How are you feeling?' he asked. Nik heard the concern in his voice. Naumann had never spoken to him like that before. And just then, images started coming came back to him: the shooting on the patio, the fear on the faces of Hannes' parents and their screams of terror and desperation.

'The boy's alive and safe,' said Naumann, as if he'd read Nik's mind.

'How is that possible?' asked Nik in a slow whisper. 'The men caught me . . . and the police at the front door were knocked out.'

'They took Hannes with them,' explained Naumann, 'but an officer found him the following evening at the edge of South Park. He was physically unharmed.'

'And how is he now?'

'Not good,' replied Naumann sadly.

Nik glanced around the room sluggishly. He was hooked up to a monitoring device and had been given pain medication. He felt exhausted and his shoulder and leg were covered in bandages.

'How long have I been lying here?'

'Two days.'

Nik felt his head with his hand. The hair above his left ear had been shaved and he could feel stitches.

'That will heal soon,' said Naumann. 'You lost a lot of blood and you suffered a craniocerebral trauma from the blow to your head. But the doctors have said you're over the worst of it.' Naumann took a step to the side, exposing a table covered in flowers and presents and a basket full of cards. A large balloon with the words 'Get Well Soon' was also bobbing above the table. 'You impressed a lot of people, Pohl.'

'Why? Because I got myself shot? Or because I didn't manage to stop Hannes from being kidnapped?'

'Because you risked your life to save the boy. Because, in spite of Greta's death, you didn't give up, and because you were right, yet again, with your assessment of the case.'

'How do you know what my assessment was?'

'I got an anonymous call from a man yesterday,' said Naumann. 'He sent me all your files.' Naumann stood in front of the bed. 'Impressive work.'

'But was any of it useful?'

Naumann shook his head dejectedly. 'We have neither a trace to Greta's murderer nor to Hannes' kidnapper.'

'Then you need to go for Olaf van Berk.'

'We did. We searched his house under false pretences.'

'Let me guess . . . you didn't find a thing?'

'No.'

'Van Berk's at the top of the top,' said Nik. 'He's not going to leave any traces.'

'We're keeping an eye on him. And we've formed two special commissions for Greta and Hannes.'

'And that's why you came here today? To tell me that?'

'I actually just wanted to come and find out how you were . . . and bring over a card from your former colleagues. But your friend Balthasar was so exhausted I said I'd stay here for the evening so he could get some sleep. He'll be so happy when he hears you're awake.'

'He's a good man.'

'And a good friend too, apparently.'

'Yes, he is,' said Nik quietly.

'You should sleep.' Naumann pulled a large mobile phone out of his pocket. 'I take my work everywhere. I'll read my emails until Balthasar gets back.' He took a gift basket off a chair and sat down, crossing his legs.

'Let me know if anything happens,' said Nik.

'Let's just concentrate on your health today, OK? And I'll fill you in on everything when you're out of here.'

Nik wanted to say something but fatigue overcame him. He closed his eyes and slipped into a deep sleep.

◆　◆　◆

'I'd like to remind you that we agreed on half an hour,' said Balthasar indignantly. He was standing beside the bed, pointing to Nik's phone. 'After that, we are hanging up and you are getting some sleep.'

'Yes, Mum,' groaned Nik.

'Don't be rude.' Balthasar lifted his finger threateningly towards Nik. 'You suffered a craniocerebral trauma so severe even *your* bullhead couldn't handle it. So, we will be keeping any exertion to a minimum.'

'Thinking isn't stressful.'

'Who is the doctor here? You or me?' asked Balthasar. 'And if you make that face at me one more time, I'll tell your nurse what's really in that bottle of apple juice. And I don't mean the pretty blonde one you've been attempting to flirt with . . . very badly.'

'How can you flirt badly?'

'*So . . . what are you doing after work?*' Balthasar mimicked in a deep voice before giving a disdainful snort. 'It doesn't get any cruder than that.'

'I'm not sure if you're the right person to be giving me advice, considering your sexual preferences.'

'Listen to me, hetero man: the principle is *exactly* the same,' said Balthasar. 'If you continue acting like that, your mini Nik is not going to be having any fun.'

Nik crossed his arms and looked away with a huff. He could hear Balthasar unlocking his phone and calling someone. Shortly after, Jon spoke over the phone's loudspeaker.

'How are you?' Jon asked.

'Well, if I don't die from the injuries, it'll be from the boredom,' answered Nik. 'Plus, I'm missing Balthasar's culinary skills.'

'Not much of a compliment really, considering the crap they serve in here,' said the pathologist. 'Anyway, bearing in mind Nik's condition, we should get straight to the matter at hand.'

'Right, well, Hannes is back with his parents, living at an unknown location,' said Jon. 'So unfortunately, I can't tell you how the poor guy's doing.'

'And the two police officers?'

'Still signed off sick,' said Jon. 'The stun grenades really took their toll on their eyes and ears, but they'll be back to work soon.'

'Then clarify for me what happened that night,' said Nik. 'I'm missing the key moments.'

'Well, as well as the damage they did, the stun grenades also woke up the entire neighbourhood in about a one-kilometre circumference. That meant there were enough witnesses to thoroughly reconstruct the attack on the Leppers' house,' said Jon. 'Four people in total were involved. You shot the man with the sledgehammer in the leg. The second guy, who you never had any contact with, was the getaway driver. He'd also thrown the stun grenades and while you were storming the house, he tied up the two disoriented police officers with cable ties. He also went to collect the guy you'd shot, and put him into the car. While all this was happening, two other men were making their way towards the back garden. At least one of them had a crowbar and the plan was to break in via the patio door.'

'I hadn't expected them to divide themselves up that way,' said Nik. 'I thought they'd come in the front door. That's why I left the guy with the hammer lying at the door . . . Thought it might make the others a bit more cautious.'

'Well, the two in the garden must have heard the shots and then, when you stormed out the patio door with Hannes, they started shooting.'

'At least nobody shot Hannes.'

'No, they wanted him alive. That's why they couldn't just shoot wildly at you.'

'Which was the downfall of one of them, right?' Nik pointed to his forehead.

'That was Vic Claes. A Belgian citizen with a record that doesn't exactly paint him in a friendly light. According to ballistics, it's him you've got to thank for the shot to the calf.'

'Any link to van Berk at all?'

'Would have been nice. But no. The second attacker shot you in the shoulder and hit you on the head with his gun,' Jon continued. 'He then went on to shoot two bullets through the patio door into the house. But Hannes' parents had stayed under cover and were unharmed. He finally picked up the boy and dragged him through the garden to the street, before shoving him into the car and driving away with the two other men.'

'And the registration number?'

'Noted down by numerous neighbours, but in the end, the car had been stolen.'

'Dozens of people must have called the police with that level of noise,' said Nik. 'Where was the police back-up?'

'There was a problem that evening.'

'Ah yeah. The hostage at the market,' Nik remembered.

'Exactly. Which, in the end, turned out to be a hoax and just a load of false reports.'

'Van Berk?' suggested Balthasar.

'Highly likely,' said Jon. 'But only two of the callers could be traced. Both of them were drug addicts who admitted during the interrogation that a man had paid them to make the prank calls.'

'That piece of shit!' Nik hit the armrest on his bed. 'And what did the forensic results have to say?'

'Nothing enlightening,' said Jon. 'No fingerprints, and the DNA from the man with the sledgehammer wasn't in the database.

Vic Claes had no links to the teenagers and he used an unregistered SIG P210.'

'And what about the stun grenades?'

'From Russian army stock,' said Jon. 'Easy to get hold of if you know the right people.'

'And the getaway car?'

'Was found burned out near Freising on the banks of the Isar.'

With a sigh, Nik let his head sink back on to his pillow. After everything that had happened, he had at least hoped for a lead to van Berk.

'And why didn't they shoot Hannes?' asked Balthasar.

'Because the kidnapper isn't afraid the boy will say anything,' explained Nik.

'So he isn't an absolute beast then.'

'It's little consolation really.'

Nik rubbed his forehead. The medication was making it difficult to think and the pain from the bullet wounds and the blow to the head also weren't helping. 'The four men were an elite group,' said Nik. 'They won't be easily found. And behind all of them is a man who moves in all the right circles and has a *lot* of money.'

'So van Berk is still our main suspect?' asked Balthasar.

'Apparently so,' said Jon. 'But other than that, we're still in the dark . . . We still don't know the reason for the abductions.'

'And we have no idea if the perpetrator has even found what they're looking for,' said Nik. 'Which brings us back to Simon.'

'Nothing new. Not on him or on Daniela Haas,' said Jon. 'I sent Naumann all our investigation files, but the CID still haven't had any success.'

'I just hope they've managed to hide and aren't lying dead in the ground somewhere.' Nik closed his eyes. 'It's been four days since Hannes was taken and we're still groping around in the dark.'

'Naumann and his men aren't giving up and neither will I,' Jon assured him. 'You can't do anything in your state so get some rest until you're back to your old self again. If anything happens, I'll let you know.'

'And with those lovely closing words,' said Balthasar, 'it's time for a midday nap! Bye for now, Jon.' He put his phone back in his pocket and squeezed Nik's hand. 'I'll be back this evening with a tub of that culinary abomination they like to call "Wurstsalat". I'll get it from your favourite butcher.'

Nik rubbed his eyes. 'Maybe my dreams will give me some insight into all this.'

'Let's hope so.' Balthasar waved goodbye on his way out the door and closed it behind him.

Not long after, Nik was asleep.

Nik woke with a start. Something had disturbed him. He reached down towards his hip to feel for his gun but then realised he was still lying in a hospital bed. A veil of moonlight glowed through the cloudless sky into his hospital room. From the corridor, he could hear the wheels of the trolley the night nurses used to distribute medication to patients. Nik was grateful he was no longer attached to the monitoring device or on a drip. The room smelled like the remains of his Wurstsalat – its packaging still lying on the side table. Just as he was about to close his eyes again, Nik noticed a quiet rustling. Somebody was standing to his right, beside the open curtain at the window.

'Good to see you're feeling better,' came the voice of a young man.

'Who's there?' He looked around for something he could use as a weapon but other than a glass water bottle, there was nothing suitable in reach.

His visitor stepped into the moonlight. 'I think you know me already.'

'Simon?' said Nik, surprised. He heaved himself up to a sitting position. 'I'm so glad you're still alive.'

'Yeah, me too.' He smiled.

'Why are you here?'

'To tell you to stop looking for me.'

'You're in a lot of danger,' said Nik insistently.

'I know that. But your search is just putting me in even more danger.'

'I don't understand.'

'I'll explain it to you some other time.'

'You have to go to the police. You won't survive this on your own.'

'It's gone pretty well until now, hasn't it?' Simon took a step closer to Nik. 'Forget about me. Please.'

'I can't do that.'

'You have to,' Simon insisted. 'You *have* to.' And with that, he turned around and walked silently towards the door. He stopped briefly to wave at Nik before slipping out into the corridor.

Nik longed to stand up but he knew he wouldn't even make it to the door without support. He sank back on to the bed and rang for the nurse, but by the time the woman had got to his room, the painkillers had set in again and he'd fallen asleep.

When he woke the next morning, he wasn't even sure Simon had really been there. He asked around, but nobody had seen a teenage boy come or leave. He must have moved like a ghost.

◆ ◆ ◆

Nik wheezed as he went up the stairs to the flat. He was sweating and his heart was racing but it felt good to be back on his legs again. Above the door hung a large sign in the shape of a red balloon with the words 'Welcome Home!' on it. As the pathologist opened the door, Kara instantly flew towards Nik, flapping her wings and squawking, before landing on his injured shoulder. She dug her claws into his skin and nipped at his ear, but for some reason, Nik took pleasure in the faint pain and stroked the parrot on the head. He pushed his suitcase into his bedroom and fell joyfully on to the couch. The seven days in the hospital had felt like an eternity. He was supposed to stay longer, but his mood had deteriorated to such an extent that it was thought better – for all parties involved – if he continued his recovery at home and received regular visits from his GP.

His eyes were almost closed when his phone rang.

'Welcome home!' said Jon.

'How did you know I was home?' asked Nik. 'I only got in two minutes ago.'

'I tracked your phone.'

'Of course you did,' Nik mumbled.

'I just wanted to tell you there's no news,' Jon continued. 'And everything else can wait until you're well rested.'

'I've been lying in bed for a week,' said Nik. 'That's more rest than I've had in the last two years.'

'Yes, and . . . ?'

'*Cui prodest scelus, is fecit*,' replied Nik.

'Excuse me?'

'It's from Seneca's tragedy, *Medea*,' explained Nik. 'For whom the crime advances, he has done it.'

'Yes, and we've been trying to come up with a solution for a long time now.'

'Van Berk's involvement only makes sense if he or his clients benefit from it. So let's forget about the children's past, who their parents are and how they came into the world. And let's focus on van Berk's motive.'

'Monitoring him is difficult because we can't get into his house,' said Jon. 'And although that email did manage to reach him, he doesn't appear to use a private computer. And the bug on his car is only partly helpful: the car wasn't used during the kidnappings and was standing in the villa driveway when all the crimes took place.'

'The CID are covering everything else,' said Nik. 'Crime scene investigations, the forensic analyses, witness interviews . . . even the search for Simon and Daniela. We wouldn't be able to do all that. So we'll just have to fill in the gaps and cover the areas where the police can't gain access.'

'Like monitoring van Berk,' concluded Jon.

'Performing a search on his house was more than we could have expected from Naumann.'

'He must be tired from the constant failures.'

'Maximum resources have already been exhausted with van Berk. Unfortunately, there's just no official reason to start surveillance procedures on him.'

'Surely we can get one or two cameras around the house. If we do that, we could at least monitor his visitors.'

'The street lamp number won't work. Van Berk's security will be too vigilant for that.'

'I know some people who could sort something out for us,' suggested Jon. 'As per usual, it's just a question of money.'

'Good. Well, I'll need various hire cars with tinted windows.'

'How many?'

'Two for every day,' said Nik. 'One for the daytime and one for night.'

'OK, but in your current condition, I think you're best not doing any long surveillance sessions.'

'Yeah, well, the cars we hire will need to be expensive so they don't stand out in the posh neighbourhood. So, if you think about it, it'll be a kind of luxury surveillance. And that won't be nearly as taxing,' said Nik. 'Plus, Balthasar wants to help out. He doesn't go back to work until next week and he's bored.'

'Balthasar isn't a trained CID agent.'

'I know. And I wouldn't ever put him in danger,' said Nik. 'He'll just do a couple of hours a day in a locked car, phone in hand and directly in front of the camera.'

'Van Berk's security people aren't squeamish, you know?'

'I *do* know. But they're not stupid either. They try to avoid any unnecessary attention.'

'And what are you hoping to achieve from it all?'

'Not a lot.' The resignation in Nik's voice was blatant. 'But I can't bear sitting around at home all day relying on the CID to find something. Monitoring the house is better than doing nothing.'

'Give me today and tonight to get organised,' said Jon. 'I'll arrange a hire car to be waiting at your front door early tomorrow morning and I'll get enough cameras set around the villa so we don't miss a thing.'

'Sounds good,' said Nik.

'Welcome back,' said Jon, before hanging up.

◆ ◆ ◆

Dana Baaken waited in the elegantly decorated living room, breathing in the aromatic scent of green tea that was steaming from the Meissen porcelain cup in her hand. She was standing in front of a painting of a birch forest in autumn that was hanging over a marble fireplace. It was perhaps less marvellous than a Rembrandt and not as surreal as something from Dali, but the picture still had a consuming magic about it. The longer you looked at it, the deeper you were pulled into the wood, where the leaves rustled under your shoes and the cool autumn breeze rushed through your hair. Dana stretched out her manicured hand, imagining she could touch the blue flowers, only to instantly pull it back as the heavy oak living room door creaked open.

An elderly man walked slowly towards her across the thick Persian rug, breathing with difficulty. His back was bent double and he was leaning on a walking stick. He was wearing a dark grey suit, a light blue shirt and shiny black leather shoes which he barely lifted from the floor. It was more of a shuffle than a walk, but he still kept his head upright and his eyes fixed on Dana, in a pathetic attempt to demonstrate his strength. He was wearing make-up and a white wig, although the wig was of such high quality and fitted him so well, barely anyone would have noticed it. But Dana had learned to be aware of such details. She had only ever seen van Berk once before. It was at a large birthday party for some industrialist near Garmisch. Back then she had been impressed by his commanding demeanour, which made seeing him so weak and helpless all the more surprising. She supposed, however, that was just the way of things.

Behind van Berk was a tall man with broad shoulders. He was looking down at van Berk's shaking hands as they grasped his stick, as though ready to catch him should his energy suddenly expire. Dana put down the cup and waited for van Berk to sit down on the couch. She then sat on a chair opposite him.

'Frau Baaken,' he began with a quiet, hoarse voice. 'Thank you for coming.'

She nodded and stroked her right eyebrow with her right hand: a nervous gesture she'd had since she was a child.

'I've heard you are among the best when it comes to finding missing people.'

'I have good employees in the right places,' she answered.

'Like your network of hotel employees?' asked van Berk.

'Yes, but that isn't my only trump card . . .' admitted Dana. 'I have lots of people on the streets: I'm in contact with security guards in clubs, and last year I managed to recruit a super recogniser.'

'Please excuse me, but I'm not aware of this modern expression.' He held his hand up to his mouth and coughed.

'A super recogniser is someone who can remember every face they have ever seen, regardless of how long ago it was. I show this person a photo and they are able to filter out thousands of others and point to the one I need.'

'A useful skill.'

'This employee has a job where he has access to all CCTV throughout Munich. None of his bosses are aware of his talent but when I'm looking for someone, he can help. He's happy to have the additional source of income.'

'And how fast can you locate someone?'

'Depends on numerous factors,' said Dana. 'The less the person goes into public spaces, the harder it is to locate them. Also, the neighbourhood in which the target is hiding plays a role. And lastly, it depends on how many other employees are deployed at the same time . . . Employees I have to acquire.'

'And if all of your employees were to be involved in the search simultaneously?'

'I've never had such a situation,' said Dana. 'The costs would be immense and . . .'

'One million straight off?' asked van Berk, interrupting the woman. 'And another million after you find the person.'

'I can work with that figure,' said Dana, trying not to show her surprise at the offer.

'My assistant will give you the first instalment when you leave the building,' said van Berk.

Dana resisted the urge to laugh out loud. She had never earned money as easily as this in her life. 'So who is it you are looking for?'

Van Berk took out a photo from his jacket pocket and laid it down on the table. It was a photo of a teenage boy. Maybe fourteen or fifteen years old.

'His name is Simon Fahl,' van Berk said. 'And if you bring him to me in the next seventy-two hours, I'll throw in the Klimt on the wall for you as well.'

Chapter 16

The last two days had done Nik the world of good. His headache hadn't been nearly as bad, which meant he'd been able to work on the case without getting tired after only an hour. Since the shot to his calf had only grazed the skin without severing any muscle, he was able to walk again, and each day, he'd gone for two walks through the nearby park, where he could enjoy the bright autumn weather. And he'd stopped sweating when walking up the stairs. But he was still taking painkillers for his left shoulder and still couldn't apply any pressure to it. Thankfully he was right-handed, so he was barely restricted by the injury.

He sat on the back seat of an SUV with soft luxury seating, watching van Berk's villa. He was using a camera that had been mounted on to a wheel arch. On the seat beside him, there was half a bar of chocolate, a Tupperware box filled with potato salad, and a bread roll. He took a sip of water from a bottle and bobbed his head to the soft rock music that was playing quietly on the radio. He had attached a clipboard with paper to the back of the driver's seat so he and Balthasar could note down any observations. Over the last two days, however, there had been barely anything to write down and between them, they hadn't even filled up one side of paper.

The song on the radio came to an end and the eight o'clock news began. It was dark now and the traffic was much quieter. The weather forecast had predicted rain and as a result, the residents of the neighbourhood had all apparently sought shelter inside their lavish houses for the evening. The only person he had seen was a man walking his German Shepherd. The man had looked at his phone the whole time and hadn't even glanced at the SUV.

Nik picked up his tablet and looked at the images being transmitted from the four cameras that Jon's useful acquaintances had installed two nights ago. Two were fixed to trees and two others to lampposts, giving them a good view of the property behind the wall.

The area surrounding the villa reminded Nik of an English garden: bursting with flowers, shrubs and trees. There was also a well in the middle and expanses of lush green grass. The upkeep costs for the garden alone would have been at least four hundred euros per month. But despite all the care and attention it had been given, the property still felt uninhabited. Once every so often, a security guard would walk around the garden unenthusiastically, usually with a cigarette in his hand, looking irritated by the surrounding beauty.

Nik took out his phone and called Jon.

'Anything new?' Jon asked after picking up.

'All quiet here,' said Nik. 'But I've got a question for you.' He scanned the paper on the clipboard. 'Have you seen van Berk on the property over the last two days?'

'Possibly,' said Jon reluctantly.

'What d'you mean possibly? Did you see him or didn't you?'

'Yesterday at midday there was movement on the patio,' said Jon. 'Somebody was rolled outside in a wheelchair by a security guard and left there for fifteen minutes. The tall beech tree was obscuring most of the view so I couldn't be sure who it was. But the white hair and dark suit definitely matched van Berk's description.'

'He uses a wheelchair?'

'Well, that's exactly why I said "possibly".'

'He didn't really appear ill in the restaurant . . . but thinking back to it now, there were a couple of signs.' Nik closed his eyes and remembered their meeting. 'I noticed he was wearing make-up but I just put that down to vanity. And his hair looked too evenly spread out for a man of his age. So that definitely could have been a wig. Plus . . . he was waiting for me in the room when I arrived and I left before he did, so if he has problems walking, I never had the chance to see them. Oh, and then there was the coughing fit. So, yes. If you put all that together, there's actually a lot to suggest he has a serious illness.'

'Maybe this is the incentive we've been looking for,' said Jon. 'He doesn't have much time left and wants to sort something out before he dies. And that something is linked to the three teenagers.'

'Then maybe the problem will solve itself.'

'No, we can't rely on that,' said Jon. 'Van Berk can easily pay people to finish the job after he's died.'

'Wait a minute . . .' said Nik, looking down at his tablet beside him. 'The gate's opening.'

'You're right.'

The men went quiet, waiting anxiously as van Berk's limousine drove out of the gate and turned left on to the street, heading in Nik's direction. Nik's hand moved automatically to his gun, preparing for an attack, but the car drove past him and turned on to the main street nearby.

'Our bug's still working,' said Jon. 'We can follow the car wherever it goes.'

'Van Berk's sitting inside.'

'How d'you know?' asked Jon. 'The back windows are tinted.'

'He was sitting up front in the passenger seat.'

'Strange,' said Jon.

'Maybe he's making himself visible on purpose,' suggested Nik. 'Do you think he found out about our surveillance?'

'Not necessarily,' replied Nik. 'But he knows I survived the night at Hannes' and he won't have been best pleased with Naumann's visit. So he'll know there's a good chance he's being watched by either the CID or myself.'

'OK. So what do we do now?'

Nik clenched his fists and tried not to let his feelings take control. How he would have loved to drive behind the car, drag van Berk from the passenger seat and beat the truth out of him. 'Is the bug definitely working?' Nik asked.

'I'm getting a clear signal.'

'Then I'll stay here,' Nik decided. 'But I need to know where he ends up.'

'He's heading towards the Altstadt right now. Anything stops longer than a red light and I'll be in touch.'

'Thanks.' Nik hung up and turned back towards the villa. 'What the hell are you up to, old man?' he mumbled to himself.

◆ ◆ ◆

Nik looked at the time again. Van Berk had been driving across Munich for the last thirty minutes and nothing had happened around the villa. His mobile phone rang, breaking the silence and causing him to jump.

'They've stopped,' said Jon.

'Where?'

'In Brunnerstraße beside Luitpold Park,' said Jon. 'But don't ask me what he's doing there.'

'Well, it's not like he's going to see the sights, is it?' said Nik.

'But he could be going up Luitpold Hill to enjoy the view one last time,' suggested Jon. 'Lots of people get sentimental when they know they're about to die.'

'Not van Berk,' responded Nik. 'For him, it'll be the opposite. There'll be a reason behind every single move he makes. He won't be wasting his energy looking at an evening view over Munich.'

'Well, the park's a terrible choice for a secret meeting.'

Just then, Nik was distracted by a black BMW speeding past him. It turned into the villa's drive.

'Who's that?' asked Jon, who had also noticed the car.

'Van Berk doesn't have any BMWs in his fleet,' said Nik.

'And the number plate doesn't match any of his registered vehicles,' said Jon as the villa gate opened.

'I don't like this,' said Nik. 'Van Berk's not home but he's getting visitors.'

'Well, now we know the trip to the park was just a distraction.'

'Yep . . . It got any possible spies out the way so the BMW could enter the premises unnoticed.'

'Van Berk's car just set off again,' said Jon. 'If they take the direct route back, they'll be home in ten minutes.'

'Are you able to zoom in on the entrance?' Nik picked up his tablet.

'No problem,' answered Jon. He zoomed in on the BMW. A man got out, opened the back door and pulled someone wearing a knitted black hat out of the car. The camera positioning wouldn't allow Nik to get a glimpse of their face but as Jon zoomed in even closer, Nik noticed the person's flapping, ripped jeans.

'It's Simon!' he called out.

'Are you sure?'

'He was wearing those trousers when he came to see me in hospital,' said Nik. 'I saw them when he was leaving the room.'

'Shit! What do we do?'

Nik went to reach for his gun but then remembered the villa's high wall and the numerous cameras mounted on the gate and doors.

'Call Naumann,' Nik said finally. 'Tell him what happened and send him the footage.'

'But those recordings were taken illegally,' Jon reminded Nik. 'And they don't prove Simon's been taken into the house against his will.'

Nik thumped his fist down on the seat beside him. Jon was right. Nik took a moment to think. 'Then just send him a picture of Simon and the car in the driveway. But before you do that, call the police anonymously and tell them you saw Simon getting kidnapped and dragged into a BMW. All of that together with the registration number surely has to be enough for a search.'

'Give me two minutes,' said Jon, hanging up.

Nik turned to look at the villa. Sitting inside the SUV doing nothing was making him go crazy, but he'd be useless to Simon in his current state. And just then, as if reminding him of his weakness, a shooting pain darted through his left shoulder. Nik put a painkiller in his mouth and washed it down with water.

'Hang in there, Simon,' he said under his breath. 'Help's on its way.'

Just as the words had left his mouth, the limousine drove past. Once again, van Berk was sitting in the front passenger seat, but this time he had a wide, contented smile on his face.

It didn't take long for the police to turn up. Two emergency vehicles headed by Naumann's private car stopped in front of the large gate. Nik's former boss stepped out of the car, rang the buzzer and showed his ID to the camera. The gate opened. Naumann's car drove in, followed by a patrol car. The second patrol car remained where it was, blocking the entrance.

Jon called. 'I'm watching,' Nik told him.

'Naumann was cooperative. He knew exactly what had to be done.'

'Second time in months I regret no longer working for the CID.'

'We'll just have to wait,' said Jon.

'Not exactly my forte,' mumbled Nik.

The time passed slowly. Nik opened the car window to let in some fresh air. He stared at the tablet, going from camera to camera, barely allowing himself to blink in case he missed something.

'You've got to be kidding me,' he said after an hour had passed. 'How long does it take to find a kidnapped child?'

'Maybe Simon had gone with them voluntarily?'

'You don't really believe that, do you?'

'Well, I doubt van Berk would have barricaded himself in.'

The front door opened and Naumann came out with the two police officers. They got back into their cars and drove through the gates – no blue lights, no sirens.

'Did you see Simon?' asked Nik.

'He wasn't with them.'

The cars drove past Nik's SUV. There was nothing to suggest they had just saved a teenager from an abduction.

'Can you get Naumann on the line?'

'Sure,' said Jon. A second later, Nik heard a beeping that was being drowned out by a loud interference.

'Heinrich Naumann,' he heard his former boss say.

'Where's Simon?' Nik asked angrily.

'He wasn't there,' replied Naumann.

'But you saw for yourself . . . He was driven into the villa by a man who certainly wasn't his best buddy.'

'No. I received an illegally shot photo of a boy about the same size and stature as Simon,' said Naumann. 'And I'm telling you, other than van Berk and two security guards, there was nobody in that villa.'

'Then they must have tied him up and hidden him.'

'We searched every inch of that house while those three people sat and waited in the living room,' said Naumann. 'Van Berk was very obliging. We were even allowed to search the summerhouse and the garage. But there wasn't a single trace of Simon.'

'He's in there!' shouted Nik.

'Then get me some better evidence! Something I can use to arrest van Berk and rip the whole house down . . . including that wall!' said Naumann. 'Until I've got that, my hands are tied, Pohl!'

'Fuck! This is bullshit!' Nik shouted, ending the call and putting his phone in his pocket. He opened the door forcefully and stomped around to the car boot.

He couldn't wait around any longer.

To free up his hands, Nik had hooked up his phone to his Bluetooth headphones. He was wearing a black woollen hat and a black jacket and carrying a large rucksack over his right shoulder.

'This is an awful idea,' said Jon.

'This was our plan B,' said Nik.

'Still doesn't mean it's a good idea. You couldn't take on those security guards even on your best day. So with your shoulder the way it is, it's a really fucking stupid idea.'

'They're going to kill him, Jon!'

'We don't know that for sure. They didn't kill Hannes.'

'Yeah, only because he can't speak.'

'That villa is a fucking fortress, Nik. You won't even get near Simon.'

'Well, then I'll die trying. But I can't stay here in this car waiting for a miracle.' Nik ran across the street and pressed himself up against the wall. 'So? Are you going to help me?'

Jon let out a loud groan. 'Of course I am.'

Nik looked up. The wall was four metres high and as smooth as a mirror. No grooves, no overhanging branches. 'Where's the best place to climb over?'

'There isn't one,' said Jon. 'There's CCTV covering the whole property. But there are a couple of points where there is just one camera, both of which are partially covered by branches. The only way this plan has any chance of succeeding is if the security guard in charge of watching the monitors isn't looking at the images too carefully at the very moment you come into the shot.'

'I've heard worse plans.'

'One of these entry points is to your right. Go to the end of the property and then four metres left. There you should see an oak tree. The plan *might* work if you're able to attach your rescue ladder to the top of the wall there, and as long as van Berk hasn't hired any extra security guards who I can't see over the cameras.'

'You should really work on your pessimism levels.'

'You'd have to ooze with optimism to assume you'd be able to get on to the property without being seen.'

Nik crept up to the corner of the wall and saw the path to the left. He couldn't see anyone, so he took four more large steps, pulled the rope ladder out of his rucksack and threw the hooks on to the top of the wall. He pulled the ladder as tightly as possible so that the pointed hooks sunk into the stone. 'Quality German workmanship right there,' Nik mumbled as he started to climb. Thanks to the painkillers, the agony in his shoulder had subsided to not much more than a light throbbing and his injured leg felt solid. Once his head had reached the top of the wall, he took out a pair of infra-red binoculars from his bag. He lifted his head until he was able to see into the garden.

'No one outside,' said Nik quietly.

'Yeah, that's why van Berk has the cameras.'

'How long will I be visible?'

'If you manage to fall behind the oak's trunk, you'll be barely visible but as soon as you deviate even slightly from there, a blind man would see you.'

'OK. And how long will I be out of the blind spots when I start to move?'

'Hard to say from here,' replied Jon. 'I reckon for the whole forty metres until the house wall.'

'That's quite a lot.' Nik pushed himself over the wall and jumped down behind the tree.

'Quite a lot? Even Usain Bolt would show up on their screens for around six or seven seconds,' said Jon.

'Then it's time for a drinks delivery, isn't it?' said Nik.

'What?'

'Find the nearest pizza delivery service where you can pay by PayPal or credit card,' said Nik. 'Order two bottles of water and transfer one hundred euros providing they set off straight away. And promise the delivery boy a hundred more if they get here in the next five minutes.'

'And why am I not ordering pizza?'

'Because someone would need to make it first and that would take too long.'

'OK. And what's the point of all this?'

'The boy will arrive and press the buzzer at van Berk's gate,' said Nik. 'And at that moment, everybody in the house will pay attention to the camera at the front door, including the security guard watching the monitors. And it's exactly at that moment when I make a run for it.'

'It could work.'

'Only one way to find out.'

'Stay on the line,' said Jon. 'I'll order the drinks.'

◆ ◆ ◆

Nik had to use every ounce of discipline at his disposal to keep his head down and wait behind the trunk. But without the distraction from the delivery boy, he didn't stand a chance. He had to wait.

'Done.' Jon was back on the line. 'What do I do if they catch you?' he asked, clearly concerned. 'Naumann won't be persuaded to search the house a third time.'

'You'll tell Daniela Haas that Simon is with van Berk in the villa.'

'Daniela Haas? How will she help you?'

'I've just got a gut feeling.'

'What do you mean you've got a fucking gut feeling?'

'I'll tell you later.' Nik heard the screeching of tyres.

'That's the delivery boy,' said Jon.

Nik looked at his watch. 'Seven minutes. Not bad.' He stood up from his crouched position and pressed himself against the tree.

'Four seconds,' said Jon. Nik tightened the straps on his rucksack and stretched out his legs. 'Go!'

Nik ran through the garden, past a fern tree and then a rose bush. Despite the tablets and the rush of adrenaline, there was still a piercing pain in his injured calf with every step. But he bit his lip and kept going. The camera attached to the gutter was aimed down precisely on his path, but he had no choice: this was the only entrance at the back of the house. In one long move, he jumped on to the patio and flattened himself against the wall.

'What's the delivery boy doing?'

'They didn't let him in,' replied Jon. 'He just put the bottles down on the ground, shrugged and left.'

'Any activity elsewhere?'

'All quiet.'

Nik examined the patio door. It looked heavy and robust, and there was no doubt it was made from bulletproof glass. There was a handle on the outside but no lock, which suggested it probably locked from the inside with a deadbolt. The curtain had been pulled closed and there was no light shining from behind it. It was possible a whole army of security guards was waiting behind that curtain, but Nik had to at least try his luck. He wrapped his fingers around the handle and pulled it carefully. The door slid open silently. Nik gave a sigh of relief; a deadlock would have made things ten times more difficult. He pulled his gun out of his holster and used the muzzle end to slide the curtain to the side. He stepped inside cautiously.

As soon as he did, he saw the shadows approaching. It was too late. Somebody sprayed tear gas in his face and something heavy thudded down on the hand holding the gun. He staggered backwards out of the door and as he did, someone grabbed his leg from underneath him and tipped him painfully on to the stone patio slabs. He brought his hands to one side and attempted to push himself up again, but it was all in vain: somebody had him in a headlock. Whoever it was pushed Nik on to his front while a second person tied his hands behind his back. Trying his best to defend himself with just his legs, he felt a sudden stabbing pain near the kidneys. His whole body shot into spasm and he cried out loudly. It was a taser gun. He lost all control over his body and slid, limp and jerking, down to the ground.

The four hands of his attackers lifted him up and carried him inside. His eyes burned and he ached to rub the liquid off his face.

But his hands were still tied. Shortly after being brought inside, he was thrown on to the floor, the impact lessened somewhat by a rug.

'Good evening, Herr Pohl,' came van Berk's voice. 'How nice of you to visit.'

Chapter 17

Nik's screams had been followed by a rattling and rustling on the line, and then he had been cut off. Jon had tried to call him back three times, each time without success. And the tracker wasn't locating the phone either. It must have been damaged.

'Fuck!' Jon jumped up and kicked his chair. He had told Nik over and over again to buy a better case for his phone so it wouldn't break. Maybe he had just tripped and his phone had fallen out of his pocket. But then, Nik's scream hadn't suggested he had merely tripped.

Jon paced back and forth. All his knowledge, all his money, all his hacking skills . . . utterly useless now. He sat back down at his computer. 'You and your fucking gut feeling!' he mumbled as he started writing an email. After clicking 'Send', he grabbed his car key and ran to a storage room at other the end of the flat. He pulled his phone out of his pocket and dialled Balthasar's number.

'What's happening?' asked the pathologist.

'I think Nik's been caught and is now sitting tied up somewhere with van Berk,' said Jon. 'And we can't rely on the police anymore.'

'OK. So what do we do?'

'I'll have to get him out of there myself.'

'How?'

'Still don't know, but I'm sure I'll think of something stupid on my way over to the villa,' explained Jon. 'You in?'

'Thought you were never going to ask.'

◆ ◆ ◆

Nik's hands had been cuffed and the men had sat him down on an armchair. As his eyes started to recover from the tear gas, the room fell into focus. In front of him was a sofa and a coffee table, and then there were the fully stacked bookcases that reached all the way to the ceiling. Licking flames crackled in the open fireplace. The man on the sofa was still blurry and vague but Nik could tell it was van Berk. He was leaning on his walking stick and breathing heavily.

'It's a shame we couldn't meet again under different circumstances,' he said with a dry voice. 'I could have put a man like you to good use.'

'I don't work for child murderers,' replied Nik.

'I never murdered Greta,' he continued, his voice grating. The man then suddenly struck his stick down on the floor, consumed by a coughing attack. If Balthasar had ever coughed and rattled in such a manner, Nik would have called an ambulance immediately. But the security guard standing beside the sofa didn't blink an eyelid. Such an attack was apparently a perfectly normal occurrence for van Berk. Nik couldn't see any other employees from where he was sitting.

Van Berk finally caught his breath. 'It was an accident.'

'Greta died from a bullet to the chest,' retorted Nik.

'The girl went for my security guard's weapon and wanted to shoot me,' van Berk continued. 'If the second man hadn't reacted as quickly as he did, I'd be dead now.'

'That's a bullshit excuse,' said Nik. 'If you hadn't kidnapped Greta, she'd still be *alive*.' Nik spat on the floor. 'She was a teenager, for fuck's sake! It might have been one of your gorillas that pulled the trigger, but her death is definitely on your shoulders.'

'Well . . . you don't need to worry yourself about seeing justice done. The cancer in my body is taking good care of that.'

'When I get out of these cuffs, it's not going to be the cancer that kills you.'

Van Berk wheezed out a laugh. 'Well, you'll need to wait a little while.' He coughed again. 'I need to deal with something else first.'

'You mean you want to know if Simon is related to you?' suggested Nik.

Van Berk looked back at Nik, pinching his eyes together.

'There's an unopened test tube on the table with a long cotton bud inside,' Nik continued. 'So, you've either got auditory canals the size of an elephant's or it's a swab for the inside of the cheek.'

'You're too clever for your own good, aren't you, Pohl?' remarked van Berk.

'That's what my teachers used to say . . . but I never used to listen to them either.' Nik leaned back in the chair. 'Finally it all makes sense,' he said. 'It wasn't the teenagers that were hiding the secrets, it was their DNA.'

'Indeed. But unfortunately, your realisation comes a little late.'

'It was *your* child that was born that night in June 2003,' Nik went on, ignoring van Berk's remark.

'My *grandchild*,' van Berk corrected Nik.

'So your son's child,' said Nik. 'And where is Elias? There's been no trace of him for years.'

'When my son found out how I earn my money, he suffered a severe morality attack,' said van Berk. 'I had got him into the best universities . . . given him everything he ever wanted, but still he renounced me.' Van Berk coughed. 'So he gave me a choice: I could either use my connections to give him a new identity, or never see him again.'

'So what did you do?'

'I gave him a new identity, of course!' answered van Berk. 'My family was always the most important thing to me.'

'And what does your son have to say about everything? To the kidnappings and murders?'

'He and his wife died a year ago in a car crash on Martinique. My grandson would also have died if they hadn't left him at home with his nanny.' Van Berk lowered his head and sighed loudly. 'So now it's just me and Elias's son, Aaron.'

'And now, right before you die, you want to proclaim that Simon is your eldest grandson,' said Nik. 'But why kidnap the teenagers? Why not put an announcement in the paper and do a DNA test with those who get in touch?'

Van Berk closed his eyes and leaned back on the couch.

Nik jiggled his legs nervously. Jon had already found out that Elias was Olaf van Berk's son and Nik now realised that the reason Jon hadn't found anything on him since 2009 was because he had changed his name. Elias wasn't married then and didn't have any children. But van Berk had just said Elias had a wife . . . So the marriage must have taken place *after* 2009.

'Oh, shit . . .' said Nik. 'His first child was born in 2003 and Aaron's a lot younger. You're scared the firstborn might make a claim to their inheritance rights.'

'That child was the result of some stupid flirtation with a whore,' said van Berk spitefully. 'Carla was a maid. Came over here from some farm in Spain. Too thick to use contraception but cunning enough to make eyes at my son.' His hands trembled as he spoke. 'It was a trap. Elias had just turned eighteen and Carla hoped she'd be able to sidle her way into higher circles by getting pregnant with his child.'

'So, let me guess . . . you planned to have the pregnancy terminated, right?'

'Elias still listened to me back then.'

'Yeah, but then Carla saw it coming and ran,' Nik concluded. 'So, it was *your* men who were at the labour ward that night. Pressurising the nurse.'

'That stupid bitch . . .'

'And what will Aaron say when he finds out his inheritance was bought with the blood of his half-brother?'

'He won't say anything because all this ends here. Come the crack of dawn, all traces will be destroyed and I'll have just the one heir.'

'A little optimistic, don't you think?' said Nik. 'The abductions are all over the media and the CID have got two special commissions on the case. Nobody's going to rest until they've found out who's behind all this.'

'The only optimist around here is you.' Van Berk pointed at Nik. 'I haven't left a single trace. I mean, the CID were just here and didn't find a thing when Simon was barely two metres away from them!' Van Berk stretched his face into an evil grimace. 'Blanket surveillance and secret soundproofed rooms certainly have their advantages.'

'And I suppose I'm one of the traces that needs to be destroyed?'

'Of course.'

'So why haven't you shot me yet?'

'Because I'm still not sure if Simon is Elias's son,' van Berk replied. 'And since you and your partners have proven yourselves rather determined opponents, you might still have some useful information. And most importantly, I want to know who your ominous hacker is.'

'Yeah, good luck with that.'

Van Berk made a dismissive hand gesture, as if to shoo away Nik's words. 'Oh yes. They're all valiant at the start. But I'm sure after my Russian friends have pulled out your fingernails, you'll tell me everything.'

Van Berk looked at his watch then shook his head, mumbling something Nik couldn't understand.

'The DNA test seems to be taking its time, doesn't it?' Nik remarked.

'Yes, well, even with the latest technology, it still takes a while,' said van Berk. 'And you should just concentrate on enjoying the last few hours of your life. And then . . . with a little bit of luck . . . my men will spare you the torture and treat you to a quick death.'

◆ ◆ ◆

Balthasar squeezed the accelerator and raced through the red light.

'If we're planning to help Nik, we should maybe try not to die first.' Jon was holding on to the door handle with both hands. He tugged once again on his belt to make sure it was definitely working.

'It's midnight. There's barely any traffic at this time of day,' said Balthasar, driving so quickly around a roundabout, Jon was slammed against his door. 'So have you thought up a plan yet?' asked the pathologist.

'I was thinking we should make some kind of diversion so Nik can free himself.'

'OK, such as?'

'When I bought Nik's weapons on the black market, I got a reserve in case he ever lost anything.'

'Are you referring to that large black box in the boot?'

Jon nodded.

'What's inside?'

'Two guns, two revolvers, one rifle and one hand grenade.'

'A hand grenade?' asked Balthasar, horrified. 'What the hell are you going to do with a hand grenade?'

'I don't know yet, but it just feels good knowing it's there.'

'Have you ever used one before?'

'No, but I thought you might know how to use them.'

'Hand grenades?' said Balthasar. 'I'm a fucking pathologist! Where the hell do you suppose I learned how to use a hand grenade?'

'You told me your dad collected weapons.'

'Antique weapons, Jon! Flintlocks, muskets, wheel-lock pistols. You couldn't kill a teddy bear with that crap!'

'But you pick locks and forge documents . . . so I just thought you'd know your way around weapons as well.'

'Jesus!' Balthasar paused for a moment. 'Well, I was a good fencer at uni. Does that count?'

'Fencing?' said Jon. 'Van Berk's men aren't pirates!'

'I didn't fence to kill people. I did it because I fancied my trainer,' said Balthasar, apparently justifying his actions.

'Well, this is going to be interesting, to say the least,' mumbled Jon.

The pathologist looked at the clock. 'We'll be at van Berk's in ten minutes. So until then, you might want to think up an alternative plan that doesn't involve hand grenades.'

Van Berk sat on the couch, staring absently at the floor and leaning on his stick for support. Every now and then he picked up his porcelain teacup and slurped at his tea. The security man standing beside him didn't move a muscle. While they were waiting, Nik moved his fingers, stretched out his legs and wriggled his toes to prevent his limbs from going numb. He had to be ready if any opportunity presented itself.

The bodyguard put his hand to his ear and listened to someone speaking before walking out of the room. After he left, van Berk reached into his jacket pocket and pulled out a gun, which he laid down beside the tea set, making sure Nik could see it. A clearly visible warning.

Not long after, Simon stumbled through the door. The security guard gave him a shove, causing him to fall to his knees. His hands were tied together with rope but he seemed unharmed. He gave Nik an acknowledging nod, as if reinforcing they were on the same side. Nik reciprocated the nod and smiled softly in an attempt to give Simon some form of encouragement in such dire circumstances. Nik considered his options. If he wanted to open his cuffs, he'd first have to get his hands to the front of his body and after that, he'd still need time to pick the lock. And even if he managed to do all that, he'd still be left facing two armed men, completely unarmed himself. Van Berk might be weak, but he would definitely be able to shoot a gun.

The bodyguard handed van Berk a piece of paper. He skimmed it over before standing up from the couch and shuffling over to Simon. He peered closely at his face. 'You remind me of him,' he said quietly. 'Elias also used to frown and purse his lips like that when he got angry. He'd usually stamp his feet and clench his fists as well, though.' Van Berk looked away from Simon and nodded to the security guard. The guard took two steps back and reached for his gun.

'Get your hands up or I'll blast a hole right through your brain!' It was a woman's voice. Daniela Haas came into the room, holding a gun that was so small it almost disappeared between her fingers. Nik recognised it immediately as a Springfield Armory 911. The handgun was useless for large distances but deadly at short range.

The sleeve on her right wrist was covered in blood but she didn't seem to be harmed.

The security guard had stopped dead in his tracks as soon as she had spoken and was now turning around slowly to look at her. When he caught sight of her gun, he raised his hands and moved to stand beside the trembling van Berk. The old man had clearly been thrown by the unexpected visitor.

'Hello, Olaf,' said the woman, keeping her gun directed towards the security guard. She nodded at Simon, who stood up and walked over to her. She took one hand from her gun and gave Simon a slap on the back of his head. 'Didn't I tell you *not* to move from the hiding place?'

Simon gave a groan of frustration before lowering his head in shame.

Van Berk looked the woman in the eyes. 'That's impossible!' he said, increasingly distraught.

'Did you really think I'd leave my son?'

He looked the woman up and down.

'Cosmetic surgery's a marvellous thing,' she said, smiling. 'A little bit more chin, a slightly smaller nose . . . ears pinned back. All of that, together with a new haircut and a different colour. Oh, and not to forget how I lost the Spanish accent. I'm basically a new person.'

Van Berk nodded.

'I also changed my name and gave up all my old friends.'

'All of them except Ismail, that is?' remarked van Berk.

'His help was vital,' said Daniela. 'I wouldn't have survived without it.'

'I didn't really have him down as a traitor. But in the end, he became a kidnapper and a murderer!'

'We didn't kidnap the children,' said Daniela. 'We protected them from you. They were doing fine.'

'Tell that to Milan, who Ismail shot through the car window,' said van Berk. 'Or Vincent Masannek, whose body was found in front of some rubbish bins.'

'They weren't humans, they were beasts,' said Daniela. 'Just like you. They would have shot any child, and done it with smiles on their faces.'

'Two deaths. Because of you.' He pointed at her. 'And now you've got Ismail on your conscience as well.'

'I tried to stop him but he wouldn't listen,' said Daniela regretfully. 'He thought it was his only option after the police rescued the children.'

'What, to kill me?'

'Of all the deaths, nobody deserves it more.'

'And going by the blood on your sleeve, I know what happened to my second bodyguard.'

She shrugged. 'Ismail taught me a lot.'

'I reinforced security precautions since he stopped working for me,' said van Berk. 'Even our former CID agent here couldn't get past it.' He nodded over to Nik. 'How the hell did you manage to get in?'

'Ismail wasn't my only friend.'

Van Berk took a moment to think. 'Arthur,' he said, sighing. 'Our forever friendly and attentive Arthur. I should've made him retire a long time ago but little Aaron loved his brioche sandwiches.'

'It was easy to get in with his security card,' said Daniela. 'And he always ironed the men's jackets, which came in pretty handy.'

In that moment, Nik realised how the tracking device had got under Masannek's collar.

'And now you're looking for revenge?' asked van Berk.

'I have *never* wanted revenge. All I wanted was for my son to grow up in peace, but you just couldn't leave him alone.'

'*Aaron* is my only heir!' said van Berk firmly.

'We don't *want* your dirty money, for God's sake!' she screamed.

'Then you're an idiot,' he answered. 'Look around you. The books in this room alone are worth more than you'll earn in your whole life. Just like that!' He snapped his fingers. 'And all your worries would be gone. You wouldn't need to go to work anymore, you could fly wherever you wanted in a private jet . . . places you've never even dreamed of!' He started to cough. 'At some point Simon will realise the value of money and he'll employ a lawyer. The proceedings will start, and greedy tax officials will start looking into how I acquired my assets. And two days later . . . the whole prosecution team will be at the door.' Van Berk shook his head. 'I will *not* let that happen.'

'There are more important things in life.'

'That's a loser's excuse.'

'What kind of person kills their own flesh and blood?'

'He isn't family!' screamed van Berk furiously. 'He's the result of some pathetic affair between an idiotic child and his idiotic servant!'

'Elias loved me,' she said quietly. 'And I loved him.' A tear ran down her cheek. 'We were young, stupid too perhaps, but our love was real and if it wasn't for you we could have had a good life together. Me, Elias and Simon.'

'But I destroyed everything because I'm a heartless bastard,' said van Berk vindictively. 'That's what you always called me, a heartless bastard.' He got up suddenly and took a step towards Daniela. 'Well then. Let's find out if I have a heart.' He straightened his back and pointed with his finger to his chest. 'This is where you need to shoot. That's where my heart should be,' he said provokingly. 'Or are you too scared? You fucking whore!' He spat on her.

Nik wanted to say something but Daniela moved the gun to point it at van Berk and pulled the trigger.

◆ ◆ ◆

Everything went quickly after that. Van Berk fell to the floor and the security guard, no longer in the line of fire, made use of the moment to jump behind the couch. Daniela pushed Simon out of the room, pulled over a heavy wooden side table and hid behind it. Nik heaved himself up with both legs and rolled over the side of the chair. A deafening shot was fired. The wooden side table splintered. Daniela crunched herself together tightly, held her head down and returned fire with her small pistol. The situation was perilous now and it wouldn't be long before the security guard shot her. Nik had to get out of the handcuffs. He pulled his aching arms underneath his backside and stepped through them. He reached underneath his top lip with his thumb and index finger and took out a narrow piece of metal which he had stuck there earlier.

'Always come prepared,' he mumbled.

Another shot sent splinters flying through the room. Nik put the piece of metal in the lock on his cuffs and turned it. Simon's mother returned the fire again.

After a couple of seconds, he had managed to get the handcuffs open. Nik waved at Daniela to get her attention. When she looked towards him, he made the sign of a gun with his fingers and signalled towards the security man. She nodded at Nik and pointed the gun.

He stuck three fingers in the air. Three, two, one. Daniela stood up quickly and pulled the trigger. The shots might not have been as loud or powerful as those from the security guard's gun but they still made him stay down. Nik ran to the couch, bent down and reached his right arm underneath. The thick upholstery made the couch heavy, but he was able to tip it over in one move.

Van Berk's security guard had not seen this coming. As the couch fell on top of him, the guard automatically lifted his arm for protection. It was a sufficient distraction to stop shooting for a moment.

And it was exactly the reaction Nik had hoped for. He kicked the gun out of the man's hand and darted behind him. The man was wearing a bulletproof vest so trying to shoot him in the torso would be futile. Instead, Nik pulled his right arm around the guard's unprotected throat and squeezed as hard as he could. Had Nik been able to use both of his arms, the bodyguard would have been unconscious within seconds. But his left arm was still weak and offered him little support. It wasn't going to be an easy fight. The man struggled into a seated position and pressed his legs into the ground. He tried to push himself up while ramming his elbows into Nik's side, but Nik held him down in the stranglehold with all the power he could muster. The pain from the blows was almost too much, but he knew if he lost this fight, he would die.

Still wrestling with the guard, Nik noticed something moving beside the couch. It was van Berk reaching for his stick. He started to climb back on to his feet.

'Are you fucking kidding me?' groaned Nik. As if responding to the remark, van Berk turned to look at Nik and pointed to his breast pocket. The bullet was stuck in the material, having made barely any impact.

'Thank you, Sir Caballero,' he mumbled.

'Fuck!' Nik screamed. Miguel Caballero was a legend. He had developed bulletproof clothes so light and so discreet that even the US president wore them. Wear a shirt or jacket from him, and any shot will only leave a tiny dent.

Daniela had also noticed Berk getting up again. She pulled the trigger but the magazine was empty. The bodyguard was gaining strength and manged to push Nik against the bookcase. Meanwhile, van Berk walked over to the couch and picked up the weapon from the floor. He calmly checked the safety catch and cocked the gun. But then, as he was turning to Nik, something solid smacked him in the jaw. The bone broke with a crunch, and he fell to the floor.

Simon looked at the man for a moment before dropping the heavy black poker to the ground and bending down to grab the gun, his hands still tied together. He pointed it at van Berk, debating whether or not to shoot his grandfather. In the end he turned to the bodyguard and aimed the gun at his head.

The man eventually stopped resisting but Nik kept his hands around his neck until he was sure he was unconscious.

Simon let the gun fall to the ground as Daniela ran over to him and wrapped her arms around him. Wheezing, Nik crawled over to them and untied the ropes around Simon's wrists.

Daniela and her son stood still, arm in arm. Daniela was crying softly, the sound drowned out by Nik's rasping breaths. Barely able to keep his head up, he noticed a dark shadow on the floor outside the room. Just as he was about to reach for a gun, a sleepy little boy with messy blonde hair and light green eyes entered the room. He was wearing white pyjamas and holding a teddy bear and looked barely five years old.

'Grandpa?' he asked cautiously, looking over at his grandfather.

Simon released himself from his mother's arms and went over to him. 'Hi, little guy. You must be Aaron.' He stroked the boy's hair.

'Is Grandpa OK?' He tried to look over Simon's shoulder but Simon moved strategically so he wouldn't be able to. 'There were so many loud bangs.'

'Your grandpa has just had a fall and needs to rest now.'

'Who are you?'

'My name is Simon. I'm your half-brother.'

'Really?' asked the boy, his eyes growing wide with astonishment. Simon nodded. 'Really.'

'My grandpa never told me I had a half-brother.'

'I was away for a long time.'

'And why are you just my *half*-brother?'

'That's because we have the same dad but different mums,' he said with a smile.

'I miss my dad.' Aaron looked at the ground.

'Me too.' Simon gave the boy a kiss on the head. 'But how about I take you back to bed now. Does that sound good?'

'Will you read me a story?'

'Of course. What would you like? Pippi Longstocking? Pinocchio?'

'Do you know Fireman Sam?' he asked excitedly.

'Of course I know Fireman Sam,' replied Simon. 'And Elvis and Penny and Station Officer Steele.'

'Grandpa gave me Tom's new helicopter last week,' said Aaron, his eyes shining. He took Simon's hand and they left the room.

Their voices soon faded into the distance.

Nik pushed open the patio door. He walked across the garden and shone his torch on the oak tree.

'You two can come out now!' he called.

'How did you find us?' asked Jon, showing his face from behind the trunk.

'Um . . .' Nik faltered. 'That trunk isn't exactly wide enough for both of your . . . um . . . full dimensions.'

'Full dimensions?' asked Balthasar, obviously offended. He stood in front of Nik with his chest out and placed one hand on his hip. 'Well, if you ask me, your hips could also do with a bit of exercise.'

Nik closed his eyes and shook his head lightly. 'What are you two doing here?'

'We actually wanted to get you out of there,' said Jon, moving to join the men.

'Well, that was very nice of you. But why have you got army camo on your faces?'

'So nobody sees us in the dark,' said Balthasar.

'And we've got revolvers.' Jon was attempting to release his gun from his trouser waistband, but the hammer had got caught in his belt. He eventually gave up.

'Why did you climb over the wall at exactly the same point as me?' asked Nik. 'That's where they spotted me.'

Jon and Balthasar looked at each other nervously, not knowing how they should best answer.

'Because your ladder was still hanging there,' answered Jon sheepishly. 'And we forgot ours.'

'How did you know we were in the garden?' asked Balthasar, changing the subject.

'Van Berk and his two bodyguards have been taken down. And Simon's safe,' said Nik. 'I actually just wanted to make sure nobody else was on the property.'

'So how is the murdering money-launderer?' asked Balthasar.

'Well, his chin got very well acquainted with a poker. So he's unconscious but still breathing.'

'OK. Then let him lie there and we can go home,' suggested Balthasar.

'It's not quite as easy as that. There have been some . . . family complications,' said Nik. 'But I'll fill you in on that at some other point,' he continued, looking at a very confused Jon. 'I called an ambulance about a minute ago. It would be slightly awkward if they find you two here wearing black clothes, with camo on your faces and pistols in your waistbands. So you need to get out of here. I'll push both your backsides up the wall, OK? You still have time to disappear.'

'Please don't push me on the backside,' said Balthasar. 'I'm a little bit sensitive there.'

'Stop complaining!' Nik moved over to the wall and made a stirrup with his hands, ready to give them a leg up. The police sirens were ringing in the distance. 'Hurry up.' A minute later, Balthasar and Jon were over the wall and on the street again. Listening to their steps as they ran away, Nik started to laugh. They might be the worst task force in the whole of Munich, but they had risked their lives for him without a flicker of hesitation. He would thank them properly at some point. Once all this insanity had passed.

Nik walked over to the villa entrance, opened the gate and waited for the patrol car. All there was left to do now was think up a believable story to tell Naumann about the fate of the stabbed man in the surveillance room. If he managed to do that, the evening might still turn out quite positively after all.

Epilogue

The English Garden was full of sun worshippers enjoying the warm autumn day. Nik sat on a park bench watching Simon and Aaron playing rugby. Simon tucked the ball under his arm and started running up the field, while Aaron tried to catch up with him. Not far away, Daniela was leaning on a tree, also watching the game and smiling serenely.

'You were right,' said Nik, without looking at Mira. She was sitting beside him on the bench.

'I didn't say anything.'

'No, but that's what you wanted to hear, wasn't it?'

She ran her fingers through her hair. 'I'll admit, I'm slightly proud of myself for convincing you not to give up the case.'

Nik smiled.

'It's what saved Simon's life in the end,' she continued. 'And on some level, it saved Aaron as well . . . Or his soul at least.'

'He has no idea what kind of man his grandfather really was,' said Nik. 'And if it was up to me, he'd never find out.' Aaron had caught up with Simon and was hanging on to his leg, trying to pull him down. 'The memories of that night at the villa will gradually disappear. And for the moment he's just happy to have a big brother. Officially too.'

'How did you manage to swing that?'

'As chance would have it, the registry office found a birth certificate stating Daniela Haas was Simon's mother and Elias van Berk was his father.'

'That was a stroke of luck.' Mira smiled and raised an eyebrow.

'Yeah, well . . . Balthasar on his own is a fantastic forger, but in combination with Jon's hacking skills, things take on a whole new dimension,' said Nik. 'And it means Simon can live with his mother now and not in the home.'

'And why did you register Elias as the father? Now Simon's reeled into Olaf van Berk's inheritance dispute.'

'I talked about it for a long time with Simon and Daniela,' explained Nik. 'Aaron doesn't have any living relatives now that his grandfather's dead. We're hoping that if Simon and Aaron are linked by having the same father, Daniela will be able to foster him.' He nodded towards the woman, her eyes full of love as she watched the children. 'The boy likes being with her and she's really taken him to her heart.'

'Must have been awful for her; being around Simon but never being able to tell anyone he was hers.'

'All those years, she was so afraid van Berk's men would find her,' Nik explained. 'And if Simon had been with her, they would've found him too. Daniela knew from the start what van Berk would've done with her son if he'd got his hands on him.'

Mira sighed. She and Nik both looked over at the boys, who were now romping around on the grass. 'Has any lawyer come forward to represent Aaron yet?'

'Van Berk would have made arrangements before he died. There's no doubt about that. But as long as the investigations are still underway, nobody's going to appear. And Jon's lawyers are ready to support Daniela when they do.'

'And what about the charges against her and Simon?'

'All been dropped. We managed to turn it around to make it look like Simon and Daniela had been kidnapped. Their actions were seen as self-defence. I put my fingerprints and the bodyguard's fingerprints on to Daniela's gun and told them it was a second weapon that I'd taken off him. Luckily, Daniela was wearing gloves so they couldn't find any gunpowder on her fingers.'

'And the security guard didn't refute that?'

Nik shrugged. 'It was his statement against those of the victims and a former CID agent. Olaf van Berk woke up after the blow from the poker but he wasn't able to speak. Two days after his death the doctors said the lack of speech had been down to a rapidly growing brain tumour.'

'So . . . everything's fine then.'

'We'll still need to be cautious – van Berk's legacy might follow us from the grave. But the prosecutor confiscated all the files in the villa and is inspecting them with a large team of analysts. Munich's underworld'll be a bit nervous about that.' He looked at Mira with a smile. 'Could have turned out a lot worse.'

'Hey!' Simon called over to Nik. 'You gonna sit around on your own all day?'

'Better go,' he told his sister. He stood up, crouched down like a rugby player and charged towards the boys.

'Get him!' cried Aaron, storming towards Nik. A second later, all three of them were scrapping after the ball on the grass.

Evening arrived and it was time for the English Garden to close. The three of them were sodden with sweat and covered in green stains but it had been a long time, far too long, since they had all smiled like they did that afternoon.

ACKNOWLEDGMENTS

Many people helped me greatly in the production of this book. My first word of thanks, of course, goes out to the wonderful team at Amazon Publishing. Your help is indispensable and it's always so much fun to see you at the book fairs.

Furthermore, I would also like to mention my two 'readers' and discussion partners, Oliver Schmitz and Ryo Takeda, without whom my readings wouldn't have been nearly as entertaining.

And in terms of specialist support, my thanks go out to Sandra Utt and Mark Fahnert, who, with their expertise, always help me to create a more believable book, as they have done again with *Blood Ties*.

ACKNOWLEDGMENTS

ABOUT THE AUTHOR

Photo © Oliver Bendig, 2014

Alexander Hartung was born in 1970 in Mannheim, Germany. He began writing while he was studying for a degree in economics and soon discovered a passion for crime fiction. He topped the Kindle Bestseller List with his Jan Tommen series and with *Broken Glass* he introduced us to Nik Pohl, the Munich detective at the centre of a gripping new investigation series. Alexander lives in his hometown of Mannheim with his wife, son and daughter.

ABOUT THE TRANSLATOR

Photo © Fiona Beaton, 2019

Fiona Beaton was born in 1984 in Dundee, Scotland. She received her degree in Translation and Interpreting with Spanish and German from Heriot-Watt University in 2007. After initially working for media monitoring companies and an investment bank, Fiona began pursuing texts of a more creative nature, where she could combine her linguistic skills with her interest in literature, film and theatre. She currently lives in Fife, Scotland.